P9-CSF-892
May 2020

Driftwood Bay

Center Point
Large Print

Books are produced in the United States using U.S.-based materials

Books are printed using a revolutionary new process called THINKtech™ that lowers energy usage by 70% and increases overall quality

Books are durable and flexible because of Smyth-sewing

Paper is sourced using environmentally responsible foresting methods and the paper is acid-free

Also by Irene Hannon and available from Center Point Large Print:

Thin Ice
Sea Rose Lane
Tangled Webs
Sandpiper Cove
Dangerous Illustions
Pelican Point
Hidden Peril

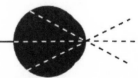

This Large Print Book carries the Seal of Approval of N.A.V.H.

Driftwood Bay

A Hope Harbor Novel

IRENE HANNON

CENTER POINT LARGE PRINT
THORNDIKE, MAINE

This Center Point Large Print edition
is published in the year 2019 by arrangement with
Revell, a division of Baker Publish Group.

Copyright © 2019 by Irene Hannon.

All rights reserved.

The text of this Large Print edition is unabridged.
In other aspects, this book may vary
from the original edition.
Printed in the United States of America
on permanent paper.
Set in 16-point Times New Roman type.

ISBN: 978-1-64358-189-7

Library of Congress Cataloging-in-Publication Data

Names: Hannon, Irene, author.
Title: Driftwood Bay / Irene Hannon.
Description: Center Point Large Print edition. | Thorndike, Maine :
    Center Point Large Print, 2019. | Series: A Hope Harbor Novel
Identifiers: LCCN 2019009283 | ISBN 9781643581897 (hardcover :
    alk. paper)
Subjects: LCSH: Large type books.
Classification: LCC PS3558.A4793 D75 2019b | DDC 813/.54—dc23
LC record available at https://lccn.loc.gov/2019009283

In loving memory of my mother,
Dorothy Hannon—my favorite
afternoon tea companion.

As I wrote this book, I thought of
all the wonderful teas we shared . . .
and our special outing on that June day six
years ago to the lovely local lavender farm
for tea and scones. That treasured memory
is tucked in my heart for always.

I miss you so much, Mom.

Every. Single. Day.

1

Chaos.

That was the only word to describe his new home.

And his new life.

Logan West ran his fingers through his damp hair, exhaling as he surveyed the mess in the kitchen.

Shredded paper towels covered the floor like springtime petals from the Bradford pear trees that had lined the streets in the small Missouri town of his youth.

Eggshells were scattered about, the residual whites oozing onto tile that had been spotless when he'd stepped into the shower less than ten minutes ago.

Soup cans, peanut butter jar, bread wrapper, OJ carton, the open container from last night's takeout dinner, and other sundry food packaging items rounded out the inventory—all of them pristine. As clean as if they'd never been used.

Meaning Toby had gotten into the trash.

Again.

The happy-go-lucky beagle might be cute as the proverbial button, but he was wreaking havoc on a life already in disarray.

Logan wiped a hand down his face.

What on earth had he been thinking when he'd decided to add a dog to the mix?

Or maybe the problem was that he *hadn't* been thinking.

Not straight, anyway.

Because getting a dog was flat-out his dumbest idea since the day he'd convinced his kid brother it would be fun to jump off the porch roof into a mound of raked autumn leaves that wasn't nearly as cushiony as it appeared.

Man, their parents had never let him forget *that* escapade—or the subsequent trip to the ER to get Jon's broken arm set.

Skirting the mess on the floor, Logan edged toward the counter as a familiar sense of panic nipped at his composure.

How could his well-ordered existence disintegrate into such bedlam in a mere four months? ER doctors were supposed to be pros at dealing with turmoil.

However . . . hospital trauma centers were *managed* chaos, with protocols for every kind of emergency, while his new life in this small town on the Oregon coast hadn't come with a procedure manual.

But who would have expected to need one this far away from the hustle and bustle of San Francisco and the complications of big-city living?

Go figure.

All he knew was that based on his first thirty-six hours in Hope Harbor, his dream of a quieter, simpler life in a small seaside town seemed destined to remain just that—a rose-colored fantasy with no basis in reality.

With a resigned sigh, he retrieved a garbage bag and began collecting the debris. Once the kitchen was clean, he'd have to round up Toby and—

A swish of movement in the doorway caught his attention.

Smoothing out the frown more than one intern had deemed intimidating, he straightened up and turned toward Molly.

The five-year-old stared back at him, eyes big, expression solemn, feet bare, her strawberry-blonde hair in desperate need of brushing, her ratty baby blanket clutched in her fist.

"Hey." The sticky goo from the eggshell in his hand leaked onto his fingers, and he tossed the fragment into the trash bag. Or tried to. He finally resorted to shaking it off. "I think you forgot your shoes." He forced up the corners of his lips.

Hers remained flat as she watched him in silence, then stuck a finger in her mouth.

His stomach twisted.

If there was a secret to coaxing a smile out of a grieving little girl, he'd yet to learn it.

He set the garbage bag on the floor, crossed to her, and dropped to one knee. Moisture spiked her thick fringe of lashes, and he swallowed past the lump in his throat.

She'd been crying again. In private—like he and his brother had always done. One more trait she shared with them, in addition to the distinctive cleft in their chin and wide-set blue eyes.

He took her small hand and gentled his voice. "Did you brush your teeth?"

She gave a silent nod.

"Why don't you put your shoes on and I'll tie them for you? Then we'll go down to the beach. Would you like that?"

She slowly removed her finger from her mouth. "Can Toby go?"

Not if he had his druthers. One glimpse of the leash at the end of their outing and the beagle would race off in the opposite direction, sand flying in his wake. After their stroll yesterday, it had taken ten minutes to corral the pup, who seemed to think they were playing a game of tag.

But if Molly's request meant she was beginning to warm up to the new addition to their family . . .

"Sure. You get your shoes while I clean up the kitchen." He stood. "Is Toby in your room?"

She shook her head.

A quiver of unease rippled through him, and once again he furrowed his brow. Come to think of it, the playful pup was uncharacteristically quiet.

"Do you know where he is?" He kept his tone casual.

Her gaze slid toward the back door.

Uh-oh.

"Molly, sweetie"—he dropped back to the balls of his feet—"did you let him out?"

She dipped her chin and wiggled her toes. "He wanted to go."

Great.

With his luck, the dog would come back covered in mud and dragging another gangly plant, as he'd done yesterday.

"We talked about this, remember? Toby has to stay in the house unless we're with him. He could get hurt if he runs around by himself."

The finger went back in her mouth.

His stomach clenched.

Again.

He was so not cut out to be a single parent.

"I'll tell you what. After you get your shoes, we'll look for him together, okay?"

Unless the dog responded to his summons, eliminating the need for a search party.

Like that would happen.

" 'Kay." The soft word found its way around the finger that didn't budge.

She retreated down the hall, trailing the bedraggled blanket behind her.

As she disappeared, Logan moved to the back door and called Toby.

11

No response.

Of course not.

That would be too easy.

Shaking his head, he shut the door, dampened a fistful of paper towels, and dropped to his hands and knees to scrub at the stubborn egg whites clinging to the tile.

They were stuck as fast as the glue he'd used in the ER to close minor lacerations.

In fact, *stuck* pretty much described the situation he'd found himself in four months ago.

But he'd made a promise—and he'd honor it.

Whatever it took.

Aha.

She'd found her culprit.

Yanking off her garden gloves, Jeannette Mason kept tabs on the dog intent on digging up yet another one of her flourishing lavender plants.

The plants she'd nurtured from tiny starts, potting and watering them with TLC until they were sturdy enough to be tucked into the beds she'd painstakingly prepared.

Based on the pup's location, the lavender now under siege was a Super French.

Lips clamped together, she tossed her gloves on the workbench in the drying and equipment shed and stormed toward the door.

Enough was enough.

If that dog kept uprooting her stock, Bayview

Lavender Farm would be out of business less than three years after she'd opened her doors.

And that was *not* happening.

She'd invested too much effort in this place to let anyone—or anything—jeopardize it.

Snatching a long-handled trowel from the tool rack as she passed, she charged out into the light rain falling from the leaden sky. She should have grabbed her coat too. Now that the sun had disappeared, it was cooler than usual for mid-April.

But coastal Oregon weather could be capricious in any season—a lesson she should have learned long ago.

Brandishing the gardening implement, she sprinted toward the tri-colored dog, weaving through the symmetrical beds.

"Hey!" She waved the trowel in the air. "Get out of there!"

The pup lifted his dirt-covered snout. Started to wag his tail. Reconsidered the scowling woman racing toward him with weapon in hand and skedaddled toward the tall hedge that separated her farm from the adjacent property.

Within seconds, the white tip of his tail disappeared as he wriggled through the dense greenery.

Huffing out a breath, Jeannette gave up the chase. The dog was gone—for now. Her time would be better spent repairing whatever destruction her unwanted visitor had wrought.

She continued to the bed, muttering as she surveyed the damage. Two of the plants had been uprooted, and the pesky beagle had started in on a third.

This was as bad as the last attack—except he hadn't absconded with one of her plants this go-round.

Gritting her teeth, she stalked back to the shed to retrieve a shovel. The ripped-up plants had to be her top priority.

But once they were back into their beds and watered, she was going to march next door and have a little chat with her new neighbors.

Shovel in hand, she retraced her steps to the pillaged bed, casting a dark look toward the hedge that hid the small house on the adjacent property.

She should have inquired about buying that lot too, when she'd purchased this one.

But the three acres she'd bought were already more than her plants and tearoom required. An acre or two would have sufficed.

However . . . none of the other parcels of land she'd viewed had had a path at the rear of the property that led to the dunes, which provided access to the vast beach and deep cobalt sea of Driftwood Bay. Plus, the microclimate in this particular sheltered spot was perfect for lavender.

So despite the excess acreage, the location had been too good to pass up—especially since the land on one side had never been developed, and the house with new owners on the other side had been occupied by an older man who kept to himself as much as she did . . . and who'd long ago planted an insulating privacy hedge.

She dug into the bed she'd augmented with truckloads of rotted fir bark and aged horse manure, casting another glance toward the shrub border.

Strange how she'd had no inkling her former neighbor had sold the property until the moving van showed up a week ago. And he'd done nothing more than flick her a brief, disinterested look as she'd driven past while he was directing the moving crew from his front porch.

Then again, she'd never gone out of her way to be sociable, either.

A twinge of self-reproach niggled at her conscience, but she quashed it as she resettled the first lavender plant in the fertile earth.

There was no reason to feel guilty. On the few occasions their paths had crossed, he'd barely acknowledged her.

And just because she didn't attempt to engage people didn't mean she was antisocial. She was always polite to her customers at the town farmer's market and in her tearoom, and she smiled and waved at familiar faces in town . . . even if she rarely stopped to chat.

But she was never *un*friendly to anyone.

Although that was about to change.

She eased the second traumatized Super French into the hole she'd dug and doused the roots with water. If fate was kind, all of the plants would recover from the shock of their abrupt extraction.

Wiping her palms on her jeans, she detoured back to the workshop, snagged her jacket, and cut across the gravel parking area at the front of her property that was empty of customers' cars on this Wednesday morning.

At least the pup hadn't launched his sneak attacks on a weekend, while she was busy serving afternoon tea to a roomful of people paying a hefty sum for a couple of hours of peace and genteel elegance.

She circled around the end of the hedge that lined her drive and strode through the adjacent yard, toward the front door of the small bungalow that could use a fresh coat—or two—of paint and some landscaping.

Maybe it was better she hadn't known it was up for sale. The temptation to buy it—and protect her privacy—would have been strong.

And more maintenance would only have added to her already long to-do list.

As she approached the door, the muffled sound of yapping penetrated the walls.

Apparently the dog was a barker as well as a digger.

That figured.

She stepped up onto the porch, took a deep breath, and pressed the bell. It was possible the new owners would be nice. Apologetic, even.

One could hope, anyway.

Confrontation wasn't high on her list of favorite activities.

But these people needed to get control of their dog—and she intended to make that crystal clear before she returned home.

Whether they liked it or not.

2

Was that the doorbell?

Cocking his ear, Logan tightened his grip on Toby, whose frantic yaps and contortionist squirms conveyed in no uncertain terms his displeasure at having the mud removed from his paws with a damp rag.

Hard as Logan listened, it was impossible to tell if someone was pressing the bell, given the din in the kitchen.

"Molly!"

The little girl peeked around the edge of the doorway, finger still in mouth.

"Would you look through the window next to the front door and see if there's someone on the porch?"

She hesitated . . . then disappeared toward the living room, dragging the blanket behind her.

Toby made another lunge for freedom.

"Not so fast, buddy. I mopped the floor once already today. You're staying on this rug until I get your paws clean."

He finished the third one as Molly reappeared in the doorway.

"Did you see anyone?" He threw the question over his shoulder.

"A lady."

Wonderful.

If ever there was an inopportune time for visitors, this was it.

Toby upped the volume of his barks and wriggled harder—but in the infinitesimal moment of peace between woofs, the bell chimed again.

Logan sighed.

Someone really wanted to talk to him.

And if it happened to be a neighbor stopping by to welcome him, he couldn't afford to be rude. At this stage, he needed all the friends he could get.

"Sorry, fella. You're stuck with me until those paws are clean." Swooping the writhing, barking beagle into his arms, he headed for the front door, flinching at every woof.

His hearing was never going to be the same.

In the tiny foyer, he wedged the pup in the crook of his arm, freeing one hand to flip the lock and twist the knob.

As the door swung wide and the female visitor came into view, Toby fell silent. As if he was dumbstruck by the vision on their doorstep.

Logan could relate.

Despite the smudge of dirt hugging the graceful curve of her jaw, the stunning woman on his porch took his breath away too.

Early thirtyish, she was six or seven inches shorter than his six-one frame, with model-like cheekbones. Her classic oval face was framed by long, light-brown hair with golden highlights.

Generous lips, big brown eyes, trim figure—she had it all.

As Toby resumed barking and wiggling, his own vocal cords kicked back in.

"Hi." He raised his voice to be heard above the yapping. "Can I help you?"

"Um . . . I'm your neighbor. Jeannette Mason." She gave him and the dog a discreet once-over as she indicated the property to her left.

"Nice to meet you. I'm Logan West. I'd offer to shake hands, but as you can see, they're occupied." He conjured up a smile.

She didn't return it.

"I noticed." She hiked up her volume too. "Actually . . . your friend there is what prompted my visit."

The corners of his lips sagged. Based on her serious demeanor, the woman hadn't stopped by to welcome him to the neighborhood.

Not even close.

"I hope he hasn't caused any trouble."

"As a matter of fact, he's been . . ." Her voice faltered, and twin creases appeared on her brow as she glanced past him.

He swiveled around.

Molly was hovering in the doorway at the end of the foyer, finger in mouth, the corner of the threadbare blanket wadded in her fist.

And there was a scratch on her cheek, oozing red.

His stomach knotted.

Where had *that* come from?

He started toward her. "Molly, what happened to—"

As if sensing his opportunity for escape, Toby twisted in his arms and leapt free. He landed on all four feet . . . slid across the plank floor, leaving a streak of mud behind from the one remaining dirty paw . . . and tore into the kitchen.

Mercifully, he stopped barking.

Logan crossed to Molly and dropped to one knee in front of her. "Sweetie, what did you do to your cheek?"

She shrugged and hung her head.

"You have a scratch." He tapped the smooth skin beside it. The scrape wasn't deep. A thorough cleaning and an application of some antibiotic ointment would suffice. But it had happened on his watch, and he didn't have a clue how.

Another indication he was in over his head with this single-parent gig.

She lifted her hand to her cheek.

Mystery solved.

All of her fingernails were too long . . . several were jagged . . . and one was streaked with crimson.

Somehow, in the craziness of packing and moving, he'd forgotten about little-girl manicures.

That chore zoomed up on his to-do list—right below rounding up Toby, finishing the canine cleanup job, and mopping the kitchen floor. Again.

The woman behind him cleared her throat.

Oh yeah.

His neighbor was standing on his porch.

"I'll fix this up for you in a minute, sweetie." He gave Molly's arm a comforting squeeze.

Her expression remained solemn as she transferred her attention to their visitor.

Logan stood and returned to the front door. "Sorry. It's been a bit crazy around here. You were saying?"

The woman rubbed her palms down her jeans, a flash of uncertainty flickering in her eyes. "Look . . . I, uh, can see you have your hands full . . . and I hate to add to your problems . . . but your dog is digging up my plants. Two today, and several yesterday—including one that disappeared."

So the leggy thing with the weird foliage that Toby had hauled home and deposited on the back porch had been from his neighbor's garden.

Not the most attractive plant he'd ever seen— but insulting this woman's garden wasn't likely to earn him any brownie points.

"I'm sorry for the inconvenience. I'll be happy to repair the damage or replace anything that was destroyed—and I'll do my best to keep Toby from escaping again."

"I'd appreciate that. And I already took care of

23

the damage. The purpose of my visit was to make sure the issue is addressed." She sent Molly a quick smile and withdrew a step. "I, uh, have to get back to work. Welcome to Hope Harbor."

With that, she turned and retreated down the walk.

He waited in the doorway until she disappeared around the hedge that separated their properties, but she never looked back.

Just as well.

Once upon a time, a beautiful neighbor would have been a major distraction. Especially if she was friendly.

But he had plenty of other distractions that took precedence these days—and Jeannette Mason hadn't exuded one ounce of friendliness.

Expelling a breath, he shut the door as Toby galloped into the foyer, skidded to a stop beside Molly, and plopped on his haunches.

The two of them watched him, as if they were waiting for the next act to begin in a three-ring circus.

An apt analogy.

And unless he managed to get a handle on all the moving parts fast, the new life he'd hoped to create on the Oregon coast could end up being a total bust.

"Jeannette! Wait up!"

At the summons, Jeannette halted her trek to

Charley's wharfside taco stand and swiveled around.

The *Hope Harbor Herald* editor jogged toward her from across the street, the sun glinting in her red hair.

Jeannette tamed the twitch tugging at her lips. As long as Marci Weber—no, Garrison now, since her marriage five months ago—was around, the town would never have an energy shortage. Nor lack for a champion. A woman who'd relaunched a defunct newspaper and spearheaded a successful campaign to save the Pelican Point lighthouse was a formidable civic asset.

The editor screeched to a stop beside her, tucking a flyaway strand of hair behind her ear. "I'm glad I caught you. I have a couple of things I wanted to talk to you about, if you can spare a minute."

Jeannette braced. When Marci had that gleam in her eye, she was usually on some sort of quest— or soliciting volunteers for her latest project.

And saying no to the vivacious redhead wasn't easy.

Which was why Jeannette had found herself attending the first lighthouse meeting last year— along with hordes of other Hope Harbor residents who'd succumbed to Marci's earnest, eager enthusiasm.

"I can give you two. Maybe even three." She tried for a teasing tone—but hopefully Marci would pick up her underlying note of caution.

"Wonderful. First, thank you for renewing your standing ad for the tearoom in the *Herald*. Without steady advertisers like you, we'd be in deep doo-doo."

"It's my pleasure—and it's a win/win situation. I can't tell you the number of customers who say they found out about me from that ad."

"Glad to hear it. Will you be back at the farmer's market in May when it opens for the season?"

"I wouldn't miss it."

"Excellent. I'm going to be doing a feature on a different vendor in each issue, and I'd love to showcase Bayview Lavender Farm."

"All publicity is accepted with thanks."

A savory whiff of grilling fish set off a rumble in Jeannette's stomach, and she slid a glance toward the white truck with colorful letters above the serving window spelling out "Charley's." She needed to get over there before the taco-making artist's muse beckoned and he closed up shop to hurry back to his studio north of town.

"Smells good, doesn't it?" Marci grinned and flapped a hand toward the truck that was a permanent fixture on the wharf.

"Better than good—and that's my next stop."

"I'm in the mood for tacos myself, but I have a standing Thursday lunch date with Ben that's sacrosanct. Sort of like our local clerics' Thursday golf game."

26

"Nice tradition."

"I agree—but it's about to come to an end, now that my husband has managed to round up a doctor to replace him as director of our urgent care center."

Jeannette arched an eyebrow. "I hadn't heard that."

"I put a small item in the *Herald* two issues ago. Easy to miss. But I'll be running a longer story once the new guy takes over. Ben's enjoyed filling in there, but he'll be happy to devote full-time to his orthopedic practice in Coos Bay."

"I can imagine." Stitching up cuts and treating stomach viruses wouldn't be much of a challenge for the former army surgeon who'd married Marci.

"Actually, I thought you might have met the new doc. He bought the place next to yours. Logan West."

Jeannette blinked.

Her new neighbor was Ben Garrison's replacement?

That was news.

She did her best to feign nonchalance. "I've met him, but it was a brief conversation. We didn't discuss our professions."

"I haven't had the pleasure myself, but Ben says he's nice." Marci gave her an expectant look, as if she was hoping for another take on the new man in town.

Not happening.

Jeannette had no opinion about her new neighbor.

At least none she wanted to share.

"As I said, we only exchanged a few words." She fingered the edge of her shoulder purse. If anyone in town knew details about the man who shared his home with a demon dog and a sad-eyed little girl, it would be Marci.

Like, say, his marital status.

Jeannette frowned at the errant thought. Where had *that* come from? It wasn't as if she had any romantic interest in the man, for heaven's sake.

Even if images of the tall, sandy-haired man with startling blue eyes *had* been popping up in her mind with annoying regularity since they'd met yesterday.

Marci exhaled, her frustration evident. "I guess I'll have to wait until I meet him myself. I have an interview scheduled next week for a personality piece, to introduce the residents to him."

Perfect. Marci was a first-rate reporter, and she'd cover all the bases in the *Herald*. No questions necessary today.

"So"—Jeannette inclined her head toward the wharf—"I better get over there before Charley decides to go paint."

"I hear you. I've almost had the window shut in my face on a few occasions. But there's someone in line today, and Charley never closes if people

28

are waiting. I won't keep you more than another minute or two, but I did have a favor to ask."

Jeannette tightened her grip on her purse.

Here it came.

"What did you need?"

If Marci noticed the wariness in her voice, she gave no indication. "You know about the refugee family the town's churches are sponsoring, right?"

"Yes." It was impossible *not* to know. Reverend Baker had been running information about the Syrian family in the Grace Christian bulletin ever since he and Father Murphy at St. Francis had cooked up the plan.

"Well, they're arriving next Tuesday, and some of us thought it would be hospitable to have a meet-and-greet for them. I ran the proposal by our clerics yesterday, and they loved it. Grace Christian is going to host the gathering in the fellowship hall a week from Saturday night, and members of both congregations will bring casseroles. But the highlight will be a 'Taste of Hope Harbor' sampling table to give them a literal flavor of the town."

Clever idea.

No wonder the PR business Marci ran on the side was successful.

"I like it—and we do have some fabulous local specialties."

"I agree. Sweet Dreams bakery is providing its

famous cinnamon rolls, Charley is bringing mini tacos, Tracy and Michael at Harbor Point Cranberries offered cranberry nut cake, the Myrtle Café is supplying meat loaf bites, and Eleanor Cooper promised to whip up one or two of her fabulous chocolate fudge cakes. I was hoping you'd bake some of your wonderful lavender shortbread to add to the table."

The request was reasonable—except she wasn't planning to attend the event. That would require socializing, and life was much more placid . . . and safe . . . when you kept to yourself.

But how could she say no, after so many residents had already done more than their share to help the family? From what she could gather, volunteers had been hard at work for weeks renovating an apartment, soliciting furnishings and clothing, stocking the kitchen, helping line up a job for the young father, and holding fundraisers to buy a used car that Marv at the body shop had fine-tuned into mint condition.

The least she could do was provide some sweets.

But perhaps she could beg off on showing up.

"I'll be happy to participate. I may drop my contribution off on Friday, though. Weekends are super busy at the tearoom. I'm always fully booked, and by the time the last person leaves on Saturday, I'm ready to fold."

Marci caught her lower lip between her teeth.

"I can understand that—but we'd love it if you could stop by to say hello. We're trying to do everything we can to make the family feel welcome, after all they've been through. They've had a really tough go of it."

Yes, they had.

She'd read the information in the bulletin about the small, shattered family that was fleeing Christian persecution. A young man with a little girl, along with his mother—the sole survivors from their family after a church bombing. They'd left the country with nothing, spent months in a refugee camp, and only by the grace of God had they connected with the two Hope Harbor churches.

Truly, it had been almost like a miracle.

If Charley hadn't heard about their plight from an acquaintance who volunteered with a humanitarian-aid organization in the Middle East, then planted the notion of rescuing them with the two clerics, the traumatized, homeless family would still be living in destitution, with no hope for a better future.

Guilt nipped at her conscience.

Everyone in town should to do their part to let these three wounded souls know that while they might be in a strange new land, they were among friends.

"If I can manage it, I'll drop in for a few minutes." It was the best she could offer on the fly.

"Awesome!" Marci beamed at her as if she'd agreed to come. "I won't delay your lunch any longer. Enjoy those tacos." With a wave, she hurried back toward the newspaper office.

Inhaling a lungful of the salt-laced air, Jeannette surveyed the picture-perfect scene as she resumed her trek to Charley's truck.

The white gazebo in the small park behind Charley's stand.

The planters separating the sidewalk from the sloping boulders that led to the water, newly filled with spring flowers.

The colorful awnings on the storefronts that faced the sea on the other side of Dockside Drive.

She paused beside one of the benches spaced along the wharf and gazed out over the deep blue water, past the boats bobbing in the placid marina, to the long jetty on the left and the two rocky islands on the right that served as a natural buffer for the protected harbor.

It was a beautiful spot.

In fact, it was this very view that had sold her on the town when she'd come west in search of refuge and a new life.

But as she'd learned, Oregon storms could be fierce. Ferocious waves could batter the rugged coast. And even in sheltered harbors like this, boats could rock dangerously if sufficient turbulence agitated the waters.

The kind produced by the type of low-hanging

gray clouds massing on the horizon that suggested some rough weather could blow into town in the not-too-distant future.

"Hi, Jeannette. May I join you for a moment to admire the view?"

Stifling her disquieting thoughts, she angled toward Charley Lopez.

Behind him, the wharfside stand was shuttered.

Drat.

She'd missed her opportunity for a taco lunch.

"Of course—although I have to admit my taste buds were clamoring for fish tacos. Can I cajole you into reopening for one more customer?"

"No cajoling necessary." Hefting a brown sack, he gave her his trademark smile, his gleaming white teeth a contrast to his sun-burnished, weathered skin. "I saw you over here and assumed you were coming my way."

"You're the best." She opened her purse to dig for her wallet.

"We can settle up on your next visit. The cash box is closed for the day."

After a brief hesitation, she re-zipped her purse. This was another thing she loved about Hope Harbor. Everyone trusted everyone else.

"Thanks." She took the bag he held out.

"My pleasure. Ignoring an obvious need would be wrong—and I could see you were desperate for a taco fix." He winked at her, adjusted the Ducks cap over the long gray hair that was pulled back into a ponytail, and shifted toward the sea to give it a long, slow sweep.

Jeannette slanted a look at him. Was that comment about ignoring obvious needs referring to more than tacos? Was he suggesting she should do her part for the immigrant family?

Crimping the top of the bag in her fingers, she rolled her eyes.

What a ridiculous stretch.

From his perch in the taco truck, there was no chance Charley could have overheard her conversation with Marci.

Her conscience was just working overtime.

Charley picked up the conversation. "I never get tired of this view. It's a balm for the soul."

She studied the scene again.

Yes, it was—most days.

But this afternoon, it did nothing to mitigate the subtle unease that had been gnawing at her since her encounter with her neighbor yesterday.

"Don't you think so?" Charley focused on her with those keen, dark eyes that seemed to have an uncanny ability to delve beneath the surface.

She had to scramble to recall his last comment.

View . . . balm . . . soul. That was it.

"I love this vista too. Although I have to admit it's not working its usual soothing magic on me today."

"I wonder why?"

She was saved from having to respond by

two seagulls that waddled over and settled at Charley's feet with a few squawks.

"Friends of yours?" She indicated the pair.

"Yes. Floyd and Gladys."

"Seriously? You name the seagulls?"

"These two are special. We go way back."

They let loose with a few more squawks.

"I think they're trying to talk to you."

"A distinct possibility." His expression grew speculative. "Curious that they'd show up now."

"How so?"

"Long story." After giving the scene another scan, he transferred his attention to her, his usual placid, pleasant demeanor back in place. "Better go eat those tacos or they'll get cold. And have some of your delicious lavender shortbread for dessert." With a jaunty salute, he ambled off.

She stared after him.

Why had he mentioned the shortbread so close on the heels of Marci's request that she provide her trademark tea pastry for the Taste of Hope Harbor table at the welcome party?

"Ignoring an obvious need would be wrong."

Turning her back on his retreating figure, she continued toward her car.

This was nuts.

Yes, Charley was an insightful man.

Yes, he'd earned his reputation as the town sage.

Yes, his comments were always thought-provoking and spot-on.

But to think his remarks had been veiled advice about the immigrant family was downright silly.

Still . . . no matter Charley's intent, as she pressed the autolock button and picked up her pace, her conscience began prickling again.

Maybe baking some shortbread for the gathering wasn't enough.

Maybe she ought to be there in person.

After all, if everyone in town dropped off their contributions and disappeared, there would be no one on hand to greet the new arrivals.

So why not show up at the last minute? She could introduce herself to the family, welcome them, and slip out before anyone cornered her—as Marci had today—and tried to extend the hand of friendship.

A very real possibility if she lingered, given the warmth of everyone she'd encountered in town.

And therein lay the problem.

She crossed Dockside Drive and slid behind the wheel.

It would be easy to establish ties in Hope Harbor, make friends, get involved in other people's lives.

But that would require opening her heart and letting herself care.

In other words, she'd have to take a risk.

And she wasn't anywhere close to making that leap yet.

Nor might she ever be.

After setting the bag of tacos on the passenger seat, she took one last look at the wharf as she started the engine.

The scene was tranquil and unchanging, peaceful and predictable.

A fair description of her life these days.

And she intended to keep it that way as long as—

A familiar yipping intruded on her thoughts, and she twisted her head toward the sidewalk.

Her new neighbor was tying the leash for his dog to the bike stand in front of Sweet Dreams bakery a few doors down—and attempting to shush the animal, based on his body language. The little girl was there too, clutching the same tattered blanket.

Finally the doctor gave up trying to silence the dog, took the child's hand, and disappeared inside.

The beagle began to yowl, ruining the usual wharfside serenity.

She was out of here.

Jeannette put the car in gear and pulled away from the curb, jacking up the volume on the classical radio station to drown out the dog's faint wails.

At the corner, she checked her rearview mirror as she hung a right.

The pup was straining at the leash—and loudly communicating his displeasure at being abandoned, based on his baying posture.

Yet another disturbing note in her day.

It was time to go home, close herself up in her workshop, and assemble some lavender sachets to supplement her stock for the opening day of the farmer's market.

And hope the relaxing scent and quiet ambiance of the farm would soothe her sudden, inexplicable apprehension that the quiet, solitary oasis she'd created in Hope Harbor was about to be disrupted.

3

This was a miracle.

Mariam Shabo smoothed out the pristine comforter on the twin bed she'd just slept in. Fingered the edge of the crisp sheet. Stroked the soft pillow.

She had a clean, safe place to live. There was a plentiful supply of food in the kitchen. They had a toilet. Running water. Electricity.

Even their pastor, Father Karam—who'd always used the term miracle sparingly—would have to agree it was accurate in this case.

Or he would have, if he was still alive.

A wave of sadness engulfed her, knotting her stomach and sucking the air from her lungs.

Despite all the months that had passed, it was hard to believe he and dozens of others had been buried beneath the rubble on that horrible Sunday morning at the church she'd attended for all of her fifty-three years.

A church that was only a distant memory now, like the life she'd once known—when being a Christian in Syria had been tolerated.

When she and Yesoph had shared laughter-filled dinners every night with their two young sons while the aroma of her grilled kufta kebabs, the lamb redolent with garlic, and her dawood basha, the meatballs tender in her secret tomato-herb sauce, whetted everyone's appetite.

When bombs hadn't been a constant threat and they could attend church without fear.

Now all that was gone.

A sob rose in her throat, but she curled her fingers until her nails dug into her palms, choking back the tears.

She must not cry.

Despite all she'd lost, God had blessed her and Thomma and Elisa, plucking them from a place of despair and destruction and giving them a new life in a town with a name that held such promise.

Hope Harbor.

How strange—and providential—was that?

"Teta?"

At the soft summons from her granddaughter, she turned toward the four-and-a-half-year-old.

Gone was the grimy waif in tattered clothing who'd shared the cramped living space at the refugee camp with her grandmother and father.

Now, Elisa's dark auburn hair was sectioned into two short ponytails on either side of her head, and her bangs were combed. The blue jeans she wore were brand new, as was the sweatshirt that featured two seagulls and the words "I ♥ Hope Harbor." Clean socks and new shoes—the laces untied—completed her outfit.

Mariam's throat tightened again. Such a sweet, beautiful child—and her future had taken a dramatic turn for the better with their arrival in Hope Harbor yesterday.

Yet her expression remained solemn.

Perhaps it always would.

The specifics of her trauma might fade as the years passed, but the effects would last a lifetime.

A wave of fresh grief pummeled Mariam.

There was nothing she could do to erase Elisa's bad memories—except pray the blessing of this second chance in a safe place would heal all of them.

She called up a smile for her granddaughter. "Do you need some help with your shoes?"

"Ee."

"No. English." They were in America now, and it was important to use the native language as much as possible—even if Thomma had yet to show any interest in learning the simple words and phrases she'd picked up in the refugee camp and taught her granddaughter.

"Yes."

"Good. Come." She patted the other twin bed in the room they shared, the comforter on this one decorated with butterflies and fanciful flower fairies designed to appeal to a little girl.

The kind people of Hope Harbor had gone out of their way to make her small family feel welcome.

Another blessing.

Elisa climbed up and traced the outline of

a flower on the quilted fabric with her finger. *"Jamila."*

"Pretty."

The child repeated the word.

"Yes. Is pretty." She needed to learn more English herself, but until she did, the bulk of her communicating would have to be done in Arabic. She switched to her native language. "Where is your father?" She tied one of Elisa's shoes.

"In his room."

"Is he up?"

"I don't know. The door is shut."

Mariam frowned.

Perhaps Thomma had had difficulty sleeping his first night in the apartment they now called home and was tired . . . or wasn't feeling well, after their long journey through multiple time zones . . . or was writing in the journal he'd begun keeping after they'd left their home for the refugee camp.

Or perhaps he was in a bad humor, as usual, and was shutting them out. Again.

She lifted her chin.

That was no longer acceptable.

All these months, she'd given him space to work through his grief. The losses he'd endured—especially a wife and young son—would bring any man to his knees, and her heart ached for him.

But he wasn't the only one grieving—and

somehow, despite their sorrow, they had to accept their new reality and move on. God had spared the three of them and given them the gift of this new life, and they needed to lean on him . . . and each other.

A lesson her son had yet to learn.

Mariam finished tying Elisa's shoes and stood. "Are you hungry?"

"Yes."

"I'll get your father, then we'll have breakfast." She pulled a picture book off a shelf filled with toys and stuffed animals and handed it to her. "I'll be back in a minute."

She closed the door behind her as she exited, crossed the hall to the other bedroom, and knocked.

No answer.

"Thomma—are you up?"

Silence.

She twisted the knob and walked in.

Her son was sitting on the side of the bed, still in his underwear, forearms on thighs, hands clasped, head bent.

He didn't look up as she entered.

She shut the door behind her. "It's morning. We have to eat."

"I'm not hungry."

He never was.

She scanned the thin frame of her once robust son, pressure building behind her eyes. The meager rations they'd subsisted on in the months following the bombing weren't the main reason for his dramatic weight loss.

Food didn't interest him anymore.

Nor did living.

In fact, there were days she feared he'd . . .

No!

She crushed the insidious thought that kept her awake more nights than she could count.

After all they'd survived, Thomma was *not* going to give up.

She wouldn't let him.

God, help me console and encourage him. Show me how to reach him. Please help him find new meaning and hope.

It was the same prayer she uttered every day.

So far, it hadn't had any effect—but perhaps here, in this small seaside town so far from everything they had known, her son's heart would begin to heal.

"You have to eat." She walked over to him.

"I told you, I'm not hungry."

"Your daughter is." If she had to use Elisa to break through his shell of grief, she would.

"The kitchen is stocked. You can feed her."

"You're her father."

"You're her grandmother."

"She needs *you,* Thomma."

"She has you. That is enough."

"No, it is not. A grandmother is not a father."

He didn't respond.

Letting out a slow breath, she lowered herself to the bed beside him. "We have all had more than our share of tragedy, my son. But Elisa has her whole life ahead of her. You and I must work together to give her the opportunity to be all that God wants her to be."

"God." He nearly spat out the Almighty's name, and a flash of fury kindled in his dull eyes. "Where was God when our church was bombed? Why did he take all the rest and leave us?"

It was a question without an answer.

"I don't know—but we must trust there is a reason."

He shot to his feet and began to pace in the small space. "Trust? You want me to trust a God who would allow terrorists to kill my wife and son and brother and father? What kind of loving deity would permit such tragedy?"

"I can't see into the mind of God, Thomma." The chronic knot in her stomach tightened. "But we cannot lose our faith along with everything else."

"I left my faith in our bombed-out church in Syria." Bitterness scored his defiant declaration.

Mariam's heart sank. He'd never before admitted what she'd long suspected.

"Whatever your personal feelings about God, you owe your daughter a fresh start."

"You can give her that as well as I can."

"No, I can't. No one can take the place of a father. You are grieving your wife, but she is grieving her mother—and she is also grieving you. If you noticed her, you would see how she watches you." Mariam swallowed, struggling to control her emotions. "She doesn't understand your distance. She yearns for your love and care, but you ignore her. It's as if you are lost to her too."

He stopped pacing and turned toward her, his face awash with anguish. "I have no love left to give. My heart is numb."

"I too am numb—but for Elisa's sake, we must try to carry on and create a home for her here."

"This will never be home, 'Ami." Weariness and dejection weighed down his words.

"Home isn't a place. It's people. And our family is here now."

He gave her an uncomprehending stare. "How can you move on so easily after everything we've been through?"

An ember of anger sparked to life deep within her. "You think this is easy for me? Nothing about starting over in a new country is easy for anyone. But no matter how much we wish it, our homeland is not the place we once loved. Nor will it ever be again. And we cannot bring back the people we have lost." Her voice broke, and tears blurred her vision.

"Ah, 'Ami." Contrition softened his features as

he crossed to her and grasped her shoulders. "I'm sorry. I know how much you must miss our old life. And I appreciate all you've done to care for me and Elisa these past months. I wish I was as strong as you are."

"Strength comes from faith—and from believing that tomorrow can be better than today." She cupped his cheeks in her hands, as she'd done when he was a young boy in need of consoling. "We must take this day by day and be grateful we have a chance to create a new life. Most of the people we left behind in that camp will never have this opportunity."

"I know." His face crumpled, and he swallowed. "But I can't help wishing everything was the way it used to be."

"I share that wish. But dwelling on the past is futile. Our future is here—and we must make it the best it can be." The doorbell chimed, and she swiped her fingers under her damp lashes. "That will be Susan. I don't know what we would have done if Father Murphy hadn't arranged for her to meet us at the airport yesterday. We would have been lost without someone who speaks Arabic."

"Why is she back?"

"She promised to show us how everything in this apartment works and to answer our questions. You will come out and speak with her?"

After a moment, he nodded.

"We'll start with the kitchen while you dress. I can explain whatever you miss later."

Without waiting for a response, Mariam opened the door and stepped into the hall.

Elisa was hovering on the threshold of their bedroom. "The bell ringed."

"Yes, I heard it. It's the lady who met us at the airport yesterday. Your father will be out in a few minutes."

Her granddaughter glanced at the bedroom door, trepidation etched on her features. "Is he mad?"

"No. Just sad. He misses our country."

"I don't." Elisa clutched the Raggedy Ann doll that had been waiting on her new bed last night, her expression fierce. "It was scary. Here is better." She hugged the doll tighter, and some of her defiance faded. "Papa won't go back and leave us, will he?"

Mariam bent down and drew her into a comforting hug. "No. This is our home now."

"For always?"

"Yes."

Whether Thomma would come to accept that remained to be seen.

But for his sake as well as theirs, she prayed her son would soon recognize and embrace all the blessings Hope Harbor had to offer.

Logan double-checked the cooking temperature

on the package of refrigerated cookie dough and set the oven to 350 degrees.

These weren't going to be anywhere near as tasty as his mom's homemade version that Molly had loved, but it was the best he could do for a special treat on this gloomy, gray Friday.

"You want to help me put these on the cookie sheet?" He opened the tube of dough and pulled a knife out of the drawer. "They're chocolate chip."

She cocked her head and studied the package as she tore the crust off the last bite of her peanut butter and jelly sandwich. "They don't look like Nana's."

No kidding.

"We might like them, though." He tried for an upbeat tone. "Want to help?"

She shrugged.

He took that for a yes as she finished her sandwich and pushed aside the plate with the crust remnants.

After skimming the directions, he began cutting the dough into slices. "Just lay these on the sheet and leave some space between them."

"Nana used a bowl and a spoon."

"This is faster. Here you go." He passed over a medallion of the sticky dough.

They worked in silence until they'd filled the pristine sheet—a gift from his mom, along with his favorite cookie recipe, when he'd taken the job in San Francisco.

Like he'd ever had a spare minute to bake anything from scratch.

Toby watched the proceedings with interest, tail wagging as he bounced around, happy yips filling the kitchen.

A common reaction to the sight of food—or to anything that caught his attention, for that matter.

Logan heaved a sigh as he slid the pan in the oven. If he didn't get the pup's barking under control soon, he was going to lose his sanity.

Too bad he hadn't read the fine print before choosing a breed. If the information he'd found the other night on Google was accurate, beagles were a wonderful family dog and good with children—but they tended to be very vocal.

He set the timer for twelve minutes and wiped down the table.

Maybe the one-year-old dog's previous owner had gotten fed up with the barking too, and that was the reason he'd sold the pooch—not because his new apartment didn't allow pets, as he'd claimed.

Didn't matter.

Toby was his problem now.

Meaning he might have to invest in some obedience training—in addition to the electronic fence scheduled to be installed in the backyard next week that would keep the dog out of his neighbor's garden.

He hoped.

"Do you want some more milk?" Logan picked up Molly's empty glass.

Another shrug.

Dodging the prancing pooch, he walked toward the fridge and forced a cheery note into his tone. "Nothing goes better with chocolate chip cookies than a glass of ice cold—"

Ding-dong.

He halted halfway across the room.

This must be the week for callers.

Or could it be his attractive neighbor again?

His pulse ticked up.

A visit from her would brighten up this dreary Friday—as long as she wasn't mad about some other transgression.

He detoured to the hall and hurried toward the door. Through the window he spied a UPS truck pulling away from the curb.

Shoot.

Not a visit from his neighbor after all.

He twisted the knob—but as he pulled the door open, a crash sounded from the kitchen. Like a chair had tipped over.

"Molly?" He swung around—and a small, wriggly body zipped past his legs.

Blast.

"Toby! Get back here!"

The dog paid him no heed.

After casting one last look at the beagle

barreling toward the hedge between his property and Jeannette's, he raced to the kitchen.

A chair *had* tipped over—but Molly appeared to be fine.

He grabbed the dog's leash from the hook by the back door, along with a handful of doggie treats. Hesitated.

Could he leave a five-year-old alone while he chased down the dog?

No.

Swooping Molly up with one arm, he dashed toward the front door as she shrieked and gripped his T-shirt with both fists.

"It's okay, sweetie. Hold on tight. We're going to follow Toby."

He tore out the door, yanked it closed behind him, and sprinted down the driveway.

If he got to the dog fast enough, maybe he could prevent him from creating any more carnage in his neighbor's garden.

If not?

Jeannette Mason was going to be back on his doorstep.

And she wasn't going to be smiling.

4

The dog had returned.

As Jeannette watched through the window of the tearoom, Toby charged around the side of the structure and hurtled toward the nearest lavender bed.

So much for Logan West's promise to keep him on a leash.

Grimacing at the inadvertent pun, she yanked a broom from the closet.

This was *not* funny.

She might feel a bit sorry for her new neighbor with the sad-looking little girl and rambunctious dog, but she was going to have to pay him another visit and lay down the law.

After all, her business was at stake, and—

"Toby! Get back here!"

Hand on the knob, she paused as Logan West careened into the garden from the direction of her driveway, Molly perched in one arm, a leash clutched in his free hand.

The dog's floppy ears perked up, and he slid to a stop, dancing in place as Logan dashed toward him.

But once the doctor drew near, the pup took off through the lavender bed, weaving among the plants.

Through the open window, Jeannette had no difficulty hearing the conversation.

"Stay here, Molly. I'm going to catch Toby." He set the girl down, keeping tabs on the dog that was watching him from the other side of the rectangular plot.

He started around the bed, pulling what appeared to be a doggie treat from his pocket. "Come on, Toby." He held it out. "See what I have?"

For a moment, it appeared the beagle was willing to be bribed.

Nope.

At the last minute, he bounded to the other side again with a playful yip.

Jeannette set the broom down to watch the antics.

The same scenario replayed twice, with the good doctor getting nowhere.

However . . . the man *was* trying. Hard. Based on the glint of desperation in his eyes, he'd clearly gotten her keep-your-dog-under-control message.

But she doubted he was going to capture the recalcitrant beagle without some help.

Since the little girl wasn't a candidate for that job, it seemed she was elected.

Jeannette opened the door, and three sets of eyes swiveled to her as she stepped outside.

Logan sent her an apologetic look. "I'm really sorry about this. I opened the door for a delivery,

54

and he darted out. I'll have this under control in a minute."

"It may be easier to round him up if we tag team this."

His features flattened—as if he was shocked by her offer. "Uh . . . okay." He glanced around the garden. "Why don't we approach him from the same direction, back him into that corner?" He motioned toward the terrace behind her adjacent L-shaped house. "Eventually he'll try to make a break for it, but if we confine him enough, one of us should be able to grab him when he tries to get past."

"Sounds like a plan."

She followed his lead, and with a fair amount of maneuvering, they managed to get Toby where they wanted him.

But the beagle was one smart pup.

Once he realized he was being set up, he made his break toward the weakest link in the two-person barricade.

Her.

She lunged for him as he drew close, seized the twenty-plus-pound mass of zooming fur, and promptly lost her balance.

Next thing she knew, she was sitting on her rump, the wriggling dog in her lap.

An instant later, her neighbor was beside her. He clipped the leash on Toby's collar and lifted him off, then hunkered down beside her, faint parallel lines etched on his forehead. "Are you all right?"

"Fine."

As she pushed herself to her feet, he took her arm in a firm grip and helped her up.

"Sorry again for all the trouble." He wound the leash around his hand as Toby began pulling. "I'm having an electric fence installed in the backyard next week, so there'll be no more escaping from that direction. And in the future, I won't answer the front door until Toby's secured in the kitchen."

The dog began to howl—almost as if he'd understood every word and knew his days of breaking free were about to come to an end.

"Does he do that often?" She upped her volume as she brushed off her jeans.

"Yeah." Logan massaged his forehead, his expression pained. "I'm going to have to find a training class for him somewhere or I'll end up with permanent hearing loss. There isn't by any chance a place like that in town, is there?"

"Not that I know of. I expect there's one in Coos Bay—but that's a bit of a hike."

"It would be worth it to get the noise under control. Besides, I'll be taking Molly to preschool there in another ten days, anyway."

He'd be taking her.

Where was the girl's mother?

She bit back the inappropriate question.

"For now, you could try giving him one of those treats." She motioned toward his pocket. "He can't bark or howl if he's eating."

"True." He dug one out and fed it to the dog.

Silence descended while Toby chomped.

"I take it you haven't had him long?"

"No. A last-minute addition to the family before we left San Francisco. I hoped a dog would help."

"With what?" *That* question came out too fast to throttle—but if he thought she was being nosy, he gave no indication of it.

Logan checked on the girl, who was watching the proceedings from a distance, and dropped his voice. "Molly's been staying with her grandmother for the past two years, but after Mom died suddenly last December, she came to live with me. It hasn't been the smoothest transition. I've never—" The barking resumed with a vengeance, and he cringed. "The story of my life."

"He *is* a loud one." Jeannette shot the dog a disgruntled look. Couldn't he have stayed quiet another sixty seconds while her neighbor finished his story—and satisfied her curiosity?

"Tell me about it. Imagine being confined in the same house with him 24/7."

She winced. "No thank you. He *is* cute, though."

"Trust me—cuteness doesn't compensate for all the noise." Logan angled toward Molly. "Come on, sweetie. Let's go back to the house."

The child trudged toward them, one finger in

her mouth, the same faded, frayed blanket she'd been clutching two days ago gripped in her hand.

Jeannette studied her as she approached. Her pants and top were mismatched but clean, and her hair had been brushed and secured into a lopsided ponytail. Someone was *trying* to look after her.

Logan?

That seemed like a safe bet.

Which would suggest the mother was AWOL—and could explain why Molly had been living with her grandmother.

Toby skipped around the child as she drew close, and she gave him a cautious, quick pat.

Not much bonding had taken place yet between girl and dog.

Nor did she and Logan seem to be close. The girl didn't appear to be wary of the man, but she kept her distance. Like he was someone she wasn't quite comfortable with or didn't know well.

And that could be the case, if he'd been an absentee father—as his comments suggested.

"We'll get out of your hair and let you get back to whatever you were doing. Sorry again for disturbing you." Logan folded the girl's hand in his and took a step toward the driveway.

"Wait." The impulsive directive spilled out as an idea popped into her mind.

He stopped and shifted toward her, eyebrows arched.

A few beats ticked by as she tried without

success to fathom why she'd wanted to delay his departure.

But whatever the reason, she was stuck now.

As the silence lengthened, she linked her fingers into a tight knot. "I, uh, have something for you, if you can wait a minute."

"Sure. As long as it's not a summons about my dog." A touch of humor glinted in his irises.

Her pulse picked up.

The man had gorgeous baby blues.

"No. Nothing like that. I'll, uh, be right back." She escaped to the tearoom kitchen.

Once inside, she gripped the edge of the counter and forced herself to take several slow, deep breaths.

She shouldn't have stopped him from leaving. It wasn't wise to prolong contact with the threesome next door if she wanted to keep her distance.

But there was no going back at this point.

Her only option was to follow through on her idea and say her good-byes as quickly as possible.

She crossed to the racks where the latest batch of lavender shortbread was cooling. After slipping six of the cookies into one of the cellophane bags she used to package her sweets for the farmer's market, she tied it with a lavender ribbon.

Molly would like that touch. After they ate the cookies, she could tie the ribbon around the stretchy band holding her ponytail in place. Most little girls were partial to ribbons.

But Molly isn't the main reason you're being kind, you know.

She exhaled.

Yeah, yeah. She knew.

Still . . . Logan and Molly were new neighbors—and it was customary to welcome newcomers with a token gift of some kind, wasn't it?

You never made a single overture of friendship to the previous owner, though.

Scowling, she snuffed out the annoying voice in her head.

This was different.

The crotchety old man who'd lived there when she'd moved in should have been the one to extend the hand of friendship to *her*.

Logan, on the other hand, was trying to be an agreeable neighbor.

The cookies were simply a considerate gesture. Nothing more.

Beribboned bag in hand, she returned to the trio on her patio and held out the package. "A belated welcome-to-Hope-Harbor present. It's lavender shortbread—a house specialty. And the pretty ribbon would be perfect for a ponytail." She winked at Molly.

The girl gave her a shy smile.

"Wow." Logan took the bag. "That's very kind of you, after all the trouble my friend here has caused." He tipped his head toward the pup.

"I appreciate your efforts to rectify the situ-

60

ation. I'm sure you'll have it under control soon."

He gave her a one-sided grin and lifted the package. "You want to hang on to these until then—just in case?"

"No. You strike me as a man who keeps his promises."

The levity vanished from his face. "Yeah. Well . . . thanks again."

With that, he tugged on Toby's leash, took Molly's hand, and led his small entourage away.

Furrowing her brow, she watched them until they disappeared around the corner of her house.

Why would he take offense at a compliment?

Clueless, Jeannette returned to the kitchen to bake another batch of shortbread for the taste-of-Hope-Harbor table tomorrow night.

But the familiar chore didn't require much concentration, and her thoughts kept drifting back to the man next door.

While Logan hadn't offered much detail about his situation during their two brief conversations, he'd said enough to intrigue her—and she was dying to know the rest of his story.

However . . . given his obvious commitment to curbing Toby's escape-artist tendencies, the pooch wouldn't give them any further reason to interact.

Plus, the tall hedge screening her property discouraged interaction with her neighbors.

She pulled some butter out of the refrigerator, weighing it in her hand.

That hedge had been a major selling point for her three years ago. The secluded acreage just outside the town limit, along with the new profession she'd chosen, had been designed to help her control—and restrict—her contact with other people.

And the whole setup had worked exactly as she'd hoped.

She had peace and quiet, and everyone respected her wish to live a solitary life. The townspeople were pleasant and gracious, and while they'd made it clear they'd welcome her into their world, no one had pushed her to leave her cocoon.

Except Marci, of course.

But she'd stuck with her original plan—and she'd been 100 percent content to keep to herself and spend most of her days alone.

She measured out the butter, but it was cold and hard. Better let it soften for a while in the warmth of the kitchen or it would be difficult to blend.

Rather than start some other chore, she wandered out and sat at the small café table on her patio. Soon, her lavender plants would begin blooming and she could bring her tea out here in the morning and enjoy the fragrance and quiet.

Her gaze strayed to the empty seat across from her. The three pieces of furniture had come as a set, and she'd never paid much heed to the extra chair.

Yet for some reason today it bothered her.

As did the quiet—although Toby's faint barks were still audible, suggesting he was dragging his feet about going back inside.

Why did the silence suddenly feel heavy rather than peaceful?

And what was that slight twinge in the region of her heart?

Could it be . . . loneliness?

She frowned.

No.

She was past that.

Wasn't she?

Yes.

Squaring her shoulders, she shifted in her seat and put her back to the hedge.

That faint, hollow echo in her heart was simple to explain. The refugee family she was baking for today was on her mind, and she felt sorry for them.

That subtle twinge had nothing to do with a handsome doctor who was trying to cope with a forlorn little girl and a mischievous dog.

It absolutely did not.

Mashing her lips together, she rose and headed back to the kitchen as the faint barks next door ceased at last.

That was her story—and she was sticking to it.

5

Something was burning.

The acrid scent that assailed Logan's nostrils when he opened the front door was his first clue—but the piercing alarm bombarding his ears clinched the deal.

"What the . . ."

Toby yanked on his leash, trying to escape the migraine-inducing screech, and Molly began to whimper as she covered her ears.

"It's okay, sweetie." He had to yell to be heard. "Everything will be fine."

Even if the haze hovering beneath the ceiling suggested otherwise.

What was going on?

He did a quick assessment. The smoke was heavier closer to the kitchen, so—

Kitchen.

The cookies were still in the oven.

That's what was burning.

He tugged Molly and the frantic dog inside. "Wait here." The house might be a touch hazy, but Toby was *not* escaping again.

After closing the front door, he sped to the kitchen.

Tendrils of smoke were seeping out of the oven from around the door.

Logan snatched up a pot holder, yanked on the door handle—and started hacking as a gray billow engulfed him.

Eyes watering, he waved the smoke aside, grabbed the edge of the cookie sheet, and stumbled toward the back door, blinking to clear his vision as he fumbled for the lock.

After several attempts, he managed to twist it, grasp the knob, and jerk the door open.

Once outside, he dropped the pan onto the concrete walk below the porch and took a deep breath.

Another.

But he didn't have the luxury of lingering until his lungs cleared.

A terrified little girl and dog were waiting for him in the foyer.

He propped open the back door, took a fortifying gulp of fresh air, and plunged back in to remove the battery from the shrieking alarm.

Blessed quiet descended.

Except . . .

Why wasn't Toby barking?

Pulse skyrocketing again, he dashed back to the foyer.

Molly was sitting on the floor, face pale, her arms wrapped around the dog, who was nuzzling her neck.

Well.

How about that?

Their cookies might be toast—literally—but

there was one positive outcome from their baking misadventure.

These two seemed to have bonded.

"Is there a fire?" Molly watched him, saucer-eyed.

"No, but our cookies got burned."

"We could eat those." She pointed to the cellophane bag Jeannette had given him, which he'd dropped on the hall table as he sprinted to the kitchen.

"Excellent idea. Are you hungry?"

She gave him her typical shrug.

"Well, I am. Let's get some milk and we'll give them a try."

Try being the operative word.

There wasn't much chance lavender shortbread would offer any serious competition to chocolate chip cookies—but his neighbor's gesture had been thoughtful.

Molly followed him into the kitchen, Toby trotting beside her. She halted in the doorway and wrinkled her nose. "It stinks in here."

"That's from the smoke. But it will smell better soon, now that the door is open." He verified the screen was locked, set the cellophane package on the table, and poured them each a glass of milk.

After taking a seat, he untied the purple ribbon and held it up. "Ms. Mason said you could use this in your ponytail. Want me to tie a bow back there for you?"

Instead of responding, she swiveled her head to give him access.

He sighed.

The child his mother had often called Miss Chatterbox was definitely MIA.

He secured the ribbon with a few deft twists. "Want to see?"

She regarded him in silence for a few moments while she chewed her lower lip, then gave a slow nod.

"Let's look in the bathroom mirror." He stood and reached for her hand, but she skirted around him and disappeared down the hall.

Trying not to take her rejection personally, he followed her to the bathroom, pulled out a hand mirror, and demonstrated how to hold it so she could see the back of her head.

It didn't take her long to get the hang of it, and a tiny smile tugged at the corners of her mouth as she examined her reflection. "Pretty."

"Yes, it is."

"I like ribbons." She fingered the dangling satin strands.

Of course she did. What young girl didn't?

He should have bought her some sooner.

Another lapse as a father.

Logan exhaled.

Would he ever get the hang of this job?

"Why don't we buy you some more ribbons on our next trip to town? Would you like that?"

She shrugged, set the mirror down, and traipsed back to the kitchen.

He raked his fingers through his hair.

If this kept up, he might have to enlist the aid of a child psychologist or counselor.

Back in the kitchen, he pulled out a cookie for each of them and handed hers over. "Let's see if we like these."

After giving his heart-shaped piece of shortbread a skeptical scan, he sniffed it.

Not as pungent as he'd expected.

In fact, the cookie's faint, pleasing aroma didn't smell anything like Gram's cloying, old-fashioned perfume—his only previous contact with lavender.

But could you bake palatable sweets from flowers?

"It's good." Molly had dived into hers with no qualms and was several bites ahead of him.

Question answered—and high praise, coming from a child who exemplified the term "picky eater."

He took a tentative nibble.

Buttery richness dissolved on his tongue, leaving a faint hint of lemon and an undertone of mint.

Whoa.

The cookie was better than good.

It was delicious.

He finished it in three bites and pulled out a

second one as Molly eyed the package. "Want another?"

She nodded.

They ate in silence for sixty seconds, until Molly spoke. "The cookie lady is nice."

"Yes, she is." At the very least.

"Could we go see her again?" Molly took a bite of her treat, watching him.

"I'll have to think about that."

"Why?"

Because Jeannette Mason was too much of a temptation for a man who needed to keep his priorities straight and get his life in order before diving into any new relationships.

But he couldn't tell that to a five-year-old.

"I think she's busy."

"Doing what?"

Of all the topics that could have prompted his niece to start asking questions, why did it have to be this one?

"Well, she grows flowers . . . and makes cookies . . . and runs her tearoom." The "and tearoom" part of her Bayview Lavender Farm sign at the entrance had finally registered as they'd walked home.

Molly's brow puckered. "What's a tearoom?"

"A place where people go to drink tea and eat little sandwiches and fancy cakes."

At least he thought that's what it was.

"Like a tea party?"

"Uh . . . yeah. I guess so."

"Nana and me had tea parties." Her face grew wistful. "They were fun."

His brain began clicking.

If Molly liked tea parties, why not take her to one? See if that would help break down the wall she'd erected between them?

But a whole afternoon of delicate china cups . . . froufrou bites of food . . . lace and lavender and clusters of ladies nibbling and chattering?

He'd rather clean a toilet with a toothbrush.

This isn't about you, West. It's about bonding and helping a little girl through her grief. Suck it up.

Right.

Shoring up his resolve, he took a swig of milk and bit the bullet. "You know, I've never been to a tea party or a tearoom. Do you think we should go to tea at Ms. Mason's?"

A tiny spark of animation lit up her eyes. "Will there be other little girls there?"

"I don't know. It may just be ladies."

She played with the crumbs on the napkin in front of her. "Do you think the cookie lady might have a little girl?"

"I doubt it. I haven't seen anyone else around her place—and I don't think she's married."

"How do you know?"

"She isn't wearing a wedding ring."

"Did you look?"

Was she kidding?

71

Any normal single man would do a ring check on someone like Jeannette within two seconds of meeting her.

However . . . the lack of a ring wasn't conclusive. Some people didn't wear rings these days—especially those who worked with their hands, as she did in the garden and kitchen.

"I noticed." Not a direct answer to the question—but not a falsehood, either.

"I wish I had a friend next door, like I did at Nana's."

"I do too—but you'll meet lots of boys and girls at the preschool I found for you."

"Will they live by us?"

Doubtful, since the program he'd enrolled her in was forty-five minutes away.

Too bad Hope Harbor didn't have anything like that for young children.

"I don't know—but we'll try to find some friends for you here in town too."

"Where?"

"Maybe at, uh, church."

She tilted her head. "Are we going to church?"

"Yeah." He may not have been the most diligent churchgoer these past few years, but now that Molly was a permanent part of his life, he ought to get back in the habit. Children should have a solid grounding in faith—and his mom had taken her every Sunday, as Molly had told him early on.

Besides, it wouldn't hurt him to reach out to

the Almighty for assistance. He could use all the help he could get with this new life he was trying to create.

"This Sunday?"

"Yes." No sense putting it off.

Toby, who'd been blessedly quiet while they ate their cookies, sidled up to his new friend, gave her a plaintive look, and began to whine.

"Can he have a cookie?" Molly petted the dog.

"No. They aren't healthy for him. But you can give him a doggie treat if you want." He fished one out of his pocket and handed it to her.

She held it out to Toby, who nibbled it from her fingers instead of snatching it away with his usual snap. As if he didn't want to scare away his new buddy.

Nice to see some progress between his niece and his dog.

Too bad the same wasn't true about the two of them.

Logan stood and began gathering up the remnants of their snack. "It's supposed to be sunny tomorrow. If it is, we could go to the beach again. How does that sound?"

"Can we take Toby?"

"Sure." He psyched himself up for another game of tag with the playful pup.

She licked her finger and pressed it against the cookie crumbs. "Could we ask the cookie lady to come?"

Logan frowned.

Why would Molly want a woman she'd seen only twice to join them?

He tried not to take offense—but he'd been busting his behind for months trying to build some rapport with his niece. Why couldn't she warm up to him like she had to his neighbor?

Get a grip, West. Be glad she warmed up to someone.

Prudent advice.

He adjusted his perspective.

"Like I said, she's busy." He picked up Molly's empty milk glass.

"She's pretty, isn't she?"

Pretty didn't come close to doing Jeannette justice.

"Uh-huh." And that was all he planned to say on the subject. "Do you want me to read you a story?"

She stared at him. "Now?"

"Yeah."

"It's not bedtime."

"I think we should have a lunchtime story today. Go pick out a book while I finish cleaning up."

She slid off her chair, gave him a wary look, and disappeared down the hall, Toby on her heels.

Saved—for now.

But he had a feeling the subject wasn't closed on his charming neighbor, who intrigued him as much as she intrigued the child who shared his home.

He rinsed out their milk glasses and set them on the counter.

Strange how little the woman had revealed about herself during their two encounters, though.

Like nothing.

He wasn't the type to run off at the mouth, either, but compared to her he'd been almost garrulous.

Was Jeannette merely reserved by nature—or was there more to her reticence than temperament?

As he pondered that question, Molly returned to the kitchen and handed him a book about a fairy princess.

Surprise, surprise.

Not.

He dried his hands on a dish towel and took it from her.

"Let's sit over there." He motioned to the cushioned window seat in the breakfast nook that offered a view of the backyard.

She climbed up beside him, keeping her distance, while Toby settled in at her heels and rested his chin on his paws.

Psyching himself up for another tale of maidens in distress and handsome princes coming to the rescue, Logan opened the book.

But as he began to read, his attention strayed for a moment to the tall hedge that separated his property from Jeannette's—and the words of an old, classic poem played through his mind.

Maybe good fences made good neighbors—but to paraphrase Robert Frost, what was Jeannette Mason walling in . . . or walling out?

6

"What do you mean, you aren't going?" Mariam stopped brushing Elisa's hair and gaped at her son from her seat on the twin bed.

Jutting out his jaw, Thomma propped a shoulder against the door frame and shoved his hands into his pockets. "You heard me. I'm not going. You and Elisa can represent our family."

"The people of this town are throwing this welcome party for *all* of us. What will they think if you don't come?"

"I don't care."

She resumed brushing Elisa's hair, trying to control her anger as she untangled the silky strands and drew them into tiny twin ponytails. "I am ashamed of you, Thomma. I did not raise you to be rude—or ungrateful."

Heavy silence filled the space between them, but she made no attempt to break it.

At last her son spoke, his tone a shade more conciliatory. "I don't know their language anyway. You can speak for me."

Mariam finished off the ponytails with two ribbons. "You don't know it because you haven't tried to learn." She glared at him, then managed to summon up a strained smile as she shifted her attention to her granddaughter. "Elisa, honey, why don't you finish your glass of milk before we leave? It's on the bottom shelf of the refrigerator. I'll meet you in the kitchen in a minute."

After giving them both an uncertain perusal, the girl edged past her father and disappeared down the hall.

"Come in and close the door." Mariam stood.

"I don't want a lecture."

"You need one. Come in."

He remained where he was, every rigid angle of his body communicating defiance.

Well, two could play that game.

She planted her fists on her hips and lifted her chin—but what recourse would she have if he refused to talk with her? He wasn't a small boy who could be forced to sit on the notorious blue chair both of her sons had come to hate after spending more time on it for various minor transgressions during their youth than either liked to remember.

He hesitated, but after she summoned up her fiercest glower, he caved.

Thank you, God!

"I'm not a little boy anymore, 'Ami." He entered and closed the door behind him.

Her lungs kicked back in. "Then stop acting like one." She had no more patience for diplomacy or kid-gloves treatment. "What will Father Murphy—and Reverend Baker—think if you don't show up? And why would you want to hurt the feelings of the wonderful people from their churches who arranged for us to come to America and gave us all this?" She swept a hand around the room.

"I'm not in the mood to be sociable."

"Neither am I. But we have an obligation to be thankful—and to show our appreciation."

His shoulders stiffened. "I don't like taking charity."

"You would prefer to have remained in that camp?"

Color suffused his cheeks. "Of course not."

"Then stop letting pride color your judgment. Take what has been generously offered and seek opportunities to repay the debt. Become part of this community. Contribute. Perhaps not with money in the beginning, but we can find other ways to give back. And one day we may be in a position to help someone else as we are being helped."

He expelled a breath. "It will be awkward. I won't be able to communicate with anyone."

"Yes you will. Susan has promised to come and translate for us. Father Murphy told everyone we don't speak English, so no one is expecting us to give a speech or have a long conversation. All we have to do is be there, greet people, and say thank you."

"I don't even know how to do that."

"It's easy." She pronounced the words in English. "Try it."

He made an attempt.

"See? It's not hard. We can learn this language."

"Who will teach us, now that the woman who had agreed to help backed out?"

"Father Murphy said he will find someone else. But I have Susan's cell phone number, and she's willing to translate until we learn enough to get by on our own."

He pinched the bridge of his nose. "I don't know how I'm supposed to do this job they lined up for me if I can't speak the language."

Ah.

Another worry that was weighing on his mind.

"You'll be fine. Father Murphy said the man who owns the charter boat knows a few words of Arabic—and sign language can be very effective. Now go put on a clean shirt and comb your hair."

"We're going to stick together, right?"

"Yes."

Three beats ticked by.

"Fine. I'll go—but I'll be glad when it's over." He twisted the knob and crossed the hall to his room.

As his door clicked shut behind him, Mariam sank back onto the bed.

Her son wouldn't be any more glad to have this over than she would be. Meeting a roomful of strangers—even kind ones—was daunting.

What if they made a bad impression, and everyone was sorry they'd sponsored a refugee family?

What if the support dried up before they became self-sufficient?

What if no one liked them or wanted to be their friend?

What if . . .

Mariam cut off the litany of doubts.

It was too late for second thoughts. They were here now, and she had to let go of her worries. Give them to God instead of letting them demoralize her. He had brought them here for a reason—and in time, he'd reveal it to them.

Until then, it was up to her to be the anchor this family desperately needed.

Even if the confidence she projected in their presence was more show than reality.

Maybe she'd skip out after all.

From the driver's seat of her Civic, Jeannette tapped a finger against the wheel and surveyed the Grace Christian fellowship hall.

She'd dropped off her contribution late yesterday—and she *had* had a full day at the tearoom. A long soak in a lavender-scented bath would be far preferable to attending this shindig.

Except when Marci had called this morning to thank her for the shortbread, the woman had managed to coax a tenuous promise out of her to show up tonight.

The *Herald* editor should have been a politician.

Heaving a sigh, Jeannette picked up her purse.

Honoring her promise didn't have to take long. All she had to do was say hello to the guests of honor.

Halfway up the walk to the hall, she slowed as the door opened.

Charley emerged, laughter and music spilling out behind him.

"Evening, Jeannette." He waved at her.

"Are you leaving?" Her spirits took an uptick. If he was cutting out already, her quick departure wouldn't be such an anomaly.

"No. I'm going over to the truck to whip up another batch of mini tacos. This is a hungry crowd—and no one's rushing to leave."

Not what she wanted to hear.

Jeannette dredged up a smile. "I'm not surprised your tacos are disappearing."

"Thank you. And your shortbread is also a hit. The little girl from the family we're sponsoring has taken several pieces." He touched the brim of his Ducks cap. "See you when I get back with my next batch of tacos."

No, he wouldn't. She intended to be long gone before he returned.

But she didn't bother to correct him as he moseyed toward the wharf.

Psyching herself up for the crush of people inside, she pushed through the door.

Based on the shoulder-to-shoulder crowd, it

seemed every single person in Hope Harbor had turned out to welcome the Shabo family.

And that worked to her advantage.

She could edge through the clusters of people, find the guests of honor, say her piece, and slip away without anyone noticing.

Tucking her purse against her, Jeannette began to weave through the mob toward the food tables near the front of the room, where she assumed the family was stationed.

Less than ten feet from her destination, a hush fell over the crowd.

Pausing, she rose on tiptoe.

Drat.

Father Murphy and Reverend Baker had separated from the crowd and were ushering the small family toward the stage.

Apparently she'd arrived just in time for the official welcome.

Jeannette cast a longing glance behind her.

The crowd had surged forward, closing up all of the gaps. Trying to backtrack now would draw too much attention.

She was stuck.

Resigned, she refocused on the elevated platform at the end of the room.

Reverend Baker took the mike first, offered a brief welcome, and handed the program over to Father Murphy.

In his usual effusive manner, the padre seconded

the welcome, offered a prayer, and introduced the family.

As he talked, Jeannette studied the Shabos, matching up the bios she'd read in the church bulletin to the real people.

Mariam, the matriarch, was fifty-three . . . but with her gray-streaked hair, lined face, and slightly stooped posture, Jeannette would have put her closer to seventy.

Understandable, given all she'd been through. The horrors—and losses—she'd endured would exact a huge physical toll on anyone.

The strain was evident in her son Thomma too. Like his mother, he appeared to be older than his age. The twenty-nine-year-old was far too thin and had a somewhat shell-shocked appearance. He acknowledged his intro with a slight dip of his chin, but unlike his mother, didn't offer a smile.

Again, understandable. There hadn't been much happiness in his life in the past couple of years.

As she turned her attention to his daughter, Jeannette's lips curved up. Holding tight to a Raggedy Ann doll and her grandmother's hand, Elisa was taking everything in with wide eyes.

Jeannette squinted, scrutinizing the child as an odd sense of déjà vu swept over her.

She'd never seen the girl before, yet Elisa reminded her of someone . . .

Wait.

It was Molly.

The two children didn't resemble each other in the least, but both had the same sad, somewhat lost demeanor.

A sudden burst of applause jolted Jeannette back to reality, and she joined in the hearty welcome the town was giving the family.

They huddled a bit closer to each other during the ovation, as if they were uncomfortable being in the spotlight. Father Murphy must have sensed that too, because he wrapped up the formalities quickly and let the family blend back into the crowd.

This was her opportunity to say hello and exit.

Jeannette worked her way through the crowd, returning greetings but maintaining a steady forward pace.

As it happened, her timing was ideal. When she broke through the throng, the family was alone except for a fortyish blonde woman she didn't recognize and Father Murphy.

"Jeannette! Nice to see you." The priest beamed at her and moved forward to clasp her hand between his. "Marci said you might come. I've already sampled your shortbread—twice—and our guests have had a taste too. Have you met them yet?"

"No. I was hoping to now."

"Come, let me introduce you." He drew her forward, mentioning that she'd baked the shortbread as he did the formalities. The blonde woman translated as he spoke.

"Happy to meet you." Mariam spoke in heavily accented English. "Alkukiz . . ." She looked to the woman the priest had introduced as Susan and raised her eyebrows.

"The cookies."

Mariam nodded. "The cookies good. Thank you."

"You're welcome."

Thomma extended his hand too. "Thank you." The man struggled even with that simple phrase.

Reverend Baker's warning to the congregation that the family's English was rudimentary hadn't been an exaggeration.

"My pleasure." She dropped to one knee, smiled at the girl, and pointed to herself. "Jeannette." Then she rested her hand on the child's arm. "Elisa."

Elisa's mouth bowed slightly, and the girl leaned forward to touch her cheek. "Pretty."

Warmth radiated through Jeannette. "Thank you." She gave the child's fingers a gentle squeeze and stood.

"There you are!" Marci materialized at her elbow, camera in hand. "I've been trying to get photos of everyone who contributed to the Taste of Hope Harbor table. Do you mind if I take a quick shot of you with the family?"

"No . . . I suppose not." A photo shouldn't delay her departure too much.

Marci took several and zipped off again.

"She's a dynamo, isn't she?" Father Murphy

grinned as he watched the redhead plunge back into the crowd.

"That's an understatement. Well . . ." Jeannette pulled out her keys. "I was sold out today, and I have another full house tomorrow. I'm ready to call it a night."

"It was kind of you to stop by after working all day. And much appreciated. I know the large turnout will help the family feel welcome."

"I hope so. After everything they've been through, they deserve all the support and compassion we can muster."

"I agree. I'm glad God gave us the opportunity to serve him in this way."

Reverend Baker beckoned the priest, and Jeannette said a fast good-bye.

After plowing through the crowd again, she made a beeline for the exit, stopping at the door to give the room one final sweep.

It was difficult to see much, but if she stood on tiptoes she could catch a glimpse of Thomma. No doubt Mariam and Elisa were close by. They'd stayed tight while she talked to them too, which wasn't surprising. The three of them were the only survivors in their family—and after enduring a significant loss, it was normal to stick close to the people you had left.

If you had any left.

A pang echoed in her heart, and Jeannette pushed through the door, into the fresh air.

Mariam and Thomma and Elisa had faced many challenges—and would certainly face many more as they adjusted to their new life in Hope Harbor—but at least they had each other to lean on. They weren't venturing into an unknown future alone.

That was a huge gift.

Her vision blurred, and Jeannette clenched her teeth, blinking away the film of moisture.

She would *not* get maudlin.

Tonight wasn't about her. It was about a family in desperate need of some TLC. And she'd done her share.

Sort of.

It didn't take much effort to bake a few dozen shortbread cookies and drop by to say hello.

But plenty of people had signed up to assist the family on an ongoing basis. They'd be well taken care of.

And now that she'd done her duty, she could slip back into her safe, quiet—solitary—life and the comforting routine that ordered her days. No further involvement with the immigrant family who now called Hope Harbor home . . . or a neighbor who seemed in over his head with a woebegone little girl and mischievous dog . . . was necessary.

From this moment on, she would retreat back into her solo world—and shore up the walls around her heart to keep any insidious emotions lurking around the edges from breaching her defenses.

7

What was that delicious scent?

As Logan drove down Dockside Drive after church on Sunday, the tantalizing aroma wafting through his window set off a rumble in his stomach.

He should have eaten a real breakfast, but getting Molly dressed, feeding her, and corralling Toby in the empty bedroom where he could do as little damage as possible during their absence had taken far longer than he'd expected.

And the untoasted bagel he'd grabbed as they left the house and scarfed down in the car was long gone.

"Are you hungry, sweetie?" He tossed the question over his shoulder, watching Molly in the rearview mirror.

She sniffed and peered through her window toward the wharf. "Yes."

He slowed as he approached the end of the street and identified the source of the appetizing aroma—the white truck he'd noticed on previous trips to town, the word *Charley's* emblazoned in colorful letters above the serving window.

On his past drive-bys, the window had been shuttered.

Today it was open.

And whatever Charley was cooking, he wanted some of it.

"Let's stop and see what that smell is." He eased back further on the gas pedal and scanned the wharf for a parking spot.

There wasn't a space to be had in front of the row of shops facing the marina—but as he circled around at the end of the street, a car pulled out of one of the few angled parking spots by the tiny park with the white gazebo.

"This must be our lucky day." He swung in, and two minutes later he had Molly free of her restraints.

Taking her hand, he led her to the line in front of the truck.

She rose on tiptoe, trying to see the serving counter, but he had the height advantage—and a clear line of sight to a ponytailed man who appeared to be Mexican working behind the counter.

Logan sniffed again.

The aroma wasn't a perfect match for Mexican food—but some of the same spices were being used.

Uh-oh.

Given how picky Molly was, spicy Mexican fare wasn't likely to appeal to her taste buds.

Maybe the guy would have some plain chicken for her.

"I bet this will be good." He gave her hand an encouraging squeeze.

"It *is* good." The woman in front of him smiled down at Molly. "If you've never been to Charley's, you're in for a treat. He makes the best fish tacos on the West Coast."

Logan smothered a groan.

No way would Molly touch a taco, let alone one with fish in it.

He'd have to fix her a sandwich once they got back to the house.

As the woman resumed her conversation with her companion, Molly wrinkled her nose. "I don't like fish."

"I know. I'll give you lunch at home." But he wasn't leaving here without some tacos for himself.

And if the guy made other versions besides fish, some plain chicken could still be an option.

While they waited their turn, Molly amused herself by watching the antics of two seagulls who were strutting around like they owned the place.

Despite the line and the relaxed conversation the cook had with every single patron, in less than ten minutes they were at the window.

Since there wasn't a menu posted on the side of the truck, he surveyed the wall behind the man.

No bill of fare there either. Instead, the space was covered with layers of pictures—all drawn by children, based on the crayoned stick figures that peopled them.

The man with the gray ponytail gave them a megawatt smile. "Good day, folks. Welcome to Charley's. You two must be hungry for tacos."

"I am." Logan nodded to Molly. "Some of us aren't partial to fish. Do you have a chicken version?"

"Can't say I do, because I don't. My specialty is fish tacos—a different version every day." The man rested his forearms on the counter and leaned down, giving Molly his full attention. "Hello, little lady."

"Hello." She studied him. "I have a ponytail too."

"I see that—and with a pretty ribbon. Purple's one of my favorite colors."

"Mine too."

"I knew you were partial to purple the minute I saw you." He winked. "Logan here says you don't like fish. Is that right?"

"Yes."

"I bet you'll like mine. It's different than any you've ever eaten. People say I have a magic touch." He flexed the fingers of his empty hand, reached behind his ear, and withdrew a shiny penny. After inspecting it, he passed it to her. "Can't imagine where that came from—but I think it's a lucky coin meant for you. Would you like to try a bite of my fish?"

She looked from him to the penny . . . and back again. "I-I don't know."

"I'll tell you what. If you don't like it, you can spit it out on the sidewalk and Floyd or Gladys will eat it." He motioned to the seagulls who were hovering nearby. "Right, you two?"

Both gulls squawked. Like they were answering him.

Logan stifled a grin.

As if.

Without waiting for a response, Charley moved to the grill, sprinkled some seasoning from a large unmarked container on the sizzling fish, and handed a small piece down to Molly on a napkin. "Tell me what you think of that."

She gave the offering a dubious scrutiny but finally picked off a section and nibbled at it.

Her eyes widened. "This is real good." She finished off the rest in a single bite. "Like those flower cookies the lady next door made."

"Two orders of tacos, coming right up." Charley set more fish on the grill and tossed some onions and red peppers on the sizzling griddle. "You wouldn't be talking about that tasty lavender shortbread Jeannette bakes, would you?"

Logan frowned. "How do you know she's our neighbor?"

For that matter, how had this stranger known his name?

Charley chuckled. "There's only one lady in

93

town I know of who bakes cookies with flowers."

Oh.

There was that.

As for knowing his name—it was possible he'd heard the new doctor in town had bought the place next to the lavender farm or read the brief article in the local paper.

"Nice woman." Charley went back to stirring the veggies, flipping the fish, and laying some corn tortillas on the grill. "I had a pleasant chat with her this morning as she was leaving the early service at Grace Christian."

So the taco chef knew his neighbor.

Would the man be willing to share a few tidbits about her?

"Seems to be. We've talked twice." He kept his tone conversational. "Does she run the farm alone?"

"Yes. Moved here about three years ago, cleared an acre of the property, built the beds, and planted every one of those lavender starts by herself. She puts a ton of TLC into that place."

No wonder she'd been upset by Toby's destructive digging.

"That's a big job for one person to take on. She must not have much downtime."

"Could be that's how she likes it."

Logan squinted at him.

Why would a person *want* to be that busy . . .

unless they had no other interests—or people—in their life?

Is that what Charley was implying?

Could he drill deeper without sounding nosy?

"She must not have many personal obligations." If there was a more discreet way to ask about the woman's relationships, it eluded him.

"If you mean family-type responsibilities, I believe that's true."

"Sounds lonely."

"I expect it is." Charley finished assembling the tacos, added some more of whatever seasoning was in that container, and wrapped them in white paper. "But sometimes people need a nudge to realize what they're missing. Here you go." He slipped the order in a brown bag and slid it across the counter.

"How much do I owe you?" He pulled out his credit card.

"No charge. First order for newcomers is always on the house. But keep this in mind for future reference." He tapped a small "cash only" sign that was taped on the side of the serving window.

"Seriously? No plastic?"

"There's too much plastic in the world already. I like to keep things simple—and real."

Not a bad philosophy.

Logan put his wallet away. "If these taste half as good as they smell, you'll have two new

95

regular customers. And thank you for the gratis dinner. This was a pleasant surprise."

"Happy to do it. As you'll discover, this town is filled with unexpected blessings." Charley flashed his white teeth again, and once more leaned on the counter to talk to Molly. "I hope to see you again soon. Maybe you can draw a picture for me to add to my collection." He swept a hand over the wall behind him.

"Would you put it up there?"

"I'd be honored. What would you like to draw?"

Her expression grew wistful. "A friend."

"That's a wonderful idea. Sometimes if we draw what we wish for, the wish comes true."

"Really?"

"Yes. Right, Floyd?" He addressed the seagulls again.

One of them squawked, while the other cackled.

"Can you talk to birds?" Molly gawked at the man, her fingers clenched around the shiny penny.

"I talk to everyone."

"Do they talk back?"

"If they're in the mood to chat."

Logan's lips twitched.

This guy was a character.

"You two enjoy those tacos." Charley straightened up and spoke over Logan's shoulder. "Be with you folks in a sec."

They must be holding up the line.

Logan took Molly's hand. "Thanks again for the lunch."

"Happy to do it. Welcome to Hope Harbor. I'll be waiting for your picture, Molly." With that, he shifted his attention to the next person in line.

They walked back to the car in silence, Logan picking up the pace as the mouthwatering aroma set his taste buds tingling.

As he pulled away from the wharf, he glanced at his passenger in the rearview mirror.

Molly remained focused on the taco stand.

Understandable.

With his magic tricks and animal friends, Charley was an intriguing personality.

He was also informative.

Logan hung a left.

In a handful of minutes, he'd learned more about his neighbor than he had during his two encounters with her.

But the new information had only generated other questions.

Like . . . why had she moved here—alone?

Why had she tackled such a huge project—alone?

Where had she come from—and who had she left behind?

What did she do in the meager free time she had—and why did she prefer to have so little of it?

He swung onto Highway 101.

Perhaps, in the weeks ahead, he'd discover some of those answers.

And when he did, might those answers lead to one of the unexpected blessings the taco man had said were standard fare in Hope Harbor?

Logan gave a soft snort as he accelerated toward home.

Entertaining such a fanciful notion was as foolish as the idea that drawing a picture could conjure up a friend.

Yet . . . somehow both had seemed plausible while they'd been speaking with Charley.

And for whatever reason, the tiny spark of hope that had ignited in his heart during their visit with the taco man refused to be extinguished.

> Many thanks to all who contributed to and attended the welcome party for the Shabo family last night. If you know of anyone who has experience teaching English, please contact Reverend Baker ASAP. The graduate student who had volunteered to instruct the Shabos had an unexpected offer of a summer internship in Europe and won't be able to assist.

Jeannette set down her mug of tea and reread the short notice in the church bulletin she'd brought home from services this morning.

The Syrian family had no one to teach them English?

This was a disaster.

Without language skills, they'd have huge difficulty functioning on their own and assimilating. That, in turn, would lead to a feeling of isolation.

A demoralizing situation for anyone, but far worse for a family already reeling from loss and trying to adjust to the shock of living in a place that was a world away—in every sense—from the home they'd left behind.

Jeannette pulled the tea bag out of the hot water before the brew got too strong and took a sip.

Chamomile was always comforting.

But less than usual today, with the faces of the family she'd met at last night's party strobing through her mind.

Based on her short encounter with them, they all appeared to have an extremely limited grasp of the language—and they couldn't hire a translator to shadow them day and night.

You could tutor them, Jeannette.

At the silent prod, her heart skipped a beat.

Yes, she could.

Who better to step forward than a former teacher who'd once volunteered to coach immigrants on language skills?

She picked up her mug. Wrapped her fingers around the warmth that had seeped through the ceramic. Read the inscription on this remnant from her old life, a gift from her parents on her twenty-first birthday.

The Best Is Yet To Come.

Pressure built in her throat.

That was how Mom and Dad had lived life, with optimism and hope and eager anticipation.

It was how they'd hoped she'd live her life too.

And she had—until the day her world changed forever.

Jeannette ran her finger around the once-smooth rim that was now marred by a couple of chips. Eyed the faint stains inside that refused to come off no matter how hard she scrubbed. Reread the sentiment that had faded a bit—on the mug, and in her heart.

Skimming the notice in the bulletin again, she took another sip of tea.

"Ignoring an obvious need would be wrong."

As Charley's comment replayed in her mind, guilt tugged at her conscience.

But that was silly. The man had been talking about tacos.

Hadn't he?

She sighed.

Hard to tell with the philosophizing artist.

Whatever his intent, though, the statement fit this situation.

The truth was, she could spare a few hours a week to help the Shabo family learn English.

And it wasn't as if she had to make a personal

investment. If she guarded her heart, a bit of tutoring shouldn't be a problem.

Still . . . there was a risk. As experience had taught her, she had a tendency to get too involved in the lives of her students.

Cradling the mug in her hand, she leaned back in her chair.

Maybe she should mull over the idea rather than dismiss it outright. That way, if she decided not to follow through after careful consideration, there might be less guilt. It would be a rational, rather than an emotional, choice. In fact, if she waited a day—or two—it was possible someone else would volunteer and she'd be off the hook.

Yes.

That was a sound plan.

Jeannette pushed back her chair and rose. Her tearoom guests would be arriving in two hours, and several chores remained on her prep list. That would keep her hands—and her mind—occupied for most of the day.

She pinned the church bulletin to her corkboard and detoured into her office to check her voicemail for any last-minute cancellations.

The light was blinking, and the digital display indicated there was one message.

She pressed play.

"Jeannette—Logan West here. After we saw you on Friday, I explained to Molly that you ran a tearoom. I have no idea if what you do is appropriate for children her age, but if it is, I'd like to bring her next weekend, assuming a reservation is available. Either day is fine. You can call me on my cell."

As he recited the number, Jeannette stared at the wall.

Logan West wanted to come to tea?

Another unsettling surprise on this Sunday.

She replayed the message and jotted down his number, then flipped open her reservation book.

There was one opening on Saturday, thanks to a cancellation.

Fate—or coincidence?

No matter.

Logan was simply another customer. He'd come to tea, eat her scones and savories and sweets, and disappear back behind the tall hedge after it was over.

Yet the mere thought of the handsome doctor sitting in her tearoom released a swarm of butterflies in her stomach.

How ridiculous was that?

Huffing out a breath, she left his number in the office and headed for the tearoom kitchen. She'd deal with his reservation later.

Like she'd deal with the item in the bulletin later.

The decision on the tea, however, was a no-brainer.

Of course she'd accept his reservation. Turning away a paying customer wasn't smart business—even if having him on her turf made her uncomfortable for reasons she didn't care to analyze.

The tutoring gig was less cut-and-dried.

She knew what she *should* do—but she wasn't yet ready to commit.

Jeannette picked up her mug to take one last sip before plunging into the final preparations for today's guests.

But the brew had gone tepid—unlike her life, which was heating up.

Too bad the reverse wasn't true. A tepid life was preferable to tepid tea any day.

Trouble was, she had the strangest feeling that trying to control this situation was going to be a losing battle.

And for a woman who'd vowed not to get tangled up in other people's lives, that was flat-out unnerving.

8

Molly was a mess.

As the preschool director brought her out by the hand to the reception area, the girl's puffy red eyes, blotchy face, and quivering lower lip spelled misery in capital letters.

Logan's stomach kinked.

What on earth had happened during her orientation day to cause a meltdown so severe the director had called him at noon on this Monday to come and pick her up?

Laura Wilson offered him an apologetic look as she approached. "I'm sorry we had to send out an SOS. That's a rare occurrence."

"No problem." He knelt in front of Molly and brushed some wisps of hair back from her tear-stained cheeks. "Hey. It's okay, sweetie. I'll fix whatever's wrong."

She hiccupped a sob and clutched his hand with her tiny, cold fingers. "I want to g-go home."

"That's where I'm taking you."

"And I don't want to c-come back here. I don't like this p-place." Another tear trailed down her cheek.

That didn't make sense.

The school had first-rate credentials. On his tour the staff had appeared to be attentive, the children happy. The facility was well-equipped and spotless.

It had seemed ideal.

"Mr. West . . . perhaps we could talk for a moment over there?" The director indicated a small seating area in the corner. "Or we could schedule a phone call later in the day."

Waiting to hear what had caused this disaster wasn't an option.

He stood, resting one hand on Molly's shuddering shoulder. "We can talk now. Do you have a few picture books Molly could page through while we chat?"

"We have a whole library. Give me two minutes." She disappeared back through the secure door.

He dropped to one knee again. "What happened, sweetie? Was someone mean to you this morning?"

"No."

"Did you fall down or get hurt?"

"No."

"Did the other children play with you?"

"I didn't want to play."

"Why not?"

Her voice dropped so low he had to lean close to hear her answer. "I was s-scared."

Logan frowned. "Why were you scared?"

"I was 'fraid m-maybe you wouldn't c-come back."

The kink in his stomach tightened. "I told you

I would. And I always do what I say, don't I?"

"Y-yes—but Nana said she'd take care of me too . . . and then she went a-away." She clutched his hand again, her grip surprisingly strong, desperation radiating from her quivering frame. "I don't want to stay here. I want to stay at your house. Please."

The door clicked behind him, signaling the director's return.

How to respond?

Hard as he tried to think of a reassuring reply, nothing came to mind.

The truth was, he had to work—and there were no preschools in Hope Harbor . . . or anywhere near the urgent care center . . . that would allow him to run over between patients and on his lunch hour until Molly was satisfied he was close at hand and could be there in minutes if she needed him.

"I'll tell you what. Let me talk to Ms. Wilson, and we'll work this out on the ride home." He shifted toward the woman, and she handed him the picture books. He led Molly to a chair where she could see them but not hear their conversation. "I'll be right over there." He indicated the chairs. "In a few minutes we'll go home and have lunch. Okay?"

She sniffled, gauged the distance between herself and the chairs, and nodded.

He followed the director over and took a seat

facing Molly, while the woman claimed one angled toward him.

"Again, I apologize for interrupting your day. We tried everything in our repertoire to console Molly, but nothing worked. Rather than further traumatize her, I made the call to have you come and pick her up."

"No apology necessary. But I don't understand what happened. Molly was in preschool in San Francisco for three months prior to our move here, and while I saw a touch of separation anxiety at the beginning, it was nothing like this."

Truth be told, it had been far easier than he'd expected. From the day he'd brought her back to the West Coast with him after his mother's funeral, she'd been docile and quiet and self-contained.

Maybe too much so, in hindsight.

She'd always done everything he'd told her to, but none of his attempts to win her trust and affection had produced results. No matter what he tried, he hadn't been able to bridge the distance between them.

Even getting a dog hadn't been the instant magic elixir he'd hoped it would be—though that, at least, was beginning to show results.

"Children can be very upset by disruptions in their world—and the more disruptions there are, the bigger the impact. It becomes harder and harder for them to adjust. Many children become clingy when their world is shaken. Have you noticed that sort of behavior recently?"

"No. Just the opposite."

The woman's brow knitted. "You mentioned Molly was in preschool for three months in San Francisco. Where was she before that?"

"With my mother, in a small town in Missouri. Mom died four months ago, and I brought her to live with me."

"I saw on the application that you're her uncle. May I ask about her parents?"

"Her mother was never in the picture after she was born." There was more to that story, but why share the details? "My brother had full custody. He tried raising Molly alone for the first two years, but he was in the military, and once he was deployed, he and Mom agreed it would be better for her if she stayed in Missouri." Logan swallowed. "He was killed in the Middle East a year ago."

The woman's features softened. "I'm so sorry for your losses."

"Thank you. I promised him I'd take Molly if anything ever happened to him and Mom couldn't be her guardian—but to be honest, I never thought I'd have to make good on that pledge."

"Had you and Molly spent much time together before she came to live with you?"

"No."

The woman glanced at his niece, who was watching them, finger stuck in her mouth. "After hearing your story, I can see why she's having some trouble. People she loved are disappearing from her life, she's been uprooted twice in less than six months, and she's living with a relative she barely knows. That would be stressful for anyone, let alone a five-year-old."

Yeah, it would.

But how was he supposed to fix this problem? He'd already changed his whole life to try and give her a more stable existence. Taken a new job with more reasonable hours, bought a house in a small town more conducive to raising a child than a large city like San Francisco, even thrown a dog into the mix. He read her fairy princess stories, was taking her to tea, catered to her food preferences. What more could he do?

Logan massaged his temple, where a jack-hammer was revving up. "I have no idea where to go from here—and I don't have long to resolve this."

Like seven days.

At this hour next week, he'd be on the job at the urgent care center.

"I understand." The woman linked her fingers in her lap. "You might want to consider a more inti-mate daycare arrangement. Perhaps you could find someone who could come to your home, or who watches only a couple of children in *her* home."

"Can you recommend anyone? I'm new to the area and haven't met many people yet."

"I wish I could, but it's against our policy—for liability reasons."

Yeah, he knew all about liability. Malpractice insurance was astronomical.

"Any other suggestions?"

She tipped her head. "If you're a churchgoer, that could be a resource. Pastors often know of reliable people who are interested in that kind of work. Of course you'd still want to vet anyone you plan to hire."

A tall order to fill in one week.

But that wasn't Laura Wilson's problem.

He stood, and she followed suit as he extended his hand. "Thank you for calling me, and for all your insights."

"I wish I could do more." She returned his shake with a firm clasp. "Molly's a sweet girl, and I know in the appropriate environment she'll thrive."

"Finding that environment will be tricky."

"I hear you. But remember, the best thing you can do for a child whose world has been rocked is love them. Let Molly know you're there for her. Cuddle her. Listen to her. Keep your promises. Eventually, once life settles into a routine, she'll respond to your attempts to win her over."

"I hope you're right. This single-parent gig is more challenging than I expected."

She smiled. "You'll get the hang of it. I talk to dozens of parents a week in this job, and I have positive vibes about you. Once you get the daycare situation worked out and Molly is comfortable, I think the two of you will do fine."

"I appreciate the encouragement."

But as he took Molly's hand and they left the building, the woman's expression of confidence wasn't enough to quell his rising panic.

Finding a daycare arrangement fast that met both his criteria and Molly's needs was a daunting task.

All he could do was pray—and hope an answer came to him sooner rather than later.

Otherwise, he'd be reporting to his first day on the job with a child in tow.

And while his experience and credentials had allowed him to negotiate a number of family-friendly job perks, onsite childcare hadn't been one of them.

Meaning the clock was ticking on finding an arrangement for Molly that didn't add more stress to her already topsy-turvy world.

So Molly was Logan's niece, not his daughter.

Jeannette sat back in her patio chair and reread Marci's *Herald* interview with the new urgent care doctor, which answered some of her questions about her neighbor.

For example—there was no wife . . . or girlfriend . . . or significant other.

Nevertheless, he'd taken on the role of Molly's guardian after his brother was killed in the Middle

East and his mother died suddenly of a heart attack.

She folded the paper and set it on the table, watching an optimistic bee flit from lavender plant to lavender plant—much too early in the season for the sweetness it was seeking. The plants weren't yet ready to nurture a large population of bees.

Kind of like Logan didn't appear ready to nurture a young niece.

Yet he was trying.

Hard.

While he'd played down his sacrifices in the article, it was clear he'd gone above and beyond to honor the promise he'd made to his brother, literally changing his life to do what he thought was best for his niece.

He'd even bought a dog that had become the bane of his existence.

The man was almost too good to be true.

Jeannette rose and wandered down one of the paths between the beds of lavender. The plants were flourishing under her tender loving care—an example of all that could be accomplished with singular devotion.

But she'd voluntarily given up her old life to relocate here and start over, making a choice she believed was in her own best interest.

Logan had upended his life for someone *else's* best interest.

His unselfishness was humbling—and did nothing to assuage the guilt that had been plaguing her since she'd read the appeal in the church bulletin two days ago for an English teacher for the Shabos.

If Logan could change his entire life for one little girl, how could she not offer to spend a few hours a week helping a family who'd suffered unimaginable trauma?

Halting in the middle of the garden, she took a steadying breath and pulled out her cell.

Forty-eight hours had passed since she'd read the appeal in the bulletin for a tutor. If no one had yet stepped forward, she had to fill that role.

Reverend Baker answered on the second ring, and once they exchanged a few pleasantries, she made her offer, giving him a quick overview of her credentials.

After she finished, the line was silent.

"Reverend Baker?"

"Yes. Yes, I'm here. I was just stunned for a moment. I had no idea someone with your background and experience was in our midst. I always think of you as the lavender lady."

"That's what I am now—and I had no plans to revisit my former life. But I understand the urgency of the situation. Unless you've already filled the job?"

"Not that I know of, but I haven't spoken with Father Murphy since Sunday. Let me give him a call and one of us will get back to you ASAP."

"No hurry on my end."

"But a big one on ours. It must be dreadful to live in a place where you can't communicate with the locals. Rectifying that situation is our top priority. Thank you, my dear, for your willingness to take this on. We'll be back in touch—and God bless you."

The line went dead, and Jeannette slid the cell back in her pocket as she headed for her work-shop. She had plenty to do to get ready for the first farmer's market on Friday, and sitting around thinking about her neighbor's sacrifices or the Shabos' plight wasn't productive.

Several minutes later, as she set to work in the small structure that was imbued with the soothing scent of lavender, Father Murphy's name popped up on the screen of her vibrating phone.

Reverend Baker had been serious about an ASAP response.

Either they'd already found someone, or the padre was anxious to sign her up before she changed her mind.

Based on the hollow feeling in the pit of her stomach, it was the latter.

His greeting confirmed that. "Jeannette! I just spoke with Reverend Baker. You are a godsend—and I mean that literally. I was beside myself trying to figure out where to find an English teacher when neither of our bulletins produced any volunteers. I was getting ready to widen the plea to neighboring parishes."

"I'm glad I could help—but please understand, I haven't done this sort of work in more than four years."

"I'm confident your skills will come back once you dive in—like riding a bicycle. How soon can you begin?"

"Uh . . . later this week?" It would take her at least that long to organize a lesson plan—and psych herself up for the job.

"Wonderful! I'll alert the Shabos. I know Susan will be happy to translate as you work out the details of a schedule. Let me give you her number, and I'll pass yours on to her. Do you have a pen handy?"

"Yes." She crossed to the counter, her pulse accelerating. This was happening much too fast. "Ready." Or not.

He recited the number, and she jotted it down. "If you incur any expense, be sure to let us know. We have a fund for reimbursements."

"There isn't usually much cost involved with tutoring."

"Well, your contribution of time and talent is sufficient. We don't expect you to dip into your personal funds too."

"If I incur any major expense, I'll let you know."

"Excellent. And I want you to know I'll be

saying a special prayer for you at all my Masses this week and asking God to bless your work."

"I appreciate that."

More than he'd ever know.

Because as they said their good-byes and the full impact of what she'd agreed to do sank in, a major case of the shakes assailed her.

For a woman who'd vowed to live a solitary life, this was a huge leap.

And a dangerous one.

Hard as she might try to keep the tutoring gig impersonal, the Shabos could end up infiltrating her heart—unless she stayed strong.

Straightening her spine, she fisted her hands.

She could manage this.

All she had to do was be pleasant and professional, help the family learn enough English to get by, and walk away once the job was over.

But in the meantime, she would take every single prayer Father Murphy was willing to say for her.

And add a few of her own.

Molly was crying.

Again.

Stomach twisting, Logan stared at the dark ceiling as her muffled sobs seeped through the wall between their bedrooms, then squinted at the digital clock on his nightstand.

Midnight.

He took a long, slow breath.

So much for the corner he'd thought they'd turned after the fiasco at the preschool yesterday. Even though she'd clammed up again on the ride home, she'd stuck close to him for the remainder of the day. She'd even let him hold her hand while he read her a bedtime story.

Today? Back to square one.

With him at least.

But the friendship she and Toby had forged continued to blossom.

Thanks to her admission yesterday at the preschool, however, he had a better grasp of why she was standoffish.

Fear could be a strong motivator.

And who wouldn't be afraid after all the people you'd loved and trusted to take care of you disappeared? How could you have any confidence it wouldn't happen again?

He totally got that.

Because the truth of the matter was, it could— not that he intended to leave the earthly realm behind anytime soon, but neither had his mom.

So how could he convince Molly it was okay to respond to his love and affection? To let herself love and trust again?

Another strangled sob ripped at his gut, and he swung his sweatpants-clad legs to the floor.

Enough.

He couldn't lie here and listen to her misery

without taking *some* action, even if she was unreceptive.

Pulling on the T-shirt he'd tossed onto his dresser last night, he padded into the hall.

Stopped.

What was he going to do once he entered her room? Nothing he'd tried so far to reach her had worked. Why should tonight be any different?

But if he didn't break through soon, he was going to have to get serious about setting up some counseling for her.

Rubbing his damp palms together, he closed his eyes.

Lord, I know I haven't been your most diligent disciple these past few years, and prayer hasn't been high on my priority list, but if you could help me out here, I'd appreciate it. I can't do this on my own. Please show me how to reach Molly, and give me words that will comfort her.

Flexing his fingers, he continued to her room and paused again.

Her sobs had stopped, but the dim light spilling in from the hall confirmed she hadn't fallen asleep. Though her eyes were closed, the sheet was clenched in her fingers, her body was rigid, and her respiration was too rapid for slumber.

She'd sensed his presence and was trying to hold herself still, hoping he'd go away, as he had last night.

Not happening.

If neither of them were going to sleep, they might as well stay awake together.

He crossed to her bed and settled on the edge beside her. Smoothed back the hair from her damp cheeks. "It's okay to be sad about Nana, sweetie." He tried for a soothing, gentle tone. "And it's okay to be scared about what could happen next. I'm sad and scared sometimes too."

She didn't speak, but a shuddering sigh quivered through her—and her eyelids flickered open.

He waited in silence, stroking her forehead, wrapping the fingers of his other hand around the tiny fist clamped on the bunched sheet.

Several minutes ticked by, the faint clatter of Toby's paws on the kitchen tile the only sound in the house as the pup did one of his nocturnal circuits.

Slowly, in tiny increments, Molly's body began to relax and her breathing evened out.

She was drifting off to sleep.

Logan waited a few minutes, then started to rise.

Instantly she groped for his hand, and her eyelids fluttered open. "Don't go."

Her request was sleep-garbled, more instinctive than intentional, but pressure built in his throat anyway.

All these months, he'd been waiting for her to say something—anything—to suggest she wanted him in her life.

This plea may have been subliminal—but he'd

take it. The subconscious was often a truer barometer of emotions than conscious behavior.

From a practical standpoint, though, he couldn't sit up all night.

He eyed the twin bed. It wasn't designed to accommodate his large frame—but Molly took up only a small part of it, and he could cope with cramped quarters for what was left of this night.

"Can I lay next to you, sweetie? It's kind of lonely in my room."

" 'Kay." She scooted over.

Another step forward.

If she let him stay with her tonight, maybe she'd be willing to sit on his lap tomorrow—or initiate *some* sort of physical affection.

After the past four tense months, any signs of encouragement were welcome.

He released her hand, circled around to the other side of the bed, and climbed in next to her. After a few moments, she scooted a tad closer to him. Not touching, but near enough that he could feel the tiny dent she made in the bed.

Within ten minutes, she was sound asleep.

He wasn't as lucky.

Half an hour later, he was still staring at the dark ceiling. Still trying to determine where to go from here.

Especially if their relationship reverted to the status quo once the sun rose on a new day.

What to do should that happen?

He was clueless.

All he knew with absolute certainty was that he was in over his head—and until he and Molly turned a definite corner, he wouldn't be able to shake the fear that he was sinking fast.

9

He was a miner, not a fisherman.

But when you were brand new in a place that had no phosphate rock to excavate, you took whatever job was offered—at least until you had a chance to get the lay of the land and decide what you wanted to do with the rest of your life.

Such as it was.

Shoulders sagging, Thomma shoved his hands in his pockets as he trod down Dockside Drive. Fortunately, the wharf wasn't far from their apartment, and he'd allowed plenty of time for the walk.

However, if all went well with the new tutor Father Murphy had lined up, he might soon be ready to take his driver's test and put the car the town had given them to use.

The sweet smell of cinnamon tickled his nose, and Thomma slowed to peer into the window of a shop with a striped awning.

It didn't take him long to spot the large tray of buns dripping with icing that was sitting on the counter.

This must be the bakery that had supplied those samples at the welcome party Saturday night.

Two customers were waiting in line as the clerk

slid a spatula under one of the rolls and deposited it into a box.

His taste buds began to tingle.

If he had the money . . . and knew the language . . . and could spare a few minutes . . . he'd buy himself one of those. The small taste he'd had Saturday night had been delicious.

But the bread and hummus and cheese he'd had for breakfast was sufficient. Lingering here was a waste of . . .

"Good morning, my friend."

He turned.

The guy with the gray ponytail who'd provided some of the food on Saturday smiled at him.

"Hello." A recent addition to his vocabulary, courtesy of his mother.

"Tempting, isn't it?" The man indicated the bakery.

Thomma furrowed his brow.

Strange.

The man was speaking English, but he got the gist of the question.

"Yes." That about used up his repertoire of English words.

"Wait here." The man held up one finger, pointed to the sidewalk, and joined the line inside.

The sounds were gibberish—but again, he understood the message.

A minute passed. Two. Thomma scanned the wharf across the street. He had to get going.

Being late the first day on the job would make a bad impression—and it could take a while to connect with the man who owned the fishing boat that was now his place of employment.

"There's always a line at Sweet Dreams in the morning." The taco guy was back, holding out a white box. "Good luck—and enjoy that." He crossed his fingers and motioned toward the wharf.

Again, Thomma got the gist of what the man had said.

Must be due to the body language his mother put such stock in.

"Thank you"—he struggled to remember the man's name—"Charley."

The guy tipped his duck-bedecked cap and continued toward the stand at the end of the wharf.

Box in hand, Thomma crossed the street and gave the waterfront a sweep. Susan had said Steven Roark would be watching for him—but they'd never met, and with all the activity down here at this hour of the morning, they could—

"Thomma?"

He swiveled around.

A tall, thirtysomething man with dark brown hair had come up behind him, silent as a ghost.

"Yes."

The guy gave him a once-over, then stuck out his hand and confirmed his identity, his grip firm. *"Aftark?"* He tapped the box.

"No." This wasn't his breakfast. He pointed toward the taco truck and hoped this man would understand it had been a gift. "Charley."

One side of his boss's mouth rose a fraction as he glanced that direction before striding down the wharf. *"Tueal maei."*

Following the broad-shouldered man's instruction, Thomma fell in behind him. His boss didn't seem like he'd be much of a talker, even if his Arabic was fluent rather than spotty—which was fine. Still, it was helpful he knew a few words.

But where had he picked them up?

Given the difficulty Susan said Father Murphy had encountered trying to find someone to translate for them, not many Americans knew his native language.

Could this man have spent time in the Middle East?

As a soldier, perhaps?

Thomma sized up Roark's confident stride.

Possible.

He had a military bearing and demeanor—and he radiated assertiveness, confidence, and decisiveness. His eyes were sharp too. Intense and discerning.

Whatever his story, Thomma should be grateful he'd been willing to give an inexperienced stranger a job—as his mother had reminded him this morning. The sole required skill, according to Father Murphy, had been the ability to swim.

126

Roark stopped beside a slip where a boat about twenty-five feet long was moored. With one lithe movement, he jumped aboard.

That was *not* a skill Thomma possessed.

As if sensing his hesitation, Roark turned back and held out his hand for the box.

Thomma passed it over. With two hands, he should be able to board without falling on his face.

He managed the maneuver, if not with grace, at least with competence. Once he was on deck, the man handed him the box, moved to the front of the boat, and picked up a large thermos.

Now what?

He stayed where he was, letting his equilibrium adjust to the gentle rocking motion of the craft. It would take some getting used to, but as far as he knew he didn't have an issue with motion sickness—and the slight undulation wasn't hurting his appetite.

Should he go ahead and eat the cinnamon roll that had jump-started his salivary glands, or wait until—

Roark pivoted around and closed the distance between them, a jacket thrown over his arm, a travel mug in each hand. He extended one.

As he took it, Thomma surveyed the dark brew. If this was anything like the weak coffee they'd served at the party Saturday night, he might not be able to stomach it.

Roark sipped from his mug, watching him.

There was only one polite response to the hospitable gesture.

Bracing, he took a tentative swallow.

Blinked.

Now *this* was coffee—thick, strong, and straight, with a hint of cardamom.

It was a taste of home.

This fisherman's usual drink—or a special treat for his new employee?

Before he could try to pose that question in sign language, Roark handed him the lined, waterproof jacket that was draped over his arm.

The man thought he needed a heavier coat?

Why, on such a warm, sunny day?

But he took it.

"Thank you."

The smell of cinnamon wafted up to him from the box, and he set down the coffee and coat. Balancing the treat in one hand, he made a motion of cutting it in half.

Roark hesitated—but after a moment he walked to the back of the boat again, flipped up the lid of a storage compartment, and returned with a knife and some paper napkins.

Thomma cut Charley's gift in half and passed a portion to the man across from him.

Roark took it and lifted his mug. "*Marhabaan bikum fi 'amrika.*"

His boss wasn't the first person to welcome him to America.

But for some reason, hearing the words from this man who'd given a stranger a job . . . holding the gift of a warm cinnamon roll in his hands . . . picturing Elisa sleeping safely in her bed, thanks to the generous people from the two churches in this town . . . brought him a measure of peace that had long been absent from his life.

And as he drank his coffee under the brilliant blue sky on this May morning . . . as he inhaled the salt-laced air . . . a tiny flicker ignited in his heart.

It felt a lot like hope.

Which was dangerous.

After everything they'd been through, it was too soon to lower his guard. To allow himself to believe their troubles were over. Healing would be a long process—and there would surely be many struggles ahead.

Yet the tiny flame continued to burn, despite his efforts to extinguish it.

He focused on the horizon, where the pink glow of morning sky met the indigo hue of the sea, and took a long, slow breath.

Maybe . . . just maybe . . . his mother was right.

Perhaps in time the hurt would diminish and he would appreciate the second chance the three of them had been given.

Right now, that seemed like a remote possibility—and he wasn't going to count on it. His grief was too raw, his loss too fresh.

But if he was meant to thrive in this new country of his, where better for that to happen than in a town whose first name was hope?

This was going to be a challenge.

Jeannette studied her three pupils seated around the kitchen table in the Shabos' apartment.

Mariam was leaning forward, face animated, hands clasped on the polished oak in front of her.

Thomma was slouched in his chair, eyes hooded, shoulders hunched forward.

Elisa was biting her lower lip and holding tight to a Raggedy Ann doll.

The age difference among her students was significant—as was their interest level.

In hindsight, she should have asked Susan to linger at this first lesson instead of assuring the translator she'd be fine. With just forty-eight hours of preparation, she felt as uncertain as she had during her early days of student teaching.

What if Father Murphy was wrong?

What if this *wasn't* like riding a bicycle?

But she was here, and she had to give it her best shot.

Propping up the corners of her mouth, she began with the little girl. "Elisa." She touched the child's arm, then pointed to herself. "Jeannette." She repeated her name and motioned for Elisa to say it.

The girl dipped her chin.

Mariam spoke in Arabic. Elisa peeked at her grandmother as the woman repeated Jeannette's name before reverting to their native language.

Gaze downcast, Elisa played with the ruffle on Raggedy Ann's white apron. "Jeannette."

"Good." Jeannette touched the girl's hand and clapped. "Thomma?"

He sighed and said her name.

Not the most promising start—but even if she only managed to teach them some basic language skills, they'd be better off than they were now.

She pulled out her old laptop. Thank heaven the apartment had Wi-Fi.

After booting it up, she opened the document she'd prepared for them containing links to photos and audio clips with the pronunciation of some common words and phrases that would help them cope with their new life.

Their first session ran for an hour. Elisa lasted longer than she'd expected, but halfway through the youngster's eyes began to glaze. Mariam remained fully engaged until the end, and Thomma appeared to be paying attention despite his reserve.

As she began to wrap up, Jeannette was as exhausted as if she'd spent an entire day on her feet teaching a roomful of rambunctious ten-year-olds.

To signal the end of the session, she closed the lid of the laptop halfway.

Mariam smiled and touched her arm. "Thank you. Good Thursday."

So the woman had retained part of today's lesson from the calendar she'd gone over with them.

Jeannette nodded her approval and motioned for Mariam and Thomma to observe how to shut down the laptop. She repeated the start-up and shutdown, and signaled for Thomma to try.

For the first time, he appeared to be completely engaged.

It didn't take him long to master the procedure—suggesting he'd had some exposure to computers.

Jeannette showed him how to open the document she'd prepared with the links to photos and pronunciation clips. "*Ealayk mumarasa.*"

Surprise registered on their faces—as if they hadn't expected her to make the effort to learn a phrase in their language.

Truth be told, she wasn't certain she'd mastered the pronunciation, but they seemed to understand her request that they practice.

"Okay." Mariam rested her fingers on the computer. "Monday? English?"

"Yes."

She would, indeed, be back on Monday. The three one-hour sessions a week she'd committed to was the bare minimum for a family who could benefit from much more intensive language training.

Digging deeper in her satchel, she pulled out the information she'd gotten from the license bureau. Thankfully, an Arabic version of the written test for a driver's license was available in Oregon, along with some basic study aids. The sooner Thomma could get a license, the sooner the family could stop relying on others for transport.

She handed them to Elisa's father.

He skimmed the heading, flipped through the pages, and gave her a small smile. His first since she'd arrived. "Thank you."

"You're welcome." She rose, tucked her purse under her arm, and walked toward the door.

Mariam followed her and pulled it open. "Good-bye."

"Good-bye." She gave the woman's arm a quick, encouraging squeeze and exited.

Clouds had rolled in during their session, and she picked up her pace as she walked toward her car. The smell of rain was in the air, and she'd rather be safely tucked back in at the farm than inching home through a downpour.

But as she drove past Charley's and the smell of his tacos drifted into the car, she eased back on the gas pedal.

Why not grab an order instead of cooking dinner? Tired as she was from her first session with the Shabos, she ought to treat herself.

Without further deliberation, she swung into an

open parking spot and jogged toward the stand. For once there was no line.

"Hi, Jeannette. I was about to close. I think we're in for some weather."

"I agree. Is it too late to place an order?"

"Never. If you catch me with the window up, I'm cooking." He set about preparing the tacos in his usual unhurried but efficient manner. "How's everything?"

"Okay, I guess."

He regarded her over his shoulder. "That sounds a mite tentative."

"I *feel* a mite tentative."

"How so?"

She frowned. Why had she admitted that? She never talked to anyone about personal subjects.

"Um . . . my routine's been a bit disrupted." True—and generic enough not to offer any real insights about the reasons for her unsettled mental state.

"Change can be unnerving, no question about it." He pulled an avocado out of the cooler and began slicing it. "On the flip side, it can also be invigorating."

"And uncomfortable." She clamped her lips together the instant the admission slipped past them.

Where had *that* come from?

If she wanted to keep her private business to herself, she should shut up.

"I hear you. Reminds me of how I felt many years ago, when I decided to leave my small village in Mexico and my grandmother, who'd raised me. She was all I had."

"If you had reservations, why didn't you stay?"

"Because of what she said one night while we were sitting outside, looking at the stars."

When he didn't elaborate, Jeannette edged closer to the window. "Are you going to tell me the rest of that story?"

"Sure." He grinned, flipped the fish, and laid out the tortillas. "She'd been encouraging me to spread my wings for months, and she brought up the subject again that night. I finally told her how I felt. She took my hand and said, 'Life is a risk, *mi cielo*. Don't let fear stop you from being everything God intended you to be. Go. Learn. Live. Love. What you and I share won't change with geography. It will always shine as bright as these stars—even after I'm gone.' "

Pressure built in Jeannette's throat, and she struggled to find her voice. "That's a beautiful thought."

"Also true. My abuela was a wise woman."

"So you left and launched a new life."

"Yes—and it's been an incredible journey filled with remarkable people who've touched my heart." He began assembling the tacos. "I'm sure you understand. You traveled far from your home and began a new life too."

135

But for very different reasons.

Charley had left his happy home in Mexico reluctantly, in search of his destiny.

She'd run away from the memories of a life that was gone, seeking to distance herself from people—not establish new relationships.

Her vision misted and she dipped her head to search in her purse for her wallet—and hide her emotions. "I do enjoy the lavender farm."

"As you should. It's a lovely, peaceful spot, and you've done a remarkable job with the tearoom. Creating a place of beauty and refreshment, along with products that feed the soul as well as the body, is a worthy occupation." He finished wrapping the tacos in paper and slid them into a bag. "Speaking of the farm—have you had a chance to get to know your new neighbors yet?"

Another subject she didn't care to discuss.

"Yes—thanks to their dog."

"Ah." Charley chuckled. "Toby can be a rascal."

"You know about Toby?" Was there anything Charley *didn't* know?

"Logan and Molly stopped by for tacos on Sunday and we had a long chat. Nice family—in need of a friend, I'd wager. Both of them."

"Once Logan starts his job and Molly's in preschool, finding friends won't be a problem."

"It's always better to have friends closer to home, though."

She scrutinized him as she handed over her money.

Was he suggesting *she* should be their friend?

Hard to tell with Charley. His manner was as pleasant and easygoing as always. That comment could have just been one of the generic platitudes he tended to toss out.

"I expect they'll both have plenty of friends soon." She picked up her bag.

"I wouldn't be surprised. Molly is a loveable child, and Logan—" He winked. "I imagine he'll be quite popular with the ladies in town. I believe he's what you women would call a good catch. Is that the correct term?"

"Yes." And for whatever reason, the notion of Hope Harbor's eligible female population descending on her neighbor wasn't sitting well.

Charley leaned out to check the sky. "I better close before those clouds open up and douse us. You have a wonderful day, Jeannette."

With that, he rolled down the window on the truck.

As if on cue, a raindrop plopped on her nose, prompting her to hurry toward her car.

But once behind the wheel, she sat and stared at the gray horizon.

Begrudging Logan West some female companionship would be uncharitable. And Molly deserved a mother. No doubt her neighbor would be open to friendly overtures.

Maybe even hers.

Except she wasn't in the market for a relationship.

Jamming the key in the ignition, she scowled at the shuttered taco stand.

This was all Charley's fault. She hadn't had any romantic fancies about her neighbor until he'd planted the seed.

Well . . . not many, anyway.

And certainly no conscious ones. It wasn't as if she could control the content of her dreams, after all.

Besides, so what if a certain handsome doctor had made more than a few appearances in her slumbering fantasies? It had to be some subliminal, instinctive female reaction. She might not be interested in a relationship with him, but no woman would be immune to the man's charisma. A few dreams didn't mean a thing.

She pulled out onto Dockside Drive, aimed the car toward home, and did her best to erase any thoughts of the doctor and his niece from her mind. She'd already stepped way outside her comfort zone with the tutoring gig, and she didn't need another disruption in her life.

Especially one that was Hollywood handsome.

Not to mention available.

10

"I appreciate your efforts, Reverend Baker. Let me think about your suggestion." Logan shifted the cell against his ear and massaged his forehead.

After spending countless hours trolling the net for a childcare setup in the area that fit his parameters—with nothing to show for his efforts—the minister had been his last hope.

So much for getting good news on this Friday afternoon.

"I know it's not ideal." The cleric's tone was commiserating. "But I'm afraid that's the best I've been able to come up with after polling the most likely members of the congregation."

"Understood. I'll give you a call later today." As he thanked him again and hung up, Toby began to bark.

The headache he'd been fighting all morning pounded harder in his temples.

What a mess.

The older woman in the Grace Christian congregation who'd offered to watch Molly until he found other arrangements might have to be an interim step—but he'd rather find a permanent solution. If his niece hit it off with her, then was yanked out in a few weeks, they could be right back where they were now—or worse.

At a slight scuffling noise behind him, he twisted in his chair at the kitchen table and looked toward the hall.

Molly was hovering on the threshold of the room, Toby at her side, one finger stuck in her mouth. Again.

Not a positive sign.

Logan relaxed his features. His niece had a remarkable ability to pick up nonverbal clues, and there was no reason for both of them to worry about the fast-approaching deadline for a childcare decision.

He picked up his car keys from the table and jingled them. "Would you like to take a ride into town? If Charley's cooking today, we could have tacos for dinner."

Instead of responding, she disappeared down the hall.

So much for that idea.

Except he had a sudden craving for tacos—and he wasn't in the mood to cook.

They were going to town.

Logan stood, snagged Toby's leash, and snapped it on. No more leaving the pup in the spare bedroom.

How the dog could have done that much damage in an empty room while they were at church was beyond him—but it wasn't happening again.

Now that the electric fence had been installed, training the dog to stay within its boundaries was his top priority. Filling holes in the yard would be much easier than repairing gouges in the drywall.

All he had to do was squeeze three fifteen-minute training sessions a day into his schedule for the next two weeks—on top of working out the daycare issue and starting a new job.

Logan leaned back against the counter, shoulders slumping.

If God was trying to test his mettle, he was doing a superb job of it.

Molly reappeared, a sheet of paper in one hand, her jacket in the other.

Huh.

She must want to go after all.

Would he ever learn to read this child who shared some of his DNA?

"What's that?" He straightened up and motioned toward the paper.

After hesitating a moment, she set her crayon drawing on the table.

Logan gave it his full attention.

The picture featured two figures, both with ponytails, holding hands and wearing dresses. There was a table and two chairs off to one side, two cups on top along with a plate of heart-shaped . . . cookies? The colors of the girls' clothing and the table were bright, and she'd drawn a sun in the sky, but the background she'd filled in was dark.

Hmm.

Too bad he wasn't a psychologist. There was probably a deep meaning here that someone like Laura Wilson could ferret out.

He'd have to rely on his niece's input for clues.

"That's a pretty picture." He smiled at Molly. "Will you tell me about it?"

She considered him, then sidled closer to the drawing. "This is me." She indicated the figure on the left with the reddish-yellow ponytail. "And this is my friend." She touched the other girl, who had darker hair. "We're having a tea party." She traced the table with her finger. "Those are cookies."

"I like this." Except for that dark sky. Keeping his inflection casual, he pointed to the background. "Is it nighttime?"

Her brow puckered. "No. The sun is out. See?" She showed him.

"Now I do."

He wasn't going to get an answer about the sky.

But maybe he didn't need to.

Maybe he just needed to keep loving her until it turned blue.

"Can we go?" She picked up her drawing.

"Yep. I'm all set. Let me help you with your jacket." While yesterday's rain had passed, coolness lingered in the late-afternoon air.

Eight minutes later, as they approached Hope Harbor, the traffic on 101 picked up—and it got heavier after he exited the highway.

Surely there wasn't an end-of-week rush hour in a town this size.

Yet something was going on.

They joined the line of bumper-to-bumper cars crawling toward the wharf—and once he reached Dockside Drive he discovered the reason for the jam.

One block of the two-block-long frontage road had been closed to traffic, and booths had been set up.

Must be some sort of festival.

He squinted at the banner in the distance.

No. Not a festival. A farmer's market.

And it was opening day for the season.

No wonder the place was packed.

"Is this a party?" Molly stretched her neck to see as Toby let out excited yips and hopped around on the back seat.

"Kind of." Savory aromas drifted in his window, along with the sound of laughter and lively music. "Want to go?" He didn't have anything else on his Friday evening agenda—except searching for more daycare options.

An unappealing prospect if ever there was one.

" 'Kay."

Her standard, pithy answer.

"Let's see if I can find a parking place." He followed the line of cars down a side street.

Three blocks later, when he spotted a guy circling the hood of a car toward the driver's side, he mashed down the brake and flicked on his blinker.

Based on the horn blast from behind him, the driver on his tail hadn't appreciated his abrupt stop.

But with parking at a premium, he wasn't giving up this spot.

The man took his sweet time pulling out—but once he did, Logan executed a fast and flawless parallel parking maneuver . . . a skill acquired during his tenure in San Francisco.

He slid out of the car and opened the back door. Molly held tight to her picture as he unhooked her restraints, helped her out, and snagged Toby's leash.

"Let's go to the taco stand first and see if Charley's open for business."

Five minutes later, he had his answer. Charley was cooking—but the line stretched down the sidewalk.

It was going to be a long wait—and patience wasn't a five-year-old's strong suit.

Ten minutes in, when Molly began to fidget, Logan expelled a breath. His heart—and stomach—were set on Charley's fare, but he might have to can the taco dinner and buy some food at one of the booths in the market.

While he debated his options, two seagulls waddled toward them.

Uh-oh.

Logan tightened his grip on Toby's leash. The beagle was always up for a new adventure.

For some reason, though, the dog didn't go berserk as the birds approached. Instead, he plopped onto his haunches and watched them in silence.

Weird.

"Is that Floyd and Gladys?" Molly studied the gulls.

"Could be." All the birds looked alike to him, but if it made her happy to think these were Charley's friends, why not play along?

Wherever the gulls had come from, they kept Molly entertained with their antics, making the long line more palatable.

"Welcome back." Charley flashed his megawatt smile as they at last stepped up to the window. "I'm always happy to see repeat customers." He leaned down, resting his forearms on the counter as he'd done during their first visit. "Hi there, Molly."

"Hi. I drawed you a picture." She held it up.

He took it and gave the rendering a thorough scrutiny. "This is wonderful. I bet you worked hard on it."

"I did."

"I see you drew that friend you mentioned." He pointed to the dark-haired figure.

"Yes." She sighed. "But I haven't found her yet."

"Well, we haven't put this on my wall yet." He rearranged a few of the pictures already on display, pinned Molly's front and center, and turned back to her. "We have to give it a chance to work. You keep wishing too."

"Okay."

"Two orders of tacos?" The man aimed the question at him.

"Yes." Logan pulled out his wallet and counted his money as Charley worked the grill and kept up a steady stream of conversation.

"Here you go." He slid a brown bag across the counter. "Have you been to the farmer's market yet?"

"No. We had dinner on our mind." Logan picked up the bag.

"I hear you. But after you eat, you should stroll through the market. We have it every Friday from four to eight during the summer months, and you'll find all kinds of goodies. You could even pick up some lavender shortbread for dessert."

Logan's spirits took a decided uptick. "Jeannette's here?"

"Every week. Her booth is always popular." Charley motioned toward the sole empty bench on the wharf, where two seagulls were perched. "Floyd and Gladys saved you the best seat in the house for dinner. Enjoy."

"Thanks." Logan took Molly's hand and eyed the bench. Given the number of people milling about, there wasn't much chance it would stay empty until they got there.

But Molly tugged him that direction, and he followed. If someone claimed the bench first, they could always take the tacos home and forget the farmer's market.

Except that would also mean foregoing a visit with Jeannette.

Not happening if he could help it.

Logan lengthened his stride until Molly had to trot to keep up with him.

Happily, the bench remained empty, and as they drew close, the two gulls vacated the seat.

Like they'd been saving it for them, as Charley had said.

Which was crazy.

Whatever the reason they'd lucked out, though, he wasn't going to complain. Eating fabulous fish tacos on a bench with an incredible view was sweet.

And for dessert?

They'd drop by Jeannette's booth, as Charley had suggested.

Also sweet.

He doled out the tacos and bit into his, scanning the festive scene behind him.

Which booth was Jeannette's—and would she be glad to see them?

Hard to say.

In all his comings and goings over the past

week, he hadn't caught a glimpse of his elusive neighbor. She must prefer to keep to herself, as Charley had implied.

Nor had he had much chance to think about her since Molly's meltdown at the preschool.

But once the daycare situation was resolved, Jeannette would be back on his mind. Guaranteed. She was an intriguing woman—and easy on the eyes too.

In fact . . . after life settled into more of a routine, maybe he'd give her the nudge Charley had said she might need to coax her out of her self-imposed isolation. See where that led.

And in the meantime, it couldn't hurt to lay a little groundwork.

11

Only an hour and a half into opening day of the farmer's market, and her booth was almost sold out.

She'd vastly underestimated the demand for her products.

Jeannette did a rapid calculation of her remaining inventory as her latest customers walked away with the items they'd purchased.

Sixteen sachets, two lavender grapevine wreaths left over from last season, five lavender scones, and three six-packs of lavender shortbread hearts.

In another half hour—or less—she'd be reduced to handing out flyers about her weekend teas.

Taking a long swig from her water bottle, she surveyed the milling crowd.

Who knew the whole town would turn out for this season's kickoff? At her first opening day last year, there'd been far fewer people, and her sales had been much more modest.

Of course, it had rained that day, while this year's ideal weather had probably brought area residents out in droves.

Lesson learned for next year.

As she spread out her remaining items to make the offerings appear less sparse, she caught sight of a family group approaching.

The Shabos had ventured to the market?

Good for them.

Smiling, she motioned them over. "Hello."

Mariam returned the greeting as they drew near. "Pretty." She swept a hand over the filmy lavender draping and large photos of the farm and her teas that decorated the booth.

"Thank you." She picked up a pack of the remaining shortbread, leaned down to Elisa, who was clutching her Raggedy Ann doll, and held it out.

The girl's eyes lit up. "Thank you."

Thomma started to pull out his wallet, but Jeannette shook her head. "Gift." She put her fingertips on her chest, then extended her hands, palm up, toward the family.

He hesitated, but after Mariam elbowed him he put his money away. "Thank you."

"Monday?" Mariam raised her eyebrows.

"Yes."

"Time . . . four?"

Someone had been practicing the material she'd left yesterday.

"Yes."

In her peripheral vision, a familiar male face and another little girl appeared.

Logan and Molly had come to the market too.

Her pulse accelerated, and she frowned.

For heaven's sake, Jeannette, get a grip. You may not be able to dictate the content of your dreams, but you ought to be able to keep your waking emotions under control.

The duo strolled over to the booth, and she gripped the edge of the counter, hiking up the corners of her mouth. "I didn't expect to see you here."

"We didn't expect to *be* here." Logan's return smile warmed her like a balmy tropical breeze— and she had to fight the urge to fan herself. "We came to town for tacos and found out there was a party."

The Shabos took a step back, and she turned to them and held up a finger before addressing Logan. *Focus, Jeannette.* "Let me introduce you to the newest arrivals in town—even newer than you." She gave him a brief explanation about their background.

"I saw a reference to them in the Grace Christian bulletin." He nodded to the family.

Logan had attended church?

Another check mark in his plus column.

He must have gone to the later service, though, or she'd have seen him.

"They know very little English, so don't expect a conversation."

"Got it."

She drew the family forward, indicating each one as she said their names, then did the same with Logan and Molly.

Logan extended his hand to Thomma. "Welcome."

The man clearly didn't understand, but he returned the shake. "Hello."

Logan also shook hands with Mariam, who bobbed her head in acknowledgment.

Molly edged close to Elisa, fairly quivering with excitement. "Hi."

"She doesn't speak our language, sweetie." Logan rested his hand on Molly's shoulder. "Elisa is from a different country. She won't understand what you say."

Molly ignored him and spoke to the girl, never breaking eye contact with her. "Elisa is a pretty name."

Thomma's daughter offered her a shy smile. "Thank you."

Molly sent Logan a boy-were-you-wrong-about-that look and refocused on the other girl.

While the two children concentrated on each other, Father Murphy strolled by and stopped to pantomime a conversation with Mariam and Thomma.

"You seem chummy with the family." Logan tipped his head toward the two adult Shabos as they tried to communicate with the priest.

"I've gotten to know them a little. I volunteered to help them learn English."

Now why had she brought *that* up?

His eyebrows arched. "I saw the appeal in the bulletin on Sunday. That's a big undertaking."

"Um . . . I have some spare time."

"Have you ever done anything like that?"

"Tutored English? Yes. A number of years ago. And as you can see, the need is great." She shrugged and changed the subject. "How's everything going on your end? Have you been settling in?"

"Trying to. The electric fence has been installed, and I'm getting ready to train our friend here." He dipped his chin toward the dog, who was bouncing around as he watched all the activity. Then he lowered his voice. "I'm having a bit of difficulty with the preschool arrangements, though. Molly didn't last in the Coos Bay facility even to the end of the orientation day—and I've got forty-eight hours left to find a new one."

"Ouch."

"Tell me about it."

"What was the problem—if you don't mind me asking?"

"The director's take was that Molly's had to cope with too many changes too fast and suggested I set up more one-on-one daycare, in our house if possible. I've spent the past four days trying to come up with an arrangement that will work."

Jeannette listened while Logan explained about the woman Reverend Baker had found, as well as his reservations.

She couldn't argue with his concerns, based on the background she'd read in Marci's *Herald* article. Molly had endured more than her share of trauma, and if she bonded with the woman the pastor had proposed, it could exacerbate her issues when Logan found a more permanent arrangement.

"I wish I could offer some suggestions, but I don't know that many people here either."

"It's not your worry—and I didn't mean to dump it on you. I'll work it out." Logan angled away to greet Father Murphy as the man spoke to him, and Jeannette checked on the two girls, who'd drawn away from the adults. They were both animated, and despite the language barrier it didn't appear they were having any trouble communicating.

"Elisa." Mariam waited until the girl responded before continuing in Arabic.

The child's face fell.

So did Molly's, after Thomma took Elisa's hand, said good-bye, and led the girl away.

Elisa kept looking back, though.

And Molly watched her until they disappeared into the crowd.

Some other customers approached the booth, and while they examined the sachets, Logan pulled out his wallet. "Charley suggested we get some short-bread for dessert, and Molly and I thought that was a fine idea. Didn't we, sweetie?" He glanced down at her, but she continued to peer into the throng, hopping up and down to see better.

"I think someone's made a friend." Jeannette watched her antics as she passed Logan a pack of the cookies.

"Yeah?" Logan handed her a few bills and squinted toward Charley's truck, his expression pensive. "She *did* have ponytails." Toby began to bark and pull on his leash, giving Jeannette no chance to follow up on his odd comment. "Our cue to exit. Come on, Molly. Let's go home and eat some cookies."

The girl at last gave up trying to catch another glimpse of her new friend, but she ignored the hand Logan extended and bent to pet Toby instead.

It seemed she was bonding better with her dog than with her uncle.

A tough situation to be in, based on the muscle that clenched in Logan's jaw and the faint furrows that scored his brow.

But when he turned back to her, he managed to lighten his demeanor. "Tell me I won't be the only man at the tea tomorrow."

Jeannette's lips twitched at the typical male reaction. "I can't promise that. Most of my customers are women—but once in a while I do get a couple, if it's a special occasion."

"That's what I figured." He sighed. "I assume tea parties are dressy affairs."

"Most people wear nicer clothes—but you don't have to dust off your tux."

155

"Could Molly wear her Easter dress and hat?"

Logan had bought his niece an Easter outfit?

Not many single guys thrust into fatherhood would have thought of that.

One more tick mark in his plus column—not that she was keeping score.

"That would be perfect for a tea party. Tell me about your hat, Molly."

The girl gave Toby one last pat and stood. "It's white and has flowers and pink ribbons."

"I can't wait to see it. It sounds beautiful."

"I liked the Easter hat Nana got me better."

Out of the corner of her eye, Jeannette saw Logan's face fall.

Her heart contracted.

The man was obviously trying hard to connect with his niece, but as far as she could see, he was batting zero.

"But a new hat is always a treat—especially one with pink ribbons."

"I like purple better. Like the one on your cookies."

Shoot.

Another kick in the shin to Logan.

"Well . . . I'll enjoy seeing your hat anyway."

Logan took her hand, his features taut despite the pleasant façade he was trying to project. "Say good-bye, Molly. We have to let Jeannette get back to work."

Molly waved. "Bye."

"Enjoy your cookies—and I'll see you tomorrow."

She watched them stroll away, Toby darting left and right to take everything in as Logan shortened his stride to accommodate his niece.

Despite the strain between them, they made an appealing, if untraditional, family group—as did the Shabos.

In fact, the two families had several things in common. They were both adjusting to life in a new place, neither had many friends, and the two men were starting new jobs. Both girls also had an air of melancholy that plucked at the heartstrings.

Except . . . neither child had seemed sad today. Just the opposite. For the few brief minutes they'd spent together, both had come alive.

As she chatted with customers, sold out her remaining inventory, and began to shut down for the night, an idea began to percolate in her mind.

Nothing might come of it—but if it worked out, maybe it would be the answer to a number of prayers.

***

"You are going to church with us this Sunday, yes?" Mariam touched Thomma's arm as he moved past her in the hall to turn in for the night, keeping her voice low so as not to disturb Elisa. "We have much to thank God for."

"I will go because the people and the priest

have been kind and I don't wish to offend them."

Not the answer she wanted to hear—but at least he was going.

And perhaps, if he continued to spend an hour a week with the Lord, he would find his way back to God in time.

"Good."

"It is nothing like St. Peter's, though."

No, it wasn't. The Mass here was much more informal, with fewer rituals and none of the chanting that were the hallmarks of the Chaldean rite she'd attended for more than half a century.

But everyone had been welcoming—and they'd been able to worship openly, without fear of bombs or other violence.

That was a huge blessing.

"We will adjust."

Thomma snorted. "You say that about everything."

"Because it is true." She touched his arm. "You haven't talked much about your job. It is okay?"

"For now."

"Your boss—he is fair?"

"Yes."

"And the work is not too hard?"

"No."

"Then all is well."

He glared at her. "How can you say that after everything we have lost?"

Without giving her a chance to respond, he

158

slipped into his room and shut the door with a sharp click.

Just as well.

She wasn't up to a debate tonight.

Shoulders drooping, she flipped off the hall light and quietly let herself into the room where Elisa was sound asleep.

After changing in silence, she crossed to her granddaughter, kissed her forehead, and tucked in the blanket. The child's slumber was peaceful, her countenance untroubled. Already she'd acclimated to this new home of theirs.

If only she and Thomma could do the same.

She climbed into the twin bed, settled into the warmth and softness, and turned on her side, toward the wall.

Only then did she let the tears come, muffling her sobs with the pillow.

Thomma might think she was strong. Optimistic. Confident about their new life in America.

But she was as scared and unsure as he was.

She missed Yesoph with an intensity that left a constant, gnawing ache in her midsection. Even now, she yearned to reach out to him, to feel his strong arms pull her close in the night and hold her . . . protect her . . . love her.

And oh, how she missed her youngest son, with his sparkling eyes and zest for life . . . and Thomma's wife, who had been like the daughter she'd never had . . . and her grandson, Elisa's brother, whose baby giggles had delighted her days.

Mariam choked back another sob.

No, this new life without so many of the family members she loved wasn't easy for her.

Nor was it easy to remain upbeat and encouraging in the face of Thomma's despair—and her doubts about her own future.

Thomma was young and smart and strong. If he gave this country a chance, he would do fine here. And Elisa's whole life stretched before her. She would send down roots in America and soon have little need of her Teta.

Mariam gripped the covers and pulled them up to her neck, her stomach churning.

She was old by Syrian standards, with few skills beyond cooking and cleaning and loving her family. Those had been sufficient—and fulfilling—in the old country, but here? She had to do more to help her family . . . and herself.

Like Thomma, she had to find her place—and her purpose . . . if there *was* a place . . . and a purpose . . . for her once she shepherded the remains of her shattered family through this transition.

What would become of her when her son and granddaughter no longer needed her?

Balling the sheet in her fists, she fought back another wave of doubt—and despair. Father Karam would not approve of such dark thinking. Nor would Father Murphy.

She had to trust in God, as she'd been admonishing her son to do.

But sometimes it was hard.

So very hard.

She stared up at the dark wall. No sound of distant bombs disrupted the stillness. No angry shouts from the street tainted the night. No flashing lights strobed through the room as emergency vehicles raced by.

If nothing else, she could be grateful for this place of refuge that had welcomed them with kindness and compassion.

As for her future—she'd have to put that in God's hands.

And pray for fortitude to endure as she struggled to find her own way in this new land that was so different from the home she had left behind.

12

Afternoon tea wasn't nearly as bad as he'd expected.

Logan lifted the dainty cup and took another sip of his Assam brew—the highest octane offering on the menu, according to Jeannette—and watched Molly play with the sugar cubes.

His niece hadn't said much, but as far as he could tell, she was enjoying herself. The bite-sized food was tasty—though he'd have to supplement it later with some serious protein. And watching their attractive hostess navigate among the tables, explaining the offerings on the three-tiered silver serving trays and the choices of tea, was enjoyable.

He could do without the scrutiny of the other patrons, however.

Every one of them was female, and from the minute he'd walked in the door holding Molly's hand, they'd been aiming discreet—and not so discreet—glances his direction.

Despite Jeannette's claim that a few men did venture here for tea, males must be a novelty at these types of genteel gatherings.

"What's this?"

At Molly's question, he studied the miniature pastry with a raspberry on top and tried to remember what Jeannette had told them about the items on the tray.

"It's a double chocolate raspberry truffle tart." She appeared beside them as if on cue. Leaning closer to the girl, she dropped her voice to a conspiratorial whisper. "If you like chocolate, you'll like that one. Promise."

"Chocolate is my bestest favorite." She reached for the tart.

"Everything okay here?" Jeannette straightened up and directed the question to him.

"Fine."

"Sorry no other men showed up today."

"I'm surviving."

Someone on the other side of the room motioned to her, then toward their teapot.

"A call for more hot water. Let me know if you need anything. Also . . . I'd like to talk with you before you leave, if you can spare a few minutes."

"Sure." All he had to do tonight was call the woman Reverend Baker had found to watch Molly and finalize the arrangements. No sense putting it off any longer. At this stage, he wasn't likely to come up with anything else suitable by Monday.

Meanwhile, why not try to enjoy the relaxing ambiance and soothing classical music in the tearoom until Molly grew bored?

An hour passed before she began to swing her legs and fidget—longer than he'd expected, but not long enough.

He could sit here all afternoon watching his neighbor flit about in her slim black skirt and figure-enhancing lavender blouse that wrapped across the front.

But since none of the other patrons seemed in a hurry to leave, he might have to catch up with her later to hear whatever she wanted to tell him.

At least it couldn't be a complaint about Toby. There'd been no more breakouts by his escape-artist dog.

"Ready to go, sweetie?" He laid his linen napkin on the white tablecloth.

She shrugged, picked up another sugar cube with silver tongs, and set it on her plate beside the other three she'd transferred. "Can I take these?"

"Sure. We'll ask for one of those boxes." He motioned toward Jeannette, who was beginning to distribute small white cartons to her patrons, many of whom hadn't consumed all of their bite-sized goodies.

He shook his head. Hard to believe every single tray wasn't bare. He'd polished off his food—and some of Molly's—in the first twenty minutes.

Jeannette stopped beside their table and inspected their empty serving tiers. "You two did very well."

"Molly has a few sugar cubes she'd like to take home, though." Logan motioned toward her plate.

"Of course." Jeannette set a box on the table and winked at the little girl. "I put an extra shortbread cookie in there for you and your uncle too."

"Thank you." Molly smiled up at her.

"I may have to touch base with you later if you want to talk. We're getting a tad restless." He indicated his niece.

"No problem. Everyone's usually gone by four. If you'll give me your cell number, I can call you as soon as I get a minute. Unless . . . did you come up with any other arrangement for Monday other than the one you mentioned?" She inclined her head toward Molly.

"No. Do you have an idea?"

"Yes."

He pulled out a pen and found an old gasoline receipt in the pocket of his sport jacket. On the back, he jotted his number and handed it to her. "I'm open to any and all suggestions. And feel free to drop by if you'd rather talk in person."

"Thanks." She took the slip of paper. "Are you ready for your bill?"

"Yes." He pulled out his credit card and handed it to her.

"Give me one sec."

She wove back through the tables, toward a doorway that must lead to the kitchen.

Logan gave the space one last sweep. The back wall of the tearoom was almost all glass, offering a view over the lavender fields that would be stunning when the flowers were in bloom. A dozen tables of various sizes offered seating for about thirty people. Other than the lavender napkins, the place was classy without being froufrou.

And unless she had help hiding in the kitchen, Jeannette ran the whole operation by herself.

Amazing.

While she only served tea two days a week, the fancy offerings on the silver trays must take an enormous amount of time and effort to prepare.

Plus, she had to tend to the plants and make the products she sold at the farmer's market.

Maybe it wasn't that she didn't *want* any downtime, as Charley had suggested, but that she simply couldn't carve any out. This place had to be a more-than-full-time job.

But why was she doing it alone?

As he pondered that question, Jeannette returned, stopping to drop other checks off at various tables while she wound through the room to them.

"We'll be home the rest of the day, whenever you have a minute—and waiting with bated breath." Logan signed the check.

"Don't get too excited until you hear my idea."

He picked up the small white box and rose. "I have a feeling that if you thought of it, I'm going to like it."

A flash of surprise flared in her eyes . . . and an instant later they shuttered.

Oops.

He must have gotten a bit too personal.

"Well . . ." She backed off a step, confirming

his conclusion. "I'll talk to you later. Bye, Molly."

Without waiting for a reply, she moved to a nearby table to deal with that check.

Curious.

His neighbor was gracious and considerate. The perfect hostess for a tearoom. But she got skittish if the conversation edged into personal territory.

Why?

And was she like that with everyone, or only him?

Could there be a failed romance in her background that had left her gun-shy of men?

Since he wasn't likely to get answers to those questions today, Logan took Molly's hand and led her out the door and around the long hedge between the properties.

As they approached their house, Toby's muffled barks seeped through the walls.

The pup did *not* sound happy.

But the crate was a necessity for short absences. No way was he letting the dog wreak further destruction in the empty spare bedroom.

It was a short-term measure, though. Once Toby got the hang of the electric fence, he'd have the run of the yard.

Which reminded him.

As soon as he talked with Jeannette, he'd better corral the pup for a training session.

And hope Toby was as diligent a pupil as he was a digger.

• • •

"Thomma? Is that you?"

He closed the front door of the apartment and shucked his jacket. "Yes. Who else would it be?" Irritation scored his words—but so be it. He'd risen at the crack of dawn and spent most of his Saturday on a fishing boat, the cold rain had seeped down his neck despite the slicker Roark had given him, and he smelled like salmon.

He wanted solitude, a hot shower, and food. In that order.

However . . . based on his mother's resolute expression when she appeared in the kitchen doorway, she had another agenda in mind for him.

Her first sentence confirmed that.

"After you take a shower, would you play a game of Candy Land with Elisa? She says her stomach hurts, and she's sniffling. I told her to stay in bed for the rest of the day. I'd play with her myself, but I'm making baklava and that will keep me busy for another forty-five minutes."

He glowered at her. "Why didn't you wait until another day to bake such a complicated dessert?"

"You like baklava. I thought it would be a special treat to celebrate the end of your first week on the job."

Her expression was guileless—but her explanation was a lie.

'Ami was worried he was neglecting Elisa, and

169

this was a setup to force him to spend more time with his daughter.

Which was the last thing he wanted to do.

Thomma balled his hands into fists . . . sucked in a breath . . . let the air hiss out through his clenched teeth.

How was he supposed to entertain Elisa when every moment he spent with her reminded him of Raca?

His daughter's dark auburn hair, big brown eyes, delicate chin—they were all inherited from the woman he'd loved and cherished with every fiber of his being.

The woman who'd added light and laughter and hope to his days.

The woman who'd filled his life with joy and given it new meaning.

His stomach twisted, as it did whenever he thought about his wife.

A huge part of him had died with her in that church.

The best part.

He drew another ragged breath . . . and admitted the ugly truth he'd been dodging for months.

Much as he loved Elisa, if he'd had to pick who would survive the bombing—his daughter or his wife—Raca would have been his choice.

Now, Elisa required more than he had to give . . . and his neglect of her was shameful. He didn't need his mother to tell him that. The guilt that gnawed at his conscience day and night was a constant reminder of his failings.

"Thomma!"

At his mother's sharp tone, he blinked and refocused. "What?"

"I asked you what is wrong."

"I'm tired." He tried to brush past her, but she stepped in front of him and pressed a hand to his chest.

"The job is too hard for you?"

"No." Compared to the backbreaking work he'd done at the mine, dealing with charter fishing customers and taking care of a boat was easy. Steven Roark was also a much better boss than his old foreman.

"Then the tiredness is from within." His mother's gaze bored into his. "That is more difficult to cure. You should talk with Father Murphy."

He snorted. "He'll just tell me to trust in God and do my best with what I have left."

"That is not bad advice."

"It doesn't bring Raca—or the others—back." He shouldered past her. "I'm taking a shower and then I'm going to rest until dinner."

She didn't say another word or try to stop him.

But the sight of his solemn-eyed daughter propped up in bed, a picture book in her lap, her hair spread on the pillow behind her, brought him to a standstill.

Elisa didn't speak. She just stared at him with

big eyes filled with sadness and longing and bewilderment.

How different this greeting was from the old days, when she'd run to him, arms upraised for a twirl as he came through the door from work, then squeal with laughter as he swung her around and nuzzled her neck.

His vision misted.

So much had changed.

Forever.

And none of it was Elisa's fault.

She didn't deserve to be dumped into the care of her grandmother, much as she loved her Teta. She was his responsibility. It wasn't her fault that every time he looked at her, he saw Raca—and a shaft of pain pierced his heart.

For the sake of compassion alone, he ought to make an effort to show some affection.

He took one step into the room. "Teta says you're sick."

She held up a tissue. "My nose runned."

"Does your tummy hurt?"

"Yes." Her voice was so soft he could barely hear it.

"You rest while I take a shower. Then we'll have dinner. Do you need anything?"

She hesitated for one second, then shook her head.

But that was a lie.

Of course she needed something.

A hug. A smile. A twirl in the air. A game of Candy Land with her papa.

Anything to reassure her that her father loved her.

Yet all he could manage was a slight flex of his lips before he escaped into the hall.

His mother was still standing at the far end, arms crossed, brow creased, her message clear.

She didn't approve of his behavior.

And he couldn't blame her.

He ought to be able to see past Elisa's resemblance to his wife, to love his daughter for herself, be grateful he had her, and give her top priority in his affections.

His head knew that—but his heart refused to cooperate.

Turning his back on his mother, he swallowed past the tightness in his throat. Fled toward the bathroom. Slipped inside and flipped the lock.

There, away from 'Ami's reproving gaze and Elisa's haunted eyes, he leaned his forehead against the door, drew in a shaky breath, and did something he'd vowed never to do again.

He prayed.

She didn't have to talk to Logan in person. A phone call would suffice.

So why was she circling around the hedge that led to his house and walking up his drive?

Jeannette halted.

This was crazy.

Paying an unnecessary visit to her neighbor broke every rule she'd imposed on herself when she'd left Cincinnati behind to start over here.

But she'd been breaking a bunch of them lately.

If she wanted to keep to herself, she shouldn't have gone to a social event like the welcome party for the Shabos. She shouldn't have offered to teach the family English. She shouldn't be initiating a visit to her new neighbor with an idea that would enmesh her even more in other people's lives.

What was going on? Why had she suddenly begun leaving her safe cocoon and connecting with the residents of this town more than her business required?

And where were those connections going to lead?

Somewhere scary.

Her pulse stuttered as the answer strobed across her mind, and she backed up a few steps.

Hesitated.

You're being selfish, Jeannette. Your neighbor is in a bind, and your idea could solve his problem.

That was true.

But she could pass it on by phone. That would be far safer.

Decision made, she pivoted and hurried back toward her house.

"Jeannette!"

As Logan called out from behind her, her step faltered—as did her heart.

Too late to run.

She swiveled toward him as he jogged down the path from the porch.

Halfway to her, he stopped and plucked a lavender ribbon from the grass.

Holding it aloft, he grinned. "Never mind. Crisis averted. I thought I might have lost this at your place and was going to ask you if I could look for it. Come on over, if you can stand Toby's barking."

She was stuck.

Smoothing a hand down her jeans, she joined him. "I'm a little later than I expected. I wanted to change first."

"That's fine. Toby was *not* happy about being confined in a cage while we were gone, and he's been barking and running around the house like he's possessed since we liberated him. He's calmed down some, but why don't we sit out here while Molly plays with him? It will be less chaotic." He motioned toward the front porch.

"Works for me."

He let her precede him, pausing at the front door as she moved toward the mesh folding chairs the former owner had left that had been there for as long as she'd lived in her house. "Let me give this to Molly and stave off a meltdown."

By the time he joined her, she'd moved the two

175

chairs farther apart and claimed one of them.

If he noticed the wider separation, he gave no indication of it. "Molly loved the tea—and we both appreciated the animal-shaped peanut butter and jelly sandwiches you added to our tray."

"I figured she'd like them better than the smoked salmon rosette and the marinated shrimp skewered on the lavender stem. Besides, that left more of the gourmet food for you—not that it filled you up, I'm guessing."

He shifted in his seat. "Everything was delicious."

"A diplomatic answer. But I have a feeling you're in the same camp as one of my male guests from Texas, who said, 'Mighty tasty, young woman—but where's the main course?'"

"Can I plead the Fifth?"

"Not necessary. Most women can't finish everything I serve and tell me they're full at the end, but their male companions don't consider my teas a meal. So you're not alone."

"Where did you learn to make all that fancy food, anyway?"

Not a subject she wanted to discuss—but she couldn't ignore the question.

"My mom was a wonderful cook. Most of the elaborate fare is self-taught, but she was my inspiration." Jeannette folded her hands in her lap and steered the conversation back on course. "Would you like to hear my idea?"

"Absolutely."

"Did you happen to notice how Molly and Elisa Shabo clicked at the farmer's market?"

"Yes."

"It occurred to me that both girls could use a friend. Given their instant rapport, I wondered if Mariam—the grandmother—might be interested in watching them in your home. That would give Molly personalized care in familiar surroundings, along with the companionship of a child she already likes."

Logan leaned forward and clasped his hands together, faint furrows creasing his brow. "Have you asked her about this?"

"No. I wanted to run the idea by you first. But I imagine the family would welcome another source of income. They came here with nothing, and Thomma isn't earning much working on a fishing boat."

"Does Mariam have any kind of childcare credentials?"

"I doubt it—but she raised two sons, and she's very loving with Elisa. Given the circumstances, it will be impossible to do any of the typical due diligence, but you could always talk to Father Murphy. Get his read."

"What's *your* take on her—and the family?"

"I don't know them that well."

"You know them better than I do—and I'd appreciate your input."

Jeannette knitted her fingers together in her lap. Back in her more sociable days, she'd been an excellent judge of character. But those skills were rusty.

As if sensing her reluctance to offer an opinion, Logan spoke again. "Whatever insights you have would be appreciated—and I won't blame you if anything goes wrong."

Given that caveat, how could she not share a few topline impressions?

"I think they're good people." She spoke slowly, choosing her words with care. "Thomma is angry, which is understandable. Mariam is trying hard to be the glue in the family and present a brave front, but I have a feeling she's hurting inside and struggling to keep it together. Elisa is like Molly—a victim of circumstance, buffeted by trauma, but like most children, she's responsive to love and very resilient."

"Does that mean you think I should give this a shot?"

"That has to be your decision. I'm just presenting it as a possible option."

"You don't think Mariam's lack of English would be a problem?"

"It's not ideal, but she has their translator's cell number. If there's a communication glitch, she can always call for clarification—and I'm next door in an emergency."

She clamped her lips shut.

Why on earth did she keep offering to get involved?

She had to stop doing that. Now.

"Do they have a car?" Logan crossed an ankle over his knee.

"Yes, but Thomma hasn't gotten his driver's license yet. Once he does, he can pick them up in the afternoon—but since he starts so early, they'd still need a ride to your house in the morning."

"Not a problem. Nothing's very far in Hope Harbor—and this arrangement would be far more convenient than the preschool in Coos Bay." He leaned back, his expression thoughtful. "I like the idea of Molly having a ready-made friend—and the daycare center director did recommend in-home care."

Jeannette remained silent while he mulled over the notion. She'd presented her case, and she wasn't going to push. She'd already far overstepped her self-imposed boundaries.

"Maybe I should run this by Molly. What do you think?" Logan looked over at her.

"I think it's always wise to involve children in decisions if possible. And given the preschool fiasco, letting her have some control over the situation could help create buy-in."

Logan hitched up one side of his mouth. "You seem to know as much about kids as Laura Wilson, the daycare center director."

She let that pass. "I'll tell you what. If you're

179

interested in considering this, why don't I contact Mariam and see if the idea appeals to her before you broach the notion to Molly? No sense getting her hopes up if this isn't going to fly—or you decide not to pursue it."

"That makes sense. Can you reach her tonight? I have to get back to the woman Reverend Baker found ASAP."

"Yes. I have the translator's cell number, and she sounded willing to help if an urgent situation came up. Given your ticking clock, I think this qualifies."

"Amen to that."

"I'll call Susan as soon as I get back to the house." She rose.

He stood too—much more slowly. As if he wasn't anxious for her to leave.

Or was that her overactive imagination at play?

"I'll tell the woman Reverend Baker lined up that I may have an alternate plan, but I'd appreciate it if you'd get back to me as soon as you hear anything."

"Why don't I call you with an update by eight o'clock at the latest?"

"Perfect."

She edged around him on the porch, doing her best to ignore the hint of spicy aftershave tickling her nose. "I'll let you get back to whatever you were doing."

"No rush on my end. I'm going to read Molly a

180

few of her fairy-tale princess books and introduce Toby to the electric fence."

"Exciting Saturday night."

"The fence part might be."

"*That* kind of excitement you could do without, I'm sure."

"True."

"This new lifestyle of yours must be a huge adjustment after leading a bachelor life in San Francisco. I bet Saturday nights there were much more . . . entertaining." As the comment tripped off her tongue, she tried not to cringe. It sounded like she was digging for information about his social life, when all she was trying to do was make conversation.

Yeah, right, Jeannette. Who are you trying to kid?

She mashed her lips together.

Fine.

She *was* digging.

But he probably wouldn't answer anyway.

"To be honest, I like Saturday nights here better." He leaned against the porch post and slid his fingers into his pockets, his casual stance at odds with his serious demeanor. "I worked a fair number of weekends in the ER, which had a dramatic impact on my social life. Since I wasn't dating anyone seriously, though, it was no big deal."

She stared at him.

Why would he share such personal information? Unless . . .

Was he trying to communicate that he was available . . . and interested in *her?*

Hard to tell. Her skills at reading those kinds of signals were too rusty.

Whatever his intention, however, the revelation was more than she'd bargained for.

And much too unsettling.

"Um . . . I'm glad it's been a positive change for you in that regard." She eased down the three steps from the porch to the walk. "I'll give you a call later."

"I'll look forward to that."

Because he was anxious to hear what Mariam had to say—or anxious to talk to her again?

It could be both.

And that was bad.

She did not want to attract attention or catch any man's eye. That was one of the reasons she'd kept to herself for the past three years.

Without looking back, she hightailed it down the drive, toward the safety of her farm behind the tall hedge. Where she belonged.

Because once you started getting involved in other people's lives, once you began to let yourself care, you opened yourself up to a world of heartache.

And that wasn't a place she intended to visit ever again.

13

"Congrats on surviving your first week on the job." Barb Meyers grinned as she flipped off the lights in the last treatment room of the urgent care center.

Logan slipped out of his white coat and hung it in the closet next to the reception desk while the nurse practitioner locked the supply room. "Thanks. It was busier than I expected."

To say the least.

A broken arm, two cases of strep throat, a gash requiring ten stitches, and a possible concussion they'd referred to Coos Bay for follow-up had kept him hopping on this warm, sunny Friday.

And the rest of the week had been just as hectic.

On the plus side, he'd been able to leave every day at five o'clock and delegate Saturday and the two-nights-a-week evening duties to Barb or Ellen, the physician's assistant—part of the deal he'd negotiated when he'd taken the job.

But it wouldn't hurt to have another pair of hands on deck—a part-time nurse perhaps.

An observation he'd pass on to the management team after he'd logged a bit more experience here.

"Any weekend plans?" Barb slid the strap of her purse over her shoulder.

"Other than training my dog—no."

"Toby sounds like a handful."

"Yeah." The staff had offered him plenty of sympathy and advice during the week as he'd shared some of the pup's escapades—like Toby's diligence in digging up the flags marking the electric fence boundary instead of learning to respect what they represented.

At this rate, he wouldn't be able to power up the fence for weeks without fear of freaking out the beagle with an electric shock.

"Hang in there. Most dogs catch on eventually."

"That's what Chuck said." Their office manager, who'd already left for the day, had been happy to share his experience with dogs in the occasional lull between patients. "See you Monday."

He checked his watch as he hurried toward the door. He was a few minutes behind schedule, thanks to that broken arm, and Mariam would be waiting for him to drive her and Elisa home so she could prepare dinner for her family.

At least the first week of his new daycare arrangement had gone smoothly. Molly and Elisa had become BFFs, and Mariam seemed caring and conscientious.

He owed Jeannette a huge thank-you for suggesting the arrangement. It had been a literal godsend.

And he'd tell her that when their paths next crossed—which could be a while, given that he hadn't caught so much as a glimpse of her since their chat on his porch last Saturday.

He swung onto 101 for the six-minute, traffic-free drive home.

Bliss, after the San Francisco rush hour.

Elbow resting on the open window, he inhaled a lungful of the fresh salt air. Maybe after dinner he'd take Molly and Toby to the beach. A quiet sunset stroll past the sea stacks arrayed offshore would be a relaxing end to the work week.

Mouth flexing into a smile, Logan turned onto his street. It wouldn't take long to run Mariam and Elisa home, and he and Molly could stop for dinner at the Myrtle Café. Within an hour, they could be at the beach and—

Logan frowned.

Why was an older model Sentra parked in front of his house?

He inspected the unfamiliar car as he drove past it and swung into the driveway. Who could have come to call—and had Mariam let a stranger in the house?

A niggle of alarm rippled through him.

That had been one of the firm rules he'd laid down the first day, and with Susan interpreting, he had no doubt Mariam had understood—and she'd promised to abide by it.

So where was the driver?

Logan pulled into the detached garage, slid out of the car, and jogged toward the back door.

Laughter, music, and little-girl giggles greeted him as he approached.

Logan exhaled.

Didn't sound as if a criminal had invaded his home after all.

He took the back steps two at a time and paused at the porch door to survey the scene in his kitchen, inhaling the tantalizing aroma wafting toward him.

Mariam was at the stove, stirring a mixture in a large pot. Thomma sat at the kitchen table playing some sort of card game with the two girls. Toby was prancing around the activity, as usual.

As soon as the pup caught sight of him, he began barking.

Thomma glanced toward the door, then aimed a forceful command in Arabic at the dog.

Toby ignored him.

Shooting the beagle a stern glance, Thomma set his cards down and held up a dog treat, called the dog over, and repeated the order while gently grasping his muzzle. After a moment he released the muzzle, pressed Toby's hind quarters into a sitting position, and said the term again. Then he gave him the treat.

The pup stopped barking and stayed where he was.

Until Logan pushed through the door.

Toby immediately scrambled to his feet and began to bark again.

Thomma rose, and Mariam swiveled away from the stove, wiping her hands on her apron.

"Hello." She motioned from the stove to him, raising her volume to be heard above the yaps. "For you. Thank you."

She'd cooked them dinner?

He pantomimed eating, and she nodded, her features taut. Like she was afraid he'd complain about having delicious-smelling food waiting for him.

"Thank *you*." He rubbed his stomach. "Hi, sweetie." He crossed to Molly and bent to give her a hug. She didn't snuggle against him—but she didn't pull away either. "What are you playing?"

"Old Maid."

If ever there was a politically incorrect name for a game, that was it. But Molly loved it—and anything that made her happy was fine with him.

Mariam walked over to him, held out a slip of paper with Susan's name and phone number on it, and motioned for him to call the woman.

There must be a message his babysitter wanted to pass on that sign language and her limited vocabulary couldn't transmit.

He pulled out his phone and sent the barking dog a disgruntled look. Too bad he didn't have Thomma's magic touch with Toby.

As if the man had read his mind, he said the word he'd used a few minutes ago. It took three tries, each one more forceful, along with the bribe of a dog treat, but at last Toby fell silent, trotted over to him—and sat as the man had taught him.

It was a miracle.

Motioning Thomma to retake his seat and resume his game, Logan tapped in Susan's number. After returning her greeting, he explained the reason for his call.

"Yes, Mariam spoke with me earlier today," Susan confirmed. "She wanted to let you know Thomma got his driver's license today and can pick them up from now on. She also wanted to tell you she prepared a thank-you dinner tonight for giving her a job and for chauffeuring them all week."

He shifted around to find Elisa's grandmother watching him and mouthed another thank-you.

Faint color stole over her cheeks, and she refocused on the stove.

"Can you do me a favor, Susan?" Logan eyed Toby, who was still sitting quietly beside Thomma.

"Sure."

"If I put Thomma on the line, will you ask him how he managed to get my dog under control— especially the barking?"

"I'll be happy to."

"Hang on a minute." He walked over to the table and held the cell out to Elisa's father. "Susan."

The man took it, had a brief conversation with the woman, and handed it back to him.

"So what's the story?" Logan watched as Mariam tasted the stew-like concoction on his stove.

"He said he likes dogs and often trained them for his friends in Syria."

"No kidding." Logan propped a fist on his hip. "I wonder if he could train Toby on the electric fence I installed. I'm getting nowhere."

"I could ask him for you. Tell me how the training works."

Logan gave her a brief overview. "Of course, I'll pay him for this."

"Why don't you give the phone back to him and I'll explain the job?"

Once again, Logan passed over the cell.

This time, Thomma had a longer conversation with the woman, doing more listening than talking, shaking his head once. Finally he handed the phone back.

It was impossible to tell from his expression whether he'd agreed to help, but the head shake wasn't promising. However, Logan was willing to up the fee to whatever the man wanted. Bringing peace and quiet to this house would be worth any price.

"What's the verdict?" Logan curled the fingers of his free hand into a tight ball and held his breath.

"He said he'd be glad to help you. He can come early in the morning before work, right after

189

work, and again in the evening—but he doesn't want to take any money. He said he'd enjoy doing it."

Thank you, God.

He refilled his lungs. "I can't let him do this for free."

"I told him you'd probably say that. He countered with the equivalent of five dollars a day for the three fifteen-minute sessions."

"Let's make it twenty-five."

"I'll leave you to negotiate that."

"Fair enough. Thanks for your help tonight."

"Anytime. But I doubt you—or the Shabos—will need me much longer. Jeannette is doing an outstanding tutoring job. I can't believe the progress they've made after just three lessons. In the meantime, though, don't hesitate to call if I can be of assistance."

After they said good-bye, Logan joined Thomma at the table. "Molly, why don't you and Elisa go play in your room for a few minutes while I talk to her daddy?"

In silence, she slid off her chair, took the other girl's hand, and tugged her down the hall.

"Toby . . . okay." Logan indicated the dog.

At the sound of his name, the dog gave a yap.

"*Kunn hadyaan.*" Thomma grasped the dog's muzzle, his tone firm.

It was the same command he'd used before—and it worked again.

Logan repeated the phonetics silently and tucked the term away in his vocabulary as he pulled up a calendar on his cell, angled it so Thomma could see, and drew a finger across the next fourteen days, beginning with tomorrow.

The other man dipped his chin in acknowledgment. "Okay."

"Good." They could deal with the money issue at the first session.

Mariam took off her apron, folded it, and tucked it inside her tote bag. "Dinner." She indicated the simmering dish emitting savory aromas, lifted a lid on a pot of rice, and motioned toward a plate of—baklava?—on the counter.

There was way too much food here for him and Molly.

He swept a hand over the Shabo family and indicated the table. "Eat?"

"No. Thank you." Mariam picked up her purse. "Monday?"

"Yes."

Thomma stood and walked to the door of the hall. "Elisa."

When the girl appeared, her father spoke in Arabic and took her hand.

Molly trailed in, dragging her feet, the corners of her lips drooping as her new friend prepared to leave.

Logan followed the family to the front door, with Molly and Toby in his wake, and watched

191

as they walked down the driveway to their car.

"Did you have fun with Elisa today?" Logan rested his hand on Molly's stiff shoulder.

"Uh-huh."

"What did you do?"

"Played."

"What did you play?"

"Games."

So much for the theory that open-ended questions stimulated conversation.

"Let me run down to the mailbox, and then we'll eat dinner. You can watch me through the window, but don't open the door or Toby might take off."

He slipped outside, pulling the door shut behind him, and jogged down the drive.

As he approached the box, Jeannette appeared on the other side of the hedge heading for *her* mailbox.

Perfect timing.

"Hi." He gave her his best smile.

She jerked and swung toward him with a soft exclamation.

"Sorry." He flattened his lips. "I didn't mean to startle you."

"That's okay. I'm, uh, not used to friendly greetings from my neighbor."

"The previous owner wasn't sociable?"

"Not very. I doubt he said more than ten words to me the entire three years we shared a property line."

"His loss."

A faint flush stole over her cheeks—but she didn't otherwise acknowledge his comment. "How's Mariam working out?"

"Couldn't be better. And I got an extra benefit. It seems Thomma has a way with dogs, and he's agreed to help me try to get Toby under control."

"That *is* a bonus." Jeannette continued to her mailbox and pulled out the letters inside.

In a minute, she was going to disappear behind her hedge again—unless he took some fast action.

He retrieved his own mail as she closed her box. "I don't know if you've already eaten, but Mariam made dinner tonight to thank me for giving her the job." He kept his manner casual, his tone straightforward rather than personal. "There's far more than Molly and I can eat—and since you were the catalyst, it's only fair we share it with you. Would you like to join us for dinner? Afterward we're going to take a walk on the beach."

Jeannette retreated a few steps toward her house—giving him her answer before she verbalized it. "I appreciate the offer, but I-I have chores to do tonight."

Don't push, West. Respect the lady's decision, even if you're tired of the silent treatment from Molly during meals and dying to share dinner with a female over the age of five.

"I hear you." He forced up the corners of his

mouth. "But if you see us pulling out of our driveway later and change your mind about the beach, flag us down." He started back toward the house.

He was eight steps away when she spoke.

"Logan."

Masking his surprise—and his hope—he pivoted back toward her.

"Um . . . you don't have to drive to get to the beach."

Not what he'd expected.

"Is there an access point around here?"

"Yes. At the back of my property there's a path that leads to the dunes overlooking the bay, and from there you can walk down to Driftwood Beach. It's not far. You're welcome to use it. Most days you'll have the beach to yourself."

She sounded a bit breathless. Like she was nervous or . . . afraid?

That didn't make sense.

Why would offering someone beach access generate a case of nerves?

Whatever the reason she found the offer distressing, why labor over it? Better to accept with gratitude. This would be much easier than loading Molly and Toby into the car.

"I appreciate that. Molly will get a kick out of walking to the beach, and Toby will love the exercise. But I promise to keep a tight hold on his leash while we're on your property."

"I'm not worried about that. It sounds like you're well on your way to corralling his canine capers. Enjoy your dinner."

With that, she disappeared behind the hedge.

Logan retraced his steps to the house more slowly.

It was a shame Jeannette had turned down his dinner invitation—but it might be for the best. If they spent any time together, he could get interested.

Make that *more* interested.

Which would not be good.

He had plenty on his plate already adjusting to a brand-new town, learning the ropes at the urgent care center, dealing with a rascally pup, and trying to learn how to be a single father and to win the trust—and love—of a little girl who'd been no more than a Facebook photo to him for most of her five years.

There wasn't room in his life for romance.

Yet even if there was, he suspected Jeannette wouldn't be interested.

And he didn't think it was personal.

A woman who ran a business out of her home and rarely left the premises wasn't interested in connecting with *anybody*.

At the foot of the porch steps, Logan gave the tall hedge a final sweep.

Maybe they were meant to be nothing more than neighbors.

But someday he was going to find out why a beautiful woman with a caring heart locked herself away on a lavender farm with only her flowers for company.

14

The crash from next door was loud—and it was followed by a little-girl wail.

Uh-oh.

Jeannette dropped her long-handled trowel in the lavender bed and sped toward the front of her house, heart pounding.

If Molly had gotten injured, it would be her fault. She was the one who'd suggested this day-care arrangement. And just because the first week had gone smoothly didn't mean there couldn't still be bumps in the road.

She rounded the bottom of the hedge at the end of her drive and picked up speed as she dashed toward Logan's backyard.

At least there were no more wails.

That could be a positive sign—or a bad one.

Please, Lord, let it be the former!

But it wasn't.

As the backyard came into view, both girls were huddled around Mariam, who was sitting on the ground. Toby lay on the grass as far away as his leash would stretch, chin on paws, watching the proceedings in silence—for once.

Mariam spotted her first and offered an apologetic shrug. "I fall."

"Yes. I see." Jeannette joined the girls, directing her question to Molly. "What happened?"

"Toby runned around her and she tripped on the leash."

That figured.

She refocused on Mariam. "Hurt?" She touched various parts of her own body.

The older woman pulled up the leg of her slacks.

Her ankle was already swelling.

Jeannette stifled a groan.

What a way to start the week.

And with Thomma out on the fishing boat, she'd have to deal with this herself.

So . . . what to do? Call 911?

Yes. Paramedics would be able to address this far better than she could.

As she pulled out her phone, Mariam squinted at her. "Who call?"

How could she communicate ambulance? That word hadn't cropped up in their vocabulary lessons yet.

"Hospital. Doctor. Police." Maybe one of those would register.

Mariam grabbed her arm, alarm strobing through her eyes. "No police. I okay." She tried to stand, grimacing as she struggled to her feet.

Since the woman was determined to get herself upright, Jeannette lent her a hand.

By the time Mariam was vertical, her complexion had lost most of its color.

She needed medical help—yet the notion of police involvement had frightened her.

Perhaps in Syria, any contact with the government was dangerous—especially if you were Christian.

But her injury required attention.

Jeannette debated her options. If she could get Mariam to the car, she could drive her to the urgent care center. Letting a doctor she knew examine her ankle shouldn't be too traumatic.

"Logan see." She pointed to the woman's ankle. "Okay?"

Mariam hesitated a moment. Shook her head. "No money."

"No worry." The churches must have made some arrangements for medical care for the family—but if not, she'd pay for the urgent care center visit herself.

Without giving the woman a chance to protest, she turned to the girls, who were holding hands and watching with saucer eyes. "Molly, you and Elisa stay here with Mrs. Shabo while I put Toby in the house. Okay?"

" 'Kay."

"Where's his cage?"

"In the empty room."

After retrieving a folding chair from the back porch for Mariam, she took Toby's leash and pulled the protesting dog toward the house. "Sorry, fella. I don't have time to play games or put up with your antics. Be a good boy and make this easy, please."

The pup actually cooperated—more or less—as she entered the house and searched for the spare bedroom.

Once she found it, however, he began barking and dug in his paws.

"Come on, Toby." She gripped his collar and joined the game of tug-of-war. "It's an emergency. We won't be gone long."

Somehow she managed to get the twenty pounds of writhing fur into the cage—but as she locked the door, he let loose with ear-splitting howls.

She winced.

No wonder Logan had complained about losing his hearing.

Back outside, she raced around the hedge to get her car, pulled into Logan's driveway, and managed to support Mariam as the woman shuffled to the vehicle.

She had no car seats for the girls, but she buckled them into the adult restraints in the back and prayed none of the Hope Harbor cops would pull her over during the short drive to town.

The ride was silent—and stressful. Tension radiated off the two girls in the back seat, and Mariam had gone from colorless to gray.

Not until she pulled up in front of the urgent care center did her pulse begin to settle back into the semblance of a normal rhythm. In less than five minutes, she ought to be able to hand this over to the experts and escape back to her peaceful farm.

"Stay here." She addressed her three passengers. "I'll get help."

With that, she slid out of the car and jogged to the door.

No one was in the waiting room when she entered, and she pressed the bell on the front desk.

A fortysomething woman appeared at the door that led to the examining rooms. "May I help you?"

Jeannette explained the situation in a few short sentences. "The patient is Logan—Dr. West's—babysitter. If he's available, you might want to let him know."

"I'll do that, get a wheelchair, and meet you at the car." The woman disappeared behind the door again.

Jeannette returned to the parking lot, dredging up a reassuring smile for the solemn occupants of her Civic as she opened Mariam's door. "Help is coming."

The woman nodded, as if she understood. And it was possible she did. All of the Shabos were progressing at a remarkable pace, and it was obvious Mariam was putting in extra hours on the vocabulary and pronunciation links she left with them after each lesson. But Elisa was advancing fastest, thanks to her interactions with Molly.

Three minutes later, Logan pushed a wheelchair

through the door and joined her beside the car. "Sorry you got pulled into this."

"Emergencies happen."

"What's the story?" He leaned down to examine Mariam's ankle.

"According to the eyewitness who speaks fluent English—that would be your niece—Toby gets the blame for this."

He sighed. "Why am I not surprised?" He finished his preliminary probing and stood. "I don't think this is too serious, but we'll take an X-ray to verify that." He positioned the wheelchair and helped the woman into it. "Where is the demon dog?"

"In his cage—and not happy about it. He was very vocal in his protests."

"I can imagine."

Jeannette shut the door behind Mariam. "Shall I bring the girls inside?"

"For now. Thomma gets off in about forty-five minutes. I'll have Susan try his cell and leave a message if he doesn't answer. He can swing by here and pick up Mariam and Elisa."

Frowning, Jeannette unbuckled the two girls. That took care of Mariam and Elisa, but Logan was stuck here until five. Molly couldn't sit in the waiting room that long . . . and he didn't know anyone else well enough yet to ask for a babysitting favor.

Except her.

And he wouldn't solicit her help. Not after she'd rebuffed his few friendly overtures.

Besides, he didn't come across as the pushy type—or the kind of person who would ever want to impose.

You could offer *to help him out, though. It wouldn't kill you to watch Molly for a few hours.*

That was true.

But Molly was a charming child—and her uncle was big-time appealing. It would be far too easy to fall under their spell. Get involved. Let them finagle their way into her heart.

And that would be scary.

Stomach roiling, she took the girls' hands and led them toward the urgent care center.

In the lobby, Logan paused. "I hate to delay you, but would you mind waiting with the girls for a few minutes while I line someone up to stay with them until Thomma gets here and try to find someone to watch Molly?"

"No problem." She took a deep breath. *Just suck it up and do the compassionate thing, Jeannette.* "But I have a better idea. I'll wait with the girls, and after the Shabos leave, I'll take Molly home with me until you get off work."

"Seriously?"

"Yes. She can help me make sachets. And I can take her and Toby down to the beach later."

"That would be great." Some of the tension in his features eased.

"I'll need a key, though. I locked your door behind me after I put Toby in the cage."

He fished out a ring, pulled a key off, and handed it over. "I owe you."

"No, you don't. This is what neighbors do." She slid the key into the pocket of her jeans and motioned toward a sitting area in the corner, where a table held an array of children's books. "We'll wait over there until Thomma gets here."

"It shouldn't be long."

As he turned his attention back to the patient, Mariam grasped her hand. "Thank you."

"You're welcome." Jeannette squeezed her fingers.

Elisa had been silent throughout the ordeal, but as Logan began to wheel Mariam into the treatment area, she whimpered and latched onto the woman's arm, tears welling in her eyes.

Mariam spoke to her in soothing tones in Arabic while Molly patted her back. "It's okay, Elisa. Teta will get better." She sent her uncle a beseeching look.

Picking up her prompt, he got down on Elisa's level and crossed his heart. "Teta okay. Promise."

Mariam spoke again in Arabic, and at last Elisa relinquished her grip.

"Come over here, girls, and we'll find some picture books." Jeannette took their hands again and led them to the corner. Elisa came without protest, but she kept looking over her shoulder until Logan and her grandmother disappeared through the door.

Jeannette did her best to entertain them—and to give Elisa an extra language lesson in the guise of fun—but it was obvious the girl was worried and having difficulty concentrating.

Yet when her father pushed through the door, she didn't rush to him for reassurance as he strode toward the reception desk. She simply sat and watched, waiting to be noticed.

Hoping to be noticed.

Jeannette wasn't surprised.

Based on what she'd observed during her tutoring sessions, Thomma was so mired in grief over the family he'd lost that he was oblivious to the needs of the loved ones he still had.

"Can I help you, sir?" The thirtyish guy now behind the desk—Chuck, according to the name-plate—rotated his chair away from the computer.

"Mariam Shabo."

"Are you related?"

It was obvious Thomma had no idea what the man had asked.

Jeannette rose. "Thomma."

He swung around, and the lines of tension in his face smoothed as he joined her. "Mother . . . here?"

"Yes. Sit." She motioned to the chair beside Elisa.

He sat, gave his daughter's shoulder a distracted pat, and said a few words in Arabic.

Not the kind of comfort the child hungered for—a hug would have been far better—but Jeannette couldn't tell this man how to love his lost little daughter. That had to come from within.

She could only pray he realized how much Elisa needed him before it was too late.

Jeannette crossed to the desk. "This is Mariam's son. Would you let Logan . . . Dr. West . . . know he's here?"

"Sure thing." He disappeared into the back.

Jeannette rejoined the small group in the corner.

"Is Mrs. Shabo better?" Molly sidled up to her.

"Your uncle will tell us that in a few minutes." The girl's ponytail had slipped sideways, and she retied the purple ribbon.

Molly leaned close to her ear. "Elisa's scared."

Remarkable how children could pick up nuances, even if they didn't speak the same language.

"I know. It's always scary if someone we love gets hurt."

"My daddy got hurt—and my Nana got sick. They both went to heaven." Her voice quavered. "Is Mrs. Shabo going to heaven?"

"No. She just hurt her ankle." Jeannette put her arm around the girl and gave her a squeeze. "Your uncle will fix her all up."

As if on cue, the door opened and Logan pushed Mariam into the waiting area. The woman's ankle was wrapped in a compression bandage and elevated, but her color had returned. Logan handed Thomma a cell phone as he joined them, and Elisa slipped out of her chair to stand beside Mariam, leaving her father sitting alone.

"How is she?" Jeannette stood.

"She'll be fine. It's a Grade 1 sprain, which is the least serious. I wrapped it to help control the swelling and decrease the pain. The treatment is simple—rest, ice, compression, and elevation. The swelling should go down within a few days. Susan's explaining that to the Shabos." He motioned toward Thomma, who was talking on the cell in low tones.

"Will she be able to watch the girls at your house?"

"I'd rather she stick close to home tomorrow. After that . . . as long as she stays off her feet as much as possible, she should be able to come. I may take Molly to their apartment tomorrow, if Mariam's up to it. Or I could see if the woman Reverend Baker found for me would be willing to come to our house for one day. In the meantime, thank you for filling in for the rest of today. You're a lifesaver."

"It's no big deal."

"It is to me." His gaze locked with hers.

She swallowed and fumbled for Molly's hand. "I, uh, guess we'll go on home. Will Toby be all right in his cage for another hour or two, while I finish up in my workshop?"

"Yes."

"I'll go over and get him after that for a walk on the beach."

"He'll love that—but be warned. If you let him off the leash, roundup can be a challenge."

"I'll keep that in mind."

"Thank you again for the offer of beach access, by the way. We've used it twice. It's much more convenient than piling into the car and driving down 101 to take a walk."

"My pleasure."

Sort of.

As Logan took the phone from Thomma and spoke with Susan, Jeannette busied herself collecting her purse.

In truth, it had been kind of bittersweet to watch through the kitchen window as the three occupants of the house next door had traipsed through her garden to the beach access.

And it had set off a powerful longing deep inside her.

One so strong it had tempted her to emerge from the shadows inside her house and see if she could finagle another invitation to join them.

But she'd resisted.

Mightily.

Her life in Hope Harbor was perfect just as it was. She'd planned every detail, built a business that suited her to a T, kept herself too busy to reminisce . . . or mourn . . . or be lonely.

So what if every day was 100 percent predict-

y

208

able? Consistency was good. Routine didn't have to be stale or boring. It could be comforting.

And after three years, she saw no reason to change a single thing.

Trouble was . . . things were changing around her.

In fact—some days it kind of felt like she was losing control.

And that was *not* comforting.

"I think we're all set." Logan pocketed the cell phone Thomma handed him and dropped to the balls of his feet in front of Molly. "Ms. Mason's going to take you home with her until I get off work, sweetie. You can call me on the phone if you want to, though. She'll help you if you ask."

Molly looked past him to the Shabos. "Is Elisa coming?"

"Not today. Her daddy's going to take her and her grandma home. But she'll be back the day after tomorrow, after Mrs. Shabo's ankle isn't as swollen." He gave her a quick hug, but the girl didn't reciprocate.

Apparently there'd been no progress on the bonding front.

Logan stood and pulled out his keys again. "Unless you have a car seat, you'll have to transfer mine to your car." He held out the ring as a new patient arrived with a blood-soaked towel wrapped around his arm. "You can just leave them at the desk."

"Thanks." She took the fob.

As Logan said a fast good-bye and disappeared into the treatment area, Mariam looked up at her. "English?"

Oh yeah.

They were scheduled for a lesson tonight.

That wasn't going to happen.

"Tomorrow? Tuesday?" This week's three lessons would be back-to-back, but that was better than skipping one.

Mariam tipped her head up toward Thomma and spoke in Arabic. He nodded.

"Okay." The woman smiled at her. "Thank you. Seven?"

"Yes." Meeting at a later time now that Mariam was working had ended up being far less disruptive to her day.

Jeannette took Molly's hand and followed the family out of the urgent care center, Thomma wheeling his mother.

After they waved good-bye to the family, she switched the car seat, buckled her charge into the restraint, dropped Logan's keys at the desk, and took the wheel. In the rearview mirror, she watched the girl tracking the progress of her friend, who was being secured into her car seat a few vehicles away.

Those two had really connected.

And despite the language barrier, they didn't seem to have any difficulty communicating.

That was a blessing for both of them.

Especially since Thomma appeared to have distanced himself from his daughter, and Molly was resisting Logan's attempts to connect.

It was also a blessing for *her*.

If the girls didn't have each other, she'd have been tempted to step in, see if she could ease the deep sadness in Molly's eyes and try to help her connect with her uncle.

Jeannette put the car in gear and backed out of the parking spot.

As it was, she could entertain Molly for a few hours this afternoon, maybe offer to watch her tomorrow if Logan couldn't find anyone else, then slip back to her side of the hedge—and the life she'd had before her new neighbors and a traumatized family had disrupted her orderly existence.

And reminded her how much she missed the loving relationships that had once brightened her world.

15

Logan crested the dune at the end of the access trail behind Jeannette's house and paused to survey Driftwood Beach.

As had been the case on his two previous visits, the vast expanse was almost deserted.

Only three figures were visible today—a little girl with a strawberry-blonde ponytail, a cavorting beagle, and a dark-haired woman trying in vain to coax the dog close enough to snap on a leash.

"Come on, Toby. Cooperate. We have to go home."

Her frustration-laced plea floated up to him as she approached the dog.

Toby hunkered down on his front paws, waited until she got within inches of reaching distance—then dashed off with a happy, catch-me-if-you-can yip to hide behind one of the large, sculpture-like pieces of driftwood arrayed behind the high-water line.

Typical.

Grinning, Logan adjusted the blanket draped over his shoulder, tightened his grip on the bags in his hands, and started down to the beach. "It might be easier to round him up if we tag team this."

As he parroted back the words she'd said to him

213

when the situation had been reversed, Jeannette whipped around, cheeks flushed. "You weren't kidding about trying to corral him."

"Nope. But let's give him a reprieve while we eat dinner. Hi, sweetie." He bent to kiss the top of Molly's head.

Jeannette's gaze moved from the blanket to the bags in his hands, brow crinkling. "Dinner?"

"Yes." He set the sacks on the sand and spread out the blanket. He wasn't taking no for an answer tonight—if he could help it. "I brought Charley's tacos and picked up some brownies from Sweet Dreams. It was the least I could do after you bailed me out with Molly today."

"I was happy to help."

"I appreciate that—but it had to be an inconvenience." He opened the bag of tacos, waved it under her nose, and motioned to the blanket. "Join us?"

She narrowed her eyes. "Not fair. That smell is hard to resist."

"Please stay." Molly edged closer to Jeannette and touched his neighbor's hand.

The brief flash of dismay on Jeannette's face was telling.

She might be able to say no to him, but she had a soft spot for his niece.

Too bad it didn't extend to him—but hey. Whatever worked to keep her here.

"I guess I can stay for a couple of tacos." She

lowered herself to a corner of the blanket and gave Toby a disgruntled look as he trotted over. "Oh, sure, now that we're staying you want to get up close and personal." She scratched behind his ear.

"With us . . . and the food." Logan claimed the other side of the blanket and patted the spot between them. "Come sit, Molly."

She dropped down beside Jeannette instead.

He tried not to let her rebuff bother him as he set the food bags in the center of the blanket and dispensed the tacos.

But it hurt.

"Milk for you"—he handed his niece a small carton with a straw attached—"and a selection for us." He lined up four soft drink cans on the blanket along with two bottles of water.

Jeannette chose a diet Sprite. "It took some effort to put this all together." The carbonation hissed out as she released the tab.

"Easier than cooking." He claimed a full-octane Coke.

"I can't argue with that—and Charley's tacos are much better than the tuna salad in my fridge that was slated to be my dinner. Let me help you with that, honey." She took the milk carton from Molly, detached the straw with one deft twist, and fitted it through the opening.

Like she'd been through that drill a million times.

Curious.

He hadn't even noticed Molly was having difficulty with the carton, and it would have taken him a moment to determine how to release the straw. Jeannette had done it on autopilot.

How did she know so much about kids? Could it be an instinctive female skill—or was there more to her story?

Molly dived into her taco. "Charley cooks good."

"Yes, he does." Jeannette took a big bite.

"I drawed a picture for him." Molly angled toward their neighbor—a clear signal she didn't intend to include him in the conversation.

Logan tried to ignore the tiny twist in his gut.

"Tell me about it." Jeannette gave the child her full attention.

Molly described her rendering in detail. "He put it on his wall and said it might help me find a friend. And it did! Do you think Charley is magic?"

Jeannette smiled. "I don't know about that—but he does have a magic touch with tacos. Don't you think so, Logan?"

"Yep." He left it at that. While he appreciated her effort to include him in the conversation, his participation could shut Molly down—and he'd rather watch her interact with his neighbor. It gave him a glimpse of the kind of relationship they could have if she ever let him into her life.

If being the operative word.

So far it had been a long, slow slog—and some days, for every step forward they took, it felt as if they slipped two steps back.

Yet as he sat here in what any third-party onlooker would assume was a family group, he didn't feel quite as dejected as usual—thanks to Jeannette.

And as the meal wound down, he wasn't ready for this interlude to end.

"Molly, would you like to play with Toby for a few minutes before we go home?" He kept his tone casual.

The dog's ears perked up, and he popped to his feet, abandoning his fruitless food-scrap vigil at the edge of the blanket.

"By myself?" Her last bite of brownie froze halfway to her mouth.

"Jeannette and I will be right here. Just stay back from the edge of the water."

She shoved the fudgy confection into her mouth and jumped up, as if she was afraid he'd change his mind.

"Come on, Toby." She raced down the beach, the dog barking happily at her heels.

Once she was out of earshot, Logan shifted his attention to Jeannette. "Any problems with her today?"

"No. She's a delightful child. But she misses her Nana."

"She talked to you about that?" In his presence,

Molly was as taciturn about personal subjects as the woman sitting across from him.

"Indirectly. While we were making sachets, she mentioned that her grandmother liked to knit—and she told me how she used to help her wind yarn into balls. She also talked about them baking chocolate chip cookies together. It's obvious your mom's death left a huge hole in her life."

"Yeah." He sighed and sifted some sand through his fingers. "One I haven't been able to fill."

"You've only had her four months—and she's dealing with a ton of heavy stuff. If you keep loving her, she'll come around."

"I don't know. I used to think that was true, but I'm beginning to wonder if love is enough. She should be talking to someone—but she clams up around me. I've been considering professional help."

"Like a counselor?"

"Yeah."

"Mmm." Jeannette watched the two small figures romping on the beach. "I suppose it wouldn't hurt—but she and Elisa seem to have become fast friends. That could make a difference."

"Maybe." He ran his palm over the sand, until the surface was smooth and unblemished again. "She likes you too. I'm the one she's having an issue warming up to."

"You took the place of her Nana. That's a challenging role to fill." Jeannette folded her napkin into a precise square, giving the task more attention than it deserved. "I got the impression it was just the two of them after her father died."

"It was."

She didn't ask any more questions—but they hung in the air nonetheless.

Logan brushed off his hands and filled his lungs with the tangy air. Why not tell Jeannette the whole story? Maybe if he shared some of his family history with her, she'd reciprocate down the road. It wasn't as if Molly's background was a state secret, after all.

He stretched out his legs and leaned back on his palms. "If you have a few minutes, I could tell you why there haven't been many people in Molly's life."

"I have to admit I've been curious about that."

"You're not alone. The local newspaper editor almost sweet-talked me into divulging details I'd decided weren't for general consumption."

Jeannette's lips flexed. "Marci is very likeable—and she manages to wheedle an incredible amount of information out of people . . . as I learned from experience."

"She did a story on you?"

"A small one, not long after I arrived."

He'd have to dig through some back issues of the *Herald* and see what he could discover about the reticent woman who'd shared dinner with him on the beach.

"I think she missed her calling. She'd have been an ace investigative reporter."

"I won't argue with that—but she loves what's she doing . . . and that's what counts."

"Agreed. And you do too. Have you always been in the hospitality or restaurant business?"

"No." She folded her legs and picked up a broken sand dollar from the beach beside her. Fingered the jagged, battered edge.

Two seagulls swooped low overhead, but she was oblivious to them.

Logan waited a few more seconds in case she decided to offer more.

She didn't.

And she might bolt if he pushed.

Better move on, much as he'd like to delve deeper into what made his companion tick.

"So in terms of—"

"In my previous—"

As their words overlapped, he closed his mouth.

"Sorry." She glanced over at him.

"No. Go ahead."

"I was going to say that in my previous life, I was an elementary school teacher."

Aha.

That would explain her comfort level around Molly and her adept handling of the milk carton.

But it didn't explain the reason behind her dramatic career shift.

"An unusual background for a lavender farm

220

and tearoom business." He kept his manner conversational. "What prompted the switch?"

She scanned the horizon, where a distant boat was silhouetted against the evening sky. "I needed a change of scene. Since I was relocating, I also decided to rethink my career. My mom and I had always talked about opening a tearoom, and years ago we visited a lavender farm together. I thought it would be fun to combine the two. Bayview Lavender Farm was the result."

"Where was home before you came here?"

"Cincinnati."

That *was* a dramatic change of scene.

"How did you end up in Hope Harbor?"

She shrugged. "After I decided to move, I did some traveling on the West Coast and stumbled onto this town. I stopped for tacos at Charley's, immediately felt at home, discovered there were microclimates here perfect for growing lavender—and the rest is history. So how did *you* find Hope Harbor? There wasn't much detail about that in Marci's article."

She was done sharing.

And that was okay—for now. She'd told him far more than he'd expected.

Yet questions remained.

Like . . . why had she needed a change of scene?

Who had she left behind?

Why did she keep to herself?

He wasn't going to get those answers today,

however. Best to follow her lead and switch gears.

"After I became Molly's guardian, it didn't take me long to realize my lifestyle wasn't conducive to raising a family. I had a studio apartment, I worked long—and odd—hours, and after living in a small town in Missouri, Molly was bewildered and intimidated by the big city. The longer she was in San Francisco, the quieter she got."

"It's not unusual for children to withdraw if their world is disrupted. Either that, or they act out."

"So I discovered after doing tons of research. I thought a smaller town, a house with a yard, and a job with more regular hours would be better for her."

"Not to mention a dog."

He grimaced. "A last-minute addition, the merits of which I'm still debating."

Jeannette turned her attention to Molly and Toby. "They seem to have bonded."

"Unlike her and me. She's been living under my roof for four months, and she talks more to you and Elisa than she does to me." He tried to keep his inflection neutral, but a tad of discouragement crept in.

"Talking to a peer is natural—and there's no risk in communicating with me. If I disappeared tomorrow, it would have zero impact on her life. You're a different story."

That was a take he hadn't considered.

"I see your point."

"You didn't tell me how you ended up here."

He pulled up his legs and rested his forearms on his knees. "A coincidence, really. After I decided to change my lifestyle, I emailed a few classmates hoping for some leads. One of them came through. His son had fallen on some rocks and had to get stitches while they were vacationing in Oregon, and the urgent care center here was the closest place that could patch him up."

"I assume your classmate found out they might be closing."

"Bingo. The nurse who stitched up his son said the doctor in charge had taken the job temporarily to buy them time to find another director. He passed on the name of the clinic, I talked to them, visited the town, applied, and voila. Here I am."

"You gave up a lot for Molly." She cradled the damaged sand dollar in her palm as she studied him. "I'm impressed."

Heat crept up his neck, and he busied himself gathering up the remains of their dinner. "I didn't have much choice. I promised my brother I'd take her in if he or Mom weren't there to raise her."

"You did way more than that. You changed your whole life."

"It was a healthy change for me too. I was becoming a workaholic. I needed to get some balance back."

Silence fell between them, broken only by the boom of the surf crashing against the offshore sea stacks and the plaintive call of the two gulls circling above.

Jeannette hadn't asked the most obvious question, but she had to be wondering where Molly's mother was—and he'd promised to tell her the story.

As if she'd read his mind, she sent him a sidelong glance. "Since you're Molly's guardian, I assume her mother isn't in the picture."

Logan stuffed their trash with more force than necessary into one of the empty bags. "No. She never has been." This was the ugly part of the story. The part he saw no reason to share with the world.

But Jeannette wasn't the world.

She was . . .

Frowning, Logan crimped the bag in his fingers. What was she exactly?

She was too new in his life to be a friend—but she felt like more than a mere acquaintance.

She felt like a woman who had potential to be—

"Sorry. I didn't mean to pry." Jeannette started to rise. "It's getting late, and—"

"Wait." He touched her arm. "I said I'd tell you the story, and I will. It's just that I haven't shared this with many people."

Like none.

She hesitated. "I won't hold you to that promise.

I understand about wanting to keep some things private."

"I appreciate that—but I'd like you to know the history. Please stay." He didn't touch her hand, as Molly had when she'd made the same plea—but the temptation to do so was strong.

So strong he gripped the bag tighter to keep his hands out of trouble.

A few beats passed, but at last she settled back onto the blanket.

He exhaled . . . set the bag beside him . . . and dived in. "My brother was a good man, but being a soldier is a lonely, nomadic business. While he was doing some training at Fort Hood, he had a brief liaison with a woman he met in a bar. She ended up getting pregnant—and she did *not* want the baby. She told my brother she intended to get an abortion, and demanded he pay for it."

"He obviously convinced her to rethink that decision."

"Yes—but it cost him. She milked his bank account dry while she was pregnant. He did have the foresight early on to hire an attorney, who drew up an ironclad agreement in which she agreed to waive her parental rights in exchange for full financial support during her pregnancy and a hefty lump sum payment. Otherwise, the whole mess could have gotten even uglier."

She shook her head. "Children too often become a pawn in a situation like that."

"True."

"Did your mom step in to help after Molly was born?"

"Not in the beginning. My brother wasn't stationed anywhere near Missouri, and he didn't expect our mom to leave the home she'd lived in all of her married life. For the first two years, he raised Molly alone and used on-base daycare. But once he got deployed, leaving Molly with Mom was the best option."

"It's obvious she loved her Nana."

"Yeah." He linked his fingers. "She would have been a better person to raise Molly through childhood and adolescence. The learning curve on this single-parenting gig is steeper than I expected—and knowing a child is relying on you for everything can be overwhelming."

He looked over at her, and for one brief, unguarded moment he caught a touch of . . . tenderness? . . . in her eyes.

She cleared her throat and fiddled with the laces on her sport shoe. "I can't begin to imagine what a challenge this has been for you. But from what I've observed, you're doing a terrific job."

Her praise warmed him—even if he wasn't certain it was warranted.

"Thanks, but some days I—"

Molly shrieked, and he vaulted to his feet. Beside him, Jeannette scrambled up too.

False alarm.

His niece had gotten a bit too close to where the surf was breaking against a large rock, and the salt spray had rained down on her.

Nevertheless, it took a few moments for his heart to downshift.

"I think that's our cue to exit. Those wet clothes will have to be changed." He cupped his hands around his mouth. "Molly! Time to go."

She swiveled toward them . . . hesitated . . . then plodded across the sand, Toby at her heels.

"You may want to have the leash ready." Jeannette scooped it up and passed it to him surreptitiously. "If I distract your canine friend, you might be able to catch him off guard."

"Good thinking."

As the two approached, Jeannette got down on one knee. "Did you get wet, boy?"

Toby trotted to her, always up for an ear rub, and as she talked to him Logan snapped on the leash.

The instant it clicked, the dog realized he'd been had and let loose with an ear-splitting howl.

"Toby." Logan fished a doggie treat out of his pocket and waited until he had the beagle's attention. "Kunn hadyaan."

The dog stopped mid-howl . . . sat on his haunches . . . and waited for the treat.

Jeannette stared at him. "What did you say to get him to do that?"

"I think it means be quiet in Arabic. It's the command Thomma uses."

"That's amazing."

"It's more than that. It's a miracle." Logan rested his hand on Molly's shoulder. "Ready to go?"

"Do we have to?"

"Yes. It's getting cooler, and your shirt's wet. Besides, Thomma will be coming soon to work with Toby on the fence." He held the leash out to Jeannette. "Will you keep a tight grip on this while I fold up the blanket?"

"Sure."

His hand brushed hers as he passed the strap over, and despite the chill in the early evening air, a little spurt of electricity zipped up his arm, warming him to the core.

The slight hitch in her breathing suggested she'd had a similar reaction.

That could be a positive omen for the future— once life quieted down.

If it ever quieted down.

After dismantling the remains of their picnic, he fell in behind Jeannette and Molly as they took the lead on the return trip.

The two of them chatted during the entire walk, but Molly fell silent once they arrived at the lavender farm.

"I meant to ask you while we were on the beach— were you able to make any arrangements for tomorrow?" Jeannette dipped her chin toward his niece.

"Not yet. It's my top priority tonight. Worst case, I can take her to the Shabos."

"Will Mariam be up to babysitting tomorrow?"

"Probably not—but I'm keeping it as a backup plan."

"I'll tell you what . . . why don't you let her come over here again? I'll be home all day. I'm not set up for a dog in the house or the workshop, but I'll be happy to walk Toby during the day."

"I couldn't impose again." Much as he'd like to take the easy way out, if he overextended his welcome he might wear it out. "I don't want to disrupt your work."

"I don't mind."

"Please, Uncle Logan."

"Sweetie, it wouldn't be—" He blinked.

Wait.

She'd called him Uncle Logan.

That was a first.

All these months, she'd avoided calling him *anything*. While she'd referred to him as her uncle to other people, she'd never addressed him with that title.

Maybe they were beginning to turn a corner.

And if they were, he wasn't going to jinx it by refusing her request—even at the risk of wearing out his welcome with Jeannette.

"Okay." The tiny smile she gave him was more than sufficient reward for capitulating. He refocused on Jeannette. "I really will owe you after this."

"No. I'll enjoy it as much as she will."

Toby tugged on the leash, obviously eager to eat his own dinner.

"I have to feed the pup. Can I drop Molly off around eight?"

"That'll be fine. Thanks for dinner."

"My pleasure." He took his niece's hand. "Time to head home, sweetie."

"I wish we didn't have to go."

That made two of them.

"You'll be back tomorrow." Toby strained against the leash again as Logan spoke to Jeannette. "See you soon."

"Very." Her lips curved up a hair. "Have a nice evening."

He set off with his little entourage, down the hedge on Jeannette's side.

As he rounded the corner at the end, toward his own driveway, he looked back.

She was standing where he'd left her, backlit by the golden sun that left her face in shadows—and unreadable.

Who knew what she was thinking?

But he did know one thing.

His evening would be much nicer if it included her.

Suggesting there could be serious potential ahead with his reclusive neighbor if she ever ventured out from behind the hedge around her property—and the walls around her heart.

16

" 'Ami!" Thomma jolted to a stop in the kitchen doorway. "You're not supposed to be putting weight on your foot."

"I always fix your breakfast."

"I don't expect you to cook with a sprained ankle—or any day at five forty-five in the morning for that matter. I told you that when I started my job. Yogurt and bread will do today."

"No they won't. Breakfast is an important meal."

He waved a hand in dismissal. "I'm not hungry anyway."

"You will eat a meal if I prepare it."

Yes, he would—especially if she'd gone to all this effort despite her injured ankle.

As she well knew.

"I wish you wouldn't feel like you have to prepare food for me." He huffed out a breath. "I'm a grown man. I can take care of myself."

She froze for an instant, the spatula in her hand suspended above the fried egg in the pan on the stove. "I know that." A quiver rippled through her words, and she gripped the edge of the counter. Flipped the egg.

Thomma frowned. "What's wrong?"

"Nothing."

But as she hobbled to the cabinet in the small

231

kitchen to retrieve a plate, the shimmer in her eyes said otherwise.

His pulse stumbled.

" 'Ami." He closed the distance between them. "What's going on? Does your ankle hurt? Do you want a painkiller?"

She angled away from him. "I'll be done here in a few minutes. Once I sit, it won't hurt."

"Why don't you sit now? I can finish up the breakfast." He pulled out a chair.

"No. I have prepared breakfast for my family while feeling much worse than this. I'll put my foot up after you're gone."

"But I can take over."

"I know. You are a grown man, as you said. You don't need me anymore." She turned toward him, her back to the window, the sky outside not yet lightened by the sun. "But this is my life, Thomma. I cook and clean and do the laundry and keep the household running and love my family." A tear leaked out of the corner of her eye, and she swiped it away. "The truth is, I need you more than you need me."

Her admission was like a sucker punch to the gut.

Despite the strong front she presented to the world, his mother too had doubts and insecurities. The life she'd known had also vanished, and like him, she was searching for meaning in this new land.

Why had he never realized that?

Because you've been selfish, and you've only paid attention to your own problems.

The rebuke from his conscience was harsh—but true.

He had to do better for this woman who'd been the glue in their family as far back as he could remember.

"You're wrong, 'Ami." He crossed to her and took the worn hands that had cared for him with such tenderness when he was a child. That were still caring for him—and his daughter. "I do need you. So does Elisa."

"For now, maybe."

"For always."

She searched his face, straightened her shoulders, and tugged her hands free, her typical strong façade slipping back into place. "Your egg will burn. Sit. The meal is ready."

He moved to the table, filled with as many of the breakfast foods from home as she could make from the ingredients she'd found at the local market. Like it had been in the old days, before terror and persecution and tragedy had driven them away from their native land.

His mother had always done her best for her family, no matter the cost to her.

Today was but the latest example.

Despite the pain in her ankle, she was cooking breakfast for her son because that's what she

233

did. Because she considered it her responsibility. Because this was what gave her life meaning.

She had to be wondering where she would find that meaning if he and Elisa had no need of her anymore.

The early hour, coupled with pain that could have disrupted her sleep, must have left her weary and disheartened—and pried open a crack in her armor, giving him a rare glimpse of the fear and vulnerability this rock of a woman usually kept under wraps.

Whatever the reason her fortitude had faltered in the pre-dawn hours of this May morning, it was an ice-water-in-the-face wake-up call. A sharp reminder that he wasn't the only one struggling.

It was also disconcerting.

If someone as strong as 'Ami could stumble, what hope was there for him?

"Eat." She set the egg in front of him and added a basket of pita bread to the plates of cheese, hummus, yogurt, stewed fava beans, and pickled eggplant in olive oil arrayed on the table—all breakfast favorites from their homeland.

This was a feast compared to the meager, basic rations in the refugee camp.

Yet even there, she'd done her best to create meals for her decimated family from the sparse, basic ingredients available.

And he'd taken it for granted.

Still took all she did for granted.

He clenched his fingers around the mug of coffee she slid toward him, and a flood of shame swept through him as another realization smacked him in the face.

Without his mother, he and Elisa wouldn't have survived in that camp.

Nor would they be here.

She was the one who'd latched on to the invitation that had come out of the blue.

She was the one who'd worked with the person from the humanitarian aid organization to complete all the necessary paperwork.

She was the one who'd pushed and prodded him every step of the way until they'd set foot in Hope Harbor.

Vision misting, he took her hand. " 'Ami . . . I'm sorry."

"For what?" She gave him a blank look.

"For not appreciating all you've done for me and Elisa. All you've done for our family my whole life."

"It's what mothers do. Eat your egg or it will get cold." She limped back to the counter, dispensed with her apron, and continued toward the hall. "I will rest now so I can return to my job tomorrow."

"You like the work you are doing?"

She shifted back. "There is a need, and I am able to help fill it. That is good for the heart—and the soul."

Her gaze locked with his, and then she continued

down the hall, resting her fingertips against the walls for support.

Thomma broke off a bite of his egg. Surveyed the table. He would eat the food his mother had gone to the trouble to prepare.

But he hadn't lied a few minutes ago.

He wasn't hungry.

His appetite had died in Syria, along with the family and the life he'd loved.

Except . . . not all of his family was gone—and 'Ami's parting message hadn't been lost on him.

There was a need—and a responsibility—in his own backyard he alone could fill, yet he'd ignored it.

His mother had soldiered on through the pain of loss in Syria, and again this morning through the pain of a sprained ankle. Doing what had to be done. Fulfilling her obligations.

She was telling him he should do the same with Elisa.

But how could he expose himself to more hurt and heartache, when he'd already exceeded the limits of his tolerance for pain?

He set his fork down, rested his elbows on the table, and dropped his face into his hands. His desperate prayer last week hadn't produced any results, but where else could he turn?

God, I don't know what to do. I wake every morning hoping the darkness will be less oppressive, but each day is as bleak as the one before.

Help me love my daughter as I should. As I know Raca would have wanted me to. Please give me the courage and strength to carry on as my mother does—and the grace to appreciate the second chance you've given the three of us.

Thomma exhaled . . . lowered his hands . . . and picked up his fork to eat the breakfast his mother had prepared for him.

As he dug into the egg, a thin ray of light from the rising sun stole through the window and slanted across the table.

He lifted his head.

Outside, the black of night was giving way to a new day. The darkness was receding, the world once again brightening.

Perhaps the same would be true of his life.

Or not.

But for today at least, he would cling to that hope.

Because if he didn't . . . if he succumbed to the fear that the shadows encroaching on his soul would plunge it into darkness forever . . . he might not make it through another day.

"I think we better start back, Molly. Your uncle will be home soon." Jeannette checked her watch as they strolled along the beach. She also had a lesson to prepare for tonight's session with the Shabos. It was going to be a busy evening—but she ought to be able to squeeze in a fast dinner too.

The girl bent to pick up a small piece of drift-wood. "Look, 'Nette. It's a heart."

Jeannette's lips bowed at the child's shortened version of her name. Much less of a mouthful than Jeannette or Ms. Mason.

"Let me see." She held out her hand.

Molly passed it over, and she examined the small chunk of sea-smoothed wood. It did, indeed, resemble a heart. "This is beautiful. You were lucky to find such a pretty piece. You can keep it for always to remind you of the people you love and our walk on the beach today." She extended it toward the girl.

"It's for you." Molly's demeanor was solemn.

Jeannette's heart contracted at the simple gesture of affection.

But Logan would appreciate such a gift too—and this was a perfect opportunity to plant that suggestion.

"That's a lovely present—and it makes me happy. Do you think your uncle might like to have it, though?"

"No." Molly gave her head an emphatic shake. "It's for you."

So much for that idea.

The topic was worth a bit more discussion, however. Hard as she'd tried all day to get a read on Molly's feelings for Logan, the child hadn't cooperated. Yet if she could gain a few insights that would be useful to him as he tried to connect with his niece, it was worth one more attempt.

"Don't you think he'd like it?" She kept her inflection conversational as they continued their side-by-side walk along the beach.

She shrugged. "I don't know."

"Most people like to get presents. Don't you?"

"Uh-huh."

"The Easter dress and hat you wore to tea were a nice present from your uncle."

"Nana got me an Easter dress and hat too—and sometimes she got me a popsicle from the truck that came to our street."

"I like ice cream trucks too." One more shot and she was calling this interrogation attempt quits. "Should we find another piece for your uncle, since I get to keep this pretty heart?"

"Why?"

"It might make him happy."

Molly's forehead wrinkled. "Why?"

"Well . . . the heart made *me* happy. I bet he'd feel the same about a present you gave him."

"Why?"

"Because he loves you."

Molly sighed and kicked at a piece of flotsam in her path. "Not like Nana did."

"How do you know?"

"Nana loved me . . . just because. She was happy I lived with her."

"Don't you think your uncle feels the same way?"

"No." She lunged for an elusive mole crab, but it vanished beneath the sand in a furious burst of digging.

Jeannette dropped down beside her and examined the smooth surface. "Those guys are fast, aren't they?"

"Yes. Toby can't catch them either."

"Why don't we sit back there on the dry sand for a minute, see if he comes out again?" Not likely, but it would give her a chance to continue the conversation. "Want to do that?"

" 'Kay." The girl moved a few feet back and sat beside her, watching the spot where the crab had vanished.

"You know . . ." Jeannette sieved the sand through her fingers. "It's kind of hard sometimes to know if someone loves you. Not everyone shows love the same way."

"Nana hugged me and tucked me in at night and read me stories and baked cookies."

"Your uncle doesn't do any of that?"

Molly's brow knotted. "Yes . . . but it's not the same. And he burned the cookies we made. The house was stinky."

"He tried, though—and trying should count, don't you think?"

"I guess. But Nana loved me a lot."

"I know she did—and I kind of thought your uncle did too. Not many uncles take their nieces to tea . . . or let them have all the chocolate cakes." She smiled at the girl and gave her a wink.

Molly poked her finger in the sand, her lips flat. "He's nice, but he doesn't want me."

Whoa!

Where had *that* come from?

"Why do you think that?" She brushed back a strand of hair that had worked loose from Molly's ponytail, her heart aching for the child whose eyes were sad beyond her years—like Elisa's.

" 'Cause."

Not helpful.

" 'Cause what?"

" 'Cause I heard him talking on the phone one night." Molly sniffed and wiped the back of her hand under her nose. When she continued, her voice was so soft Jeannette had to lean close to hear it above the crashing surf. "He said he promised my daddy and Nana he'd take care of me, but he didn't know what to do with a little girl and wished I was still with Nana. He sounded m-mad."

O-kay.

That kind of overheard conversation would be enough to make anyone feel unwanted, let alone a child who'd lost everyone in the world she knew and loved.

Be careful how you respond, Jeannette.

"How long ago did you hear that, honey?"

Another lift of her thin shoulders. "At the beginning. In the other place we lived." She hung her head. "I wet the bed one night, and after he changed everything, I heard him on the phone." She gave Jeannette a sidelong glance, expression earnest. "But I don't wet anymore. I'm a big girl."

Pressure built in Jeannette's throat. "I can see that. And you're also brave. It's hard when everything in your life changes, and the people you love go away." The last few words rasped, and she swallowed.

Molly scrutinized her. "Are you sad too, 'Nette?"

"Sometimes. I miss the people I loved too."

The girl took her hand. "I'll be your friend. And I gave you the heart I found. Maybe it will help you not be sad."

Mercy.

Now Molly was consoling *her.*

How had this conversation gotten so off track?

She had to regroup and focus on Logan's niece.

"I'm sure it will help me feel better. Thank you." She squeezed the girl's hand. "And you know what? I think your uncle might be sad sometimes too. Nana was his mommy, and your daddy was his brother. He must miss them."

"He never says so."

Another insight to pass on to her neighbor on the QT.

"Sometimes people don't talk about what's in their heart. And sometimes, if everything changes, people don't know how they feel. It takes them a while to figure it all out. I bet he was trying to do that the night you heard him on the phone. What do you think?"

That earned her another shrug.

"Well, all I know is what I see since you came to Hope Harbor—and I think he loves you. Why else would he take you to tea and get you a dog and buy you ribbons for your hair?" She reached over and tweaked the yellow one Molly was wearing today.

"I s'pose." The girl fingered the silky strands.

But all of that didn't erase the overheard conversation—or its effects.

It might be best to try a different tack.

"Can I tell you something? I have a feeling your uncle is glad you came to live with him. Being all by yourself can get lonesome."

Molly rose, walked over to where the crab had disappeared, and poked at the sand with a stick—but the crustacean continued to hide. "He told me that one night."

Jeannette's eyebrows rose.

Kudos to him—and so much for the conventional wisdom that said men didn't share their feelings.

"There you go."

Molly swiveled toward her. "Do you need someone to love too?"

Whoops.

That wasn't a subject she wanted to discuss with Logan's niece.

From up near the dunes, Toby began to bark.

Yes!

For once, the dog's timing was impeccable.

Jeannette stood and brushed the sand off her jeans. "Toby! Here, boy!"

The dog ignored her.

Of course.

Apparently another game of chase the beagle was on her agenda.

"We're going to have to round him up again, Molly."

"He likes the beach."

"I do too—but we can't live down here. If he comes toward you, try to grab him."

" 'Kay."

They separated as they approached the dog— but instead of watching them with the typical roguish gleam in his eye as he planned a last-second escape, his attention remained fixed on whatever had caught his interest on the beach.

Even when they were a mere six feet away, he stayed hunkered down, gaze riveted on the sand in front of him.

Highly suspect.

But Jeannette wasn't about to question her good fortune.

She swooped in and snapped on his leash.

Only then did she check to see what had distracted him.

"Oh!" Molly breathed the word as she squatted

down on the sand beside a tiny, quivering kitten.

Too tiny to be roaming about without its mother.

Jeannette tugged the dog back. "Sit, Toby—and be quiet." Too bad she couldn't remember that Arabic phrase Logan had used yesterday.

Didn't matter.

The beagle plopped down and fell silent—as if he'd done his job of calling the kitten's plight to their attention and was happy to hand off the problem to them.

But she wasn't much better equipped to deal with an abandoned kitty than her five-year-old companion.

"I think he's lost." Molly touched the baby feline's fur. "What do we do?"

Good question.

Jeannette wracked her brain, trying to call up any stray piece of dusty information filed there about how to deal with a situation like this.

Hadn't she read somewhere once that the best plan with an abandoned kitten was to back off and see if the mother returned?

However . . . the sun was dipping, the temperature was dropping, and the kitten was already shivering.

It needed warmth, and most likely food.

Fast.

As her mind raced, she scanned the area. The mother was probably a feral cat. It was possible she had a litter nearby—though the open, unprotected expanse wouldn't be the usual spot for that.

A tiny meow refocused her.

"I think he's cold, 'Nette." Molly stroked his fur again, grooves denting her forehead.

"I think you're right."

She couldn't leave him here. He'd die of exposure, or be swooped up by a raptor. There were plenty of falcons and hawks and owls at the Bandon Marsh, and that wasn't far away.

"Can we take him home with us?" Molly touched his tiny nose.

What choice did she have?

"I guess we'll have to. I don't see his mommy around anywhere."

She gave the area another sweep.

Nothing.

If the mother was in the area, she was hiding.

And this kitten couldn't wait for her to mosey back to rescue him.

Jeannette unzipped her shoulder tote and pulled out the small towel she'd brought along in case anyone got wet feet. "Can you carry my bag home, honey? I know it's kind of big."

"I can do it."

Jeannette slipped the strap across the girl's chest, created a pouch out of the towel, and scooped up the kitty, nestling it inside.

The tiny ball of fur couldn't weigh even a pound.

Cradling the kitty in one arm, she took a firm

grip on Toby's leash. "Let's get this little guy home and try to warm him up."

With Molly on one side of her and Toby trotting along on the other, Jeannette set as brisk a pace as the youngster could handle.

Rescuing a kitten had not been in her plans for today—or for her life—and the sooner she could wash her hands of this, the better.

"Are you going to keep the kitty, 'Nette?"

"No." She wanted no connections of any kinds—human or feline. "I don't know how to take care of a baby kitten. I'm going to find someone who does."

And who didn't mind getting emotionally invested in an animal's welfare.

One phone call should solve the problem. She could drop the kitty off wherever they said and continue on to the Shabos' for their English lesson.

"Where?"

"Uh . . . at the Humane Society, I guess." If there wasn't one in Hope Harbor, there had to be one in a nearby town.

"Will they help him?"

"Sure." Of course they would. Assisting abandoned animals was what they did.

Wasn't it?

Or did they restrict their intakes to older animals that required less nurturing and attention?

"Uncle Logan is here." Molly pointed toward the lavender farm in the distance.

Her neighbor was on the patio at the back of the house, fists propped on hips, watching their approach.

Either he was early or they'd lingered on the beach too long.

He met them at the back of the property. "Hi. I had a feeling you were down at the beach." He smiled at her as he gave Molly a squeeze and took Toby's leash, leaning closer to see what was tucked in her arm.

"Sorry we were delayed." She breathed in a lungful of his subtle but potent aftershave. "We got distracted by this abandoned kitty."

"He's a tiny one. No sign of the mother?"

"No."

"What are you going to do with him?"

"Turn him over to whoever tends to animals like this—the Humane Society, I guess."

Twin furrows creased his brow. "I don't think most places have the staff to care for a critter this small." He assessed the cat. "A kitten that age would require frequent feedings."

Not what she wanted to hear.

"Then what am I supposed to do with it? I have to be at the Shabos' by seven." Despite her attempt to remain calm, a thread of panic wove through her voice.

She did not want this kitten in her life. If she tended to it night and day, she could get attached—and that was against all her rules.

Logan must have sensed her panic, because when he spoke, his tone was calm and soothing. No doubt the same one he used with freaked-out patients.

"We'll work it out." He carefully lifted the tiny bundle from her arm. "You get ready for the Shabos and I'll warm this little guy up and see what resources I can find for abandoned critters."

"Seriously?"

"Yeah. Molly will help me. Right, sweetie?"

"Uh-huh."

"Why don't you stop by after your lesson with the Shabos and we'll regroup? Thomma's coming back again too to work with Toby on the electric fence. That will give the two of us a quiet few minutes to come up with a plan for this kitty."

"You're a lifesaver."

He grinned. "Just returning the favor."

Jeannette removed her tote bag from across Molly's chest. "I should be back by eight-fifteen."

"Don't rush. We'll be here all evening. Come on, sweetie. Let's go feed Toby."

The dog's ears perked up, and he began straining at the leash.

"Bye, 'Nette."

"Bye, honey." She gave the girl a hug, and bent low to whisper in her ear. "Thank you again for the heart."

"Maybe we could go back to the beach and look for more pretty pieces of wood."

Not a promise she was willing to make, despite the girl's hopeful expression.

Babysitting for her neighbor in an emergency was one thing.

Regular involvement with the duo next door was another.

"Mrs. Shabo will be staying with you from now on."

And there would be no reason in the future for her to interact much with her charming neighbors.

Which was perfect.

Except if that was true, why was there a hollow feeling in the pit of her stomach as she watched Logan take Molly's hand and lead her down the long hedge on the left, then disappear around the edge?

She should be glad they were gone.

Yet that tiny twinge deep inside felt like . . . yearning. Like a part of her wished she belonged to the family next door.

Bad news.

She turned her back and escaped to the peaceful, solitary haven she'd created, where there would be no new loss or grief.

And if this burgeoning feeling of loneliness was the price she had to pay to protect her sanctuary?

So be it.

Because it was better to be lonely than risk another broken heart.

17

"They're here!"

At Molly's excited announcement, Logan took the last plate from the dishwasher, slid it into the cabinet, and joined her in the small foyer.

Thomma's Sentra was pulling up his driveway, but there was no sign of his neighbor's car.

"Did you see Jeannette?"

"Yes. She drove behind the big bushes." Molly turned away from her post beside the front door. "Is she coming over?"

"In a few minutes." After spending all day in her company, his niece had been more talkative than usual at dinner—and much of her conversation had been about 'Nette.

"Can me and Elisa go see her tomorrow?"

"She has to work, sweetie."

"She worked today too. I helped her. We won't get in the way. Please? I like being there."

"I know—but today was special. It was an emergency. Tomorrow Mrs. Shabo will be back, and her foot will be hurting. She can't walk very far."

"Well . . . when *can* I see her again?"

He was saved by a knock on the back door.

"We'll talk about it later." He retraced his steps to the kitchen.

She followed along behind him, stopping at the table to peer into the box where the sleeping kitty lay nestled in a soft towel.

Logan handed Toby off to Thomma as the doorbell rang.

"That's 'Nette!" Molly zipped back to the front of the house.

Logan joined her as she twisted the knob.

"Come on in." He smiled at his neighbor and pulled the door wide. "How did the lesson go?"

"Great. They're all progressing at a remarkable pace." She entered and lowered herself to Molly's level. "How's the kitty?"

"We got him some milk, but he doesn't like it."

"That's strange. I thought all kittens liked milk." Jeannette stood and shifted her attention to him. "What's the status?"

"We made a fast run for some supplies while you were gone."

Her eyes narrowed. "Why do we need supplies?"

"Let's talk in the kitchen while I try to coax him to take some formula."

Without giving her a chance to reply, he ushered her toward the back of the house.

She waited beside the table while he tested the temperature of the formula he'd been heating in a pot of water, watching as he positioned the kitten on its stomach inside the blanket, tipped up the bottom of the bottle, and gently rubbed the nipple back and forth across tiny cat's lips and gums.

The kitty was having none of it, even though he had to be hungry.

"Why won't he eat?" Jeannette frowned.

"You've got me. Want to try?" He held out the bottle.

After a moment, she took it, picked up the towel-swaddled bundle, and sat in a chair with the kitten on her lap. As she mimicked Logan's actions with the nipple, she spoke in soothing tones and stroked her fingers over the feline's exposed head.

Half a minute in, the cat latched onto the nipple and began to suck.

"He's eating!" Molly hopped from one foot to the other.

"I bow to your bedside manner." Logan grinned at Jeannette.

"Don't be too hasty. I think hunger finally won out. So what's the story on all the supplies?" She motioned toward the counter, where another bottle, several nipples, and the box of formula were lined up.

Logan pulled out the chair beside her and sat. "My earlier suspicions were correct. No organization wants to take a cat this young."

Dismay darted through her eyes. "So what are we supposed to do?"

"Find someone to take care of him—or do it ourselves."

She exhaled. "That won't work with your schedule."

"No—and I don't know anyone in town well enough to ask them to tackle a job like this. Based on the markers I found online, this little guy's about three weeks old. That means he'll have to be bottle-fed every four to five hours for another week or two, at which point he can start eating canned food. He won't be ready for adoption for five to seven weeks."

"Wow."

"That was my reaction too. Do you know any cat lovers who might be willing to step in?"

"No."

That didn't surprise him.

Jeannette may have been in town longer than him, but odds were he'd soon know more people than his reclusive neighbor did.

"I guess we can both ask around—and in the meantime, I'll see if Mariam will feed him while she's here."

Not ideal, since Toby and the two girls were a handful without the addition of a helpless kitten—but what other choice did he have if Jeannette didn't volunteer?

She focused on the task of feeding the abandoned kitty for a few silent seconds before she spoke. "It's not fair to dump this on you. I'm the one who hauled him home."

"I would have done the same if I'd found him."

"But you didn't. And I have more flexibility in my schedule—along with fewer care-and-feeding responsibilities." She sighed. "I'll take him."

"Can I come see him?" Molly edged closer to Jeannette.

A few beats ticked by. "Um . . . he'll probably sleep most of the day."

Her message was clear—to him anyway.

She didn't want to commit to regular visits. She'd done him a favor yesterday and today, but she was more than ready to retreat to her solitary world.

Somehow he managed to resist the temptation to let Molly exploit the soft spot Jeannette had for her. "He has to get bigger before we bother him too much, sweetie. Baby kittens that young are too little to play with."

"I could just look at him."

"Let's see how he does for a few days. Why don't you go put on your pajamas and brush your teeth?"

"Do I have to?"

"Yep. It's bedtime. Toby can keep you company as soon as Thomma is finished with him."

As if on cue, a knock sounded at the back door.

Logan rose, crossed the room, and twisted the knob.

Thomma handed him Toby's leash. "He learn."

"Good." The sooner he could relinquish his walk-the-dog duties, the better. "Thank you."

"Tomorrow?"

"Yes."

Thomma nodded at Jeannette and retreated down the porch steps.

Logan closed the door, unclicked the leash—and the pup dashed over to Jeannette to inspect the bundle on her lap.

"Keep your distance, buddy, or you'll freak out our friend here." She twisted away from the curious dog.

"Molly, take Toby with you while you change into your pjs." Logan grasped the beagle's collar and tugged him back.

"Come on, Toby." Molly headed toward the hall.

The pup swiveled his head both directions, as if debating whether to follow, but in the end he trotted after her.

"He's better behaved than he used to be." Jeannette checked on the kitten's progress with the formula.

"Thanks to Thomma. He's also getting the hang of the fence. The installer said training should take about two weeks, and we seem to be tracking to that schedule." Logan tapped the bottle. "He's about done, isn't he?"

"Yes." She removed the nipple.

"You can burp him by patting him on the back right where he is."

"You must have done some research while I was gone—or is that your medical knowledge speaking?"

"Nope. We didn't cover cats in med school."

Her lips flexed up. "Thanks for running out to get the supplies too."

"No problem. If you want me to take a rotation on night duty, I'm willing."

"That's okay. Unlike you, I can sleep late if necessary." She continued to pat the kitty, lowering her voice as a door closed down the hall. "I had an enlightening conversation with Molly today. I can fill you in if we relocate to the porch once our friend here is done digesting his dinner."

"Sure. Give me ten minutes to tuck her in, and I'll join you out there. Would you like some coffee?"

"No thanks. I won't be staying long."

Too bad. Spending a few extra minutes in his neighbor's company would be a pleasant way to end this day.

He rose and moved toward the hall, glancing back as he reached the doorway.

Jeannette was watching him.

But she yanked her gaze back to the kitten immediately, a soft blush coloring her cheeks.

Telling.

The lady might be determined to keep her distance, but it wasn't due to lack of interest.

She liked him.

As much as he liked her, unless his instincts were failing him.

So why was she holding back?

There wasn't much chance he'd get an answer

to that question tonight—but he wasn't giving up.

No one had ever called Logan West a quitter.

After getting Molly settled as fast as he could and dispensing with her usual bedtime story, he found Jeannette waiting for him on the front porch, as she'd promised—the mesh folding chairs once again pushed farther apart than usual.

He sat, letting the furniture rearrangement pass, as he had during their last tête-à-tête in this spot.

"Is she down for the night?" Jeannette crossed her legs.

He tried not to be distracted by their nice line, shown off to perfection by her snug black leggings.

"For now." He leaned back and laced his fingers over his stomach, transferring his attention to two gulls soaring overhead. "But it may not last. Sometimes I hear her crying later through the wall between our rooms." He swallowed. "Those nights are hard."

"I can imagine." Sympathy softened her sable irises. "What do you do?"

"The first few times it happened, I went in and tried to talk to her, but she shut me out. Last round, I said I was lonesome and asked if I could stay with her."

"Ah. That must have been what she was referring to today. She said you told her once you were lonely. Not a bad strategy to build rapport."

"That's what I thought—and I hoped it would

be a turning point. She did let me stay . . . but the next day we were back to the status quo. No matter what I try, I can't break through the barrier she's erected between us."

"I may have an insight about the source of that."

He hitched up one side of his mouth. "I'm not surprised she confided in you. In case you haven't realized it, she likes you."

"It's mutual." She folded her hands. "I want to phrase this diplomatically, because I can see how hard you're trying to win her over."

"Don't worry about diplomacy. Just give it to me straight." He braced. "Did she tell you she hates me?"

Her eyebrows peaked. "No. Nothing like that. Why would she hate you?"

"Because I took the place of her Nana? Because I made her leave the only home she remembers? Because I don't have a clue how to raise a little girl?" He blew out a breath. "There could be a dozen reasons."

"She doesn't hate you. But she doesn't think you want her."

"What?" He stared at her. "Why would she think that? I've done everything I can to make her feel wanted and loved."

"She overheard a phone conversation that wasn't meant for her ears."

Logan listened as Jeannette relayed the story Molly had shared with her about the night he'd been beside himself trying to figure out how to deal with a five-year-old bed-wetting child who was lost and grieving and uncommunicative.

When she finished, he wiped a hand down his face. "I was venting to a friend. I had no idea she'd heard any of that."

"Kids have incredible audio powers."

"I've learned that in the past four months. The incident she talked about happened during the first two weeks she was with me. Months ago. I don't know what else I can do to convince her I love her and want her beyond what I'm already doing."

"May I offer a suggestion?"

"Please."

"Tell her how you feel about the loss of your mom and brother. She said you never talk about them, so she may be reluctant to bring up her own grief. If she knows you have sorrow in common, she may open up about that—and other subjects. Shared experiences can create strong bonds."

"That makes sense." He leaned back and crossed an ankle over a knee. "I thought Molly and I should establish a comfort level before we got into heavier issues, but maybe talking about those would help *build* that comfort level."

"It might."

"Any other insights or tips you can share?"

"No." She checked her watch. "And it's getting late. I better take the kitty home and get set up for some midnight feedings." She stood.

He rose more slowly, trying to come up with a logical reason to delay her.

Unfortunately, nothing convincing came to mind.

"I'll help you gather up the supplies." He opened the door and followed her to the kitchen.

She stopped in the center of the room, eyeing the counter and the kitten. "This will require two trips."

"I'd offer to help, but I don't want to leave Molly alone."

"No worries. It's not a long walk." She flashed him a smile as she picked up the box with the sleeping kitty. "I'll be back in a few minutes."

"I'll put all the supplies in a bag for you while you're gone."

He held the door for her as she left, gathered up the formula, extra bottle, nipples, and the care instructions he'd printed off the net, and was waiting on the porch when she returned.

She took the bag he handed her. "Thanks for all you did tonight. I'm sure the care and feeding of an abandoned kitten wasn't on your evening agenda."

"Watching Molly wasn't on yours for today either."

"I enjoyed having her." She descended the steps, angling back at the bottom to look up at him. "I'll text you with updates on how he's doing."

In other words, she didn't want them to come over to her place.

Didn't mean he couldn't try to push for an invite, though.

"Thanks—but I don't know if that will satisfy Molly."

She edged farther away, into the shadows beyond the pool of light from the porch. "I can bring him back for a visit in a week or two."

"Or we could walk over. I'd call first, to see if it was convenient."

"That would work."

Not if she didn't answer the phone—and he had a sneaking suspicion she'd let any calls from him roll to voicemail.

But pushing harder could backfire.

"Let me know if you need any help."

"I will. Thanks again." With that, she turned away and disappeared down the dark drive.

Logan pushed through the door, locked it, and shoved his hands in his pockets as he wandered down the hall to see if Molly had fallen asleep.

At the door to her room, he paused. Toby lifted his head from his prone position beside her bed but stayed where he was. Molly's eyes were closed, her breathing even, and the slight snuffling sound suggested she was in a deep sleep.

Maybe she'd stay that way through the night.

He returned to the kitchen and straightened up the counter and table, weighing Jeannette's advice about broaching the subject of loss and grief with Molly. His neighbor struck him as a sharp, insightful, intuitive, and caring woman who probably had keen insights about kids, based on her teaching experience.

Why not try her suggestion? It wasn't as if he had anything to lose, given the poor results with his current approach.

He nuked the cup of coffee that had cooled during Jeannette's visit and strolled out to the back porch. Propping a shoulder against the post, he sipped the java and scanned the vast, star-bedecked heavens. It was the same view he used to enjoy with his mom and brother and dad as they tried to spot the constellations in their backyard on a summer night while fireflies flitted around them.

The sky hadn't changed—but everything else had.

And all at once, a soul-deep wave of loneliness crashed over him.

Those had been good days.

Happy days.

But now they were only a memory.

His mom was gone.

His brother was gone.

His father had died long ago.

All he had was a little girl who didn't particularly like him and a dog he wasn't that fond of—although the beagle was growing on him.

Swallowing past the tightness in his throat, he perused the tall hedge on the left of his property.

His nuclear family might be gone, but as far as he could tell, he had more companionship in his life than the woman next door. Jeannette appeared to be totally alone.

The question was why.

He took a speculative sip of coffee, squinting at the faint glow of light visible above the hedge where her house stood.

If Molly had opened up to his neighbor today, could Jeannette have told his niece a few bits and pieces about her background too? More than had been in the *Hope Harbor Herald* article she'd mentioned, which he'd accessed in the paper's online archives?

Unfortunately, her interview with the local paper hadn't offered much new information. All Marci Weber had been able to wheedle out of Jeannette was her hometown and college. The lavender lady must have managed to keep their conversation centered on her new life and business here in Hope Harbor.

It couldn't hurt to put out a few feelers with Molly tomorrow in case his niece had learned anything of interest.

Because unless Jeannette had a change of heart about offering him a peek into her past, that could be his best chance of unearthing a few clues about what made his appealing neighbor tick.

18

EEEEEEEEEEEEEEEEEE!

As the piercing alarm jolted Mariam awake, she bolted upright in bed, trying to clear her sleep-fogged brain.

What in heaven's name was making that sound?

Elisa shrieked, threw off the covers, scurried across the room, and burrowed in beside her with a whimper.

Seconds later, the door to their room flew open and Thomma flipped on the light, hair disheveled, face white. "Are you both all right?"

"Yes." Mariam swung her legs to the floor and grabbed her robe from the foot of the bed, pulse racing. "What's going on?"

"I don't know. But be prepared to leave fast. I'll check the hall."

He disappeared again, and Mariam stood, balancing herself for a moment on the headboard. After five days, her ankle was feeling better, but it was still tender and she didn't yet trust it to support her.

"Put on your shoes, Elisa." She did the same as she spoke.

Moving on autopilot, she pulled a suitcase out of their closet and threw some clothes into it.

How many times over the past few years had

she been through this drill after the blaring air-raid sirens had awakened them in the middle of the night?

Too many to count.

But those days *had* prepared her for whatever emergency they faced tonight.

She hurried to Thomma's room, Elisa clinging to the hem of her robe and clutching her doll, and added a few items to the bag for him too.

He was back in less than five minutes. "I can't understand most of what the other residents are saying, but I think there's a fire. We have to evacuate."

"We're ready." She zipped up the bag.

He grasped it with one hand, swept Elisa up into his other arm, and crooked his elbow. "Hold on. I don't want you to fall."

"I can manage. Take care of Elisa."

"I can help you both. Hurry."

No sense wasting time arguing.

She took his arm.

In the hall, they merged with other sleepy residents who were filing out of the building, some of them grumbling. As if this was a huge inconvenience rather than a possible life-threatening situation.

At home in Syria, they'd always taken warning sirens seriously.

Yet here, they were the only ones carrying a suitcase.

Perhaps they'd overreacted.

But as they hurried down the hall, Mariam caught the faint scent of smoke.

Perhaps not.

They joined the group assembled outside as the first blush of Saturday morning tinted the eastern sky. Two police cars arrived, sirens screeching. A few minutes later, a fire truck roared up, lights flashing and sirens blaring.

It was impossible to follow all that was being said. The three of them were learning English faster than she'd expected, but no more than a few words registered here and there amid the shouts and barked commands.

"Thomma—we should call Susan. Ask her to talk with someone in charge and find out what's going on."

"It's too early to call anyone."

"This is an emergency."

He hesitated . . . but at last he set Elisa on the ground and pulled out his phone. "I'm going over there, where it's less noisy." He motioned to the sidewalk across the street.

Mariam put her arm around Elisa, and her granddaughter huddled against her, silent as she watched the goings-on with big eyes. She was too young to remember much about her life in Syria, but there could be some subconscious memory of terror in the night after sirens had gone off.

Who'd have thought they'd be reminded of it here, though?

Mariam sighed.

Would life ever smooth out?

She murmured soothing reassurances to Elisa, keeping an eye on Thomma. He gave the crowd a sweep as he talked on the phone, homing in on the woman police chief who'd been at their welcome party at the church. Lexie something or other. He wove toward her through the clusters of people, motioned to the cell, and held it out.

The woman took it, and after a short conversation, handed it back to Thomma. He put it to his ear, listening as he returned to them and ending the call before he arrived.

"What's the story?" Mariam stroked Elisa's quivering shoulder.

"The noise we heard was the fire alarm. They're trying to determine if it's real or if there was a malfunction."

"I smelled smoke as we left."

"I did too. The police chief said they won't be letting people back in for hours if it's real. Maybe not even then, depending on the amount of damage."

"What are we going to do?"

He squinted at his watch in the dawn light. "Susan is calling Father Murphy to see what he thinks. In the meantime, I have to go to work.

Roark is counting on me. He has a full boat of charter customers today."

"I packed your work clothes." Mariam indicated the suitcase.

Relief chased some of the tension from his features. "Thank you. I can change in the restroom at the Myrtle Café." He dropped to the balls of his feet and rummaged through the suitcase. "I'll leave my cellphone with you. Roark's number is on speed dial. I'll tell him you'll be calling me with updates." He stood and handed it to her. "Will you be all right by yourself?"

"I have lived through much worse alone. But some of us haven't." She dipped her chin toward Elisa.

Thomma frowned . . . exhaled . . . and lowered himself to her level. "Be good for Teta, okay?"

She nodded.

Mariam nudged him with her knee. The child needed a hug from her father, not instructions.

Thomma ignored her message. He stood and fussed with the clothing he'd draped over his arm, not meeting her gaze. "Call Roark as soon as you know anything. I'll see you both later."

He turned and fled.

Mariam pulled Elisa close again, stroking her hair as she watched her son disappear.

If he didn't come around soon, he was going to lose his daughter forever.

But what could she do except pray God would see fit to show him the error of his ways before it was too late?

"Come on, kitty. Eat. Please. Don't pick today to be difficult." Jeannette pushed her hair back and massaged the bridge of her nose. After four days, the sleep-disrupting every-five-hour feedings were catching up with her—and she had a full house for her Saturday tea. She had to finish the last-minute preparations and be ready to greet her guests in one hour.

She nudged the kitten's mouth with the nipple, and he finally started to suck.

Thank you, God.

If he'd continued to balk, she would have been forced to enlist Logan's aid. The cat couldn't wait another four hours for a feeding, and she'd be too busy during the tea to attend to it.

But nothing short of desperation would compel her to initiate more contact with her charming neighbor and his loveable niece. Being around them planted dangerous notions in her head.

She sat with the kitten in her lap until he finished the bottle, burped him, and nestled him back in the folds of the soft blanket in the box. Now she could focus on the tearoom. He'd probably sleep almost until it was time for another feeding.

After cleaning the bottle, she shifted into high

gear and was ready to greet her first guests with all of five minutes to spare.

Many of the customers' faces were familiar from town or church, and some were regulars—including Eleanor Cooper and Luis Dominguez. With his usual solicitude, the Cuban refugee guided the ninety-one-year-old Hope Harbor native who'd taken him into her home to their usual table.

"I'm looking forward to the first blooms, Jeannette." Eleanor scanned the garden from her seat beside the window. "It's so beautiful to see that carpet of lavender stretching into the distance."

"I agree." Luis took his seat. "And it is always a pleasure to enjoy your wonderful food too."

"Thank you." Jeannette offered them each a menu with the selection of teas.

Eleanor waved it off. "Surprise me, my dear. But pick one that's soothing. After all the excitement in town this morning, I could use a nice, peaceful afternoon sipping a fine cup of tea."

"What sort of excitement?" Jeannette smoothed out a crease in the linen tablecloth, mentally organizing her to-do list for *tomorrow's* tea—including a quick run to Coos Bay after the early service at Grace Christian to buy more sugar cubes. Somehow her supply had run low. And she also—

". . . had a fire. Thank goodness no one was hurt."

She tuned back in to the end of Eleanor's reply.

There'd been a fire in town?

Where?

But how could she ask without it being obvious she'd zoned out for most of Eleanor's explanation?

As if sensing her dilemma, Luis stepped in. "House fires are always frightening, but in an apartment building the danger is much higher. At least only two units were damaged. It is a shame, though, that our Syrian family has suffered yet another challenge after all they have been through."

There'd been a fire in the Shabos' apartment?

A jolt of shock ricocheted through her.

"What happened?"

"There was an electrical fire in an adjacent unit. Both units will have to be vacated for repairs."

As a paramedic with contacts in the emergency community, Luis would know the details of the fire—but was he privy to information about the Shabos' status?

"Where are they staying?"

Eleanor rejoined the conversation. "Anna Williams is giving them her annex for a week. It's booked after that, but hopefully they'll be back in their apartment by then. You know Anna, don't you, my dear?"

An image of an older woman materialized in her mind. "I think we've met. She's involved with the Harbor Point cranberry nut cake business, isn't she?"

"She's more than involved. She runs it. I don't know what Tracy would do without her. The farm is more than enough to keep that young woman busy." Eleanor touched her arm. "I understand you've taken on the task of teaching our adopted family English. God bless you, my dear."

"I will second that." Luis laid his napkin in his lap. "It is hard to be in a new country and not know the language."

"I was happy to do my part. So many people had already pitched in to help."

"And now Anna is filling the latest need. What a blessing it is to live in a town where people care about each other."

"Amen to that." Luis lifted his empty china teacup.

Eleanor hoisted her cup too. "Let's just hope the apartment is ready for the Shabos before Anna's paying guests arrive. Otherwise, our wonderful clerics will be scrambling to find them new accommodations."

"I'm sure it will all work out." Jeannette forced up the corners of her mouth. "Now let me get your tea brewing."

She retreated to the prep area and went about filling the tea orders—but the rote task left her mind free to mull over the conversation with Eleanor and Luis.

At this point, the Shabos must be feeling like Job had in the midst of his trials.

She could relate—although the breadth of their losses was even more immense than hers had been.

And they didn't need any more challenges or disruptions in their life—or their living quarters.

You could offer them a place to stay if they end up homeless again, Jeannette.

Her stomach knotted.

Yes, she could. There was a futon in her otherwise empty spare bedroom, and her couch had a hide-a-bed. Her home wasn't set up to welcome visitors—but she could accommodate two adults and a child in an emergency.

Except she didn't want anyone invading her house—or her heart.

She stuck another china teapot under the spigot on the hot water dispenser, flipped the switch . . . and took a deep breath.

There was no reason to get anxious about this situation yet. The Shabos' unit might be ready for occupancy sooner than anyone expected.

So why not put this dilemma on the back burner, see what happened over the next week? This whole thing could blow over.

And if it didn't?

She'd deal with it then.

The boiling water splashed, burning her hand, and she jerked the teapot back as she flipped off the spigot.

An omen for what might happen if she continued to get involved in other people's lives, perhaps?

No.

Those kinds of superstitions were foolish.

Yet the warning did seem providential.

These past few weeks had thrown her a series of curves. Disrupted her placid existence. Awakened longings she thought she'd long ago put to rest.

And she didn't like it.

Not one bit.

She set the pot down and picked up another one to fill.

For three years, she'd kept to herself—and she had no regrets. The quiet life she'd created suited her perfectly. She hadn't wanted a handsome new neighbor or appealing little girls or shell-shocked refugees or abandoned kittens complicating her world.

So how had she gotten herself into this mess, anyway?

"Ignoring an obvious need would be wrong."

She turned on the spigot again as Charley's comment from weeks ago echoed in her mind—and gave her the answer. He may have offered that sentiment as a philosophical musing, but the truth was, that's how she was wired. She hadn't been born a recluse—and she'd been raised to help those facing hardship.

That was why she was getting tangled up in a bunch of people's lives.

And unless she wanted to walk away from everything she believed, she was stuck for now. She'd have to pitch in. Do what had to be done.

But after all this was over—and it would be soon—she was going to return to a life centered on her farm, where her days were quiet and safe and predictable . . . and there was no more danger of losing anyone she loved.

She turned off the water and removed the pot from under the spigot, careful this go-round to pay attention and avoid any more splashes.

Getting burned was the pits.

And while she'd always liked Tennyson's poetry, she no longer believed in his most famous sentiment.

It wasn't better to have loved and lost than never to have loved at all.

19

"Why are we going to church so early?"

As Molly posed the question for the third time in the past hour, Logan unbuckled her harness and helped her out of the car.

She must not be buying his explanation.

But he couldn't tell her the truth.

Admitting he'd risen early to see Jeannette at church might not be smart, given his niece's constant chatter about 'Nette since they'd spent last Tuesday together.

Molly could get the wrong idea.

Or the right one.

And he didn't want to encourage any matchmaking from a five-year-old.

However . . . he hadn't caught sight of Jeannette once since the night she'd taken the abandoned cat home, and while she'd sent a few text messages and photos, she hadn't issued an invitation for them to visit . . . or answered her phone when he'd called to ask if they could drop by . . . or offered to bring the cat over to his house.

Bottom line, he wanted to see her.

Molly might even be able to charm her into suggesting a get-together.

Yet another reason for their early church

attendance—and another admission he didn't intend to make.

"I told you, sweetie—I have a long list today and I want to get an early start."

"What do you have to do?"

She would ask that.

"I have to cut the grass and clean up the house and . . . uh . . . a bunch of other stuff. We could take Toby for a walk on the beach later too, if you'd like."

"Can 'Nette come?"

"You could ask her if we see her."

"Is she here?"

He was counting on it.

"She may be."

Molly stretched her neck to search the crowd as they wound through the vestibule and down the aisle to find a seat.

"I don't see her."

Neither did he.

But Charley had mentioned once that he'd run into her after the early service, suggesting she was a regular churchgoer. And with her afternoon tea schedule, this timing would better suit her.

He chose a seat that gave him a line of sight to the door, and five minutes before the service was scheduled to begin, she entered.

"She's here!" Molly tugged on his arm, her stage whisper drawing a few glances from those seated around them.

"Yes. I see her."

"Can we talk to her after church?"

"We'll try."

But she might slip away fast . . . perhaps during the final hymn.

Not much he could do about that—unless he could somehow communicate to her that Molly wanted to say hello.

He caught her eye as she settled into a pew near the back. Smiled.

She returned it—though hers seemed tentative.

Molly waved.

Her smile broadened.

Logan pointed at his niece, then at Jeannette, and made the familiar talking gesture with his thumb and four fingers.

A few beats passed, but at last she dipped her head, then redirected her attention to the front as the organ struck up the notes of the opening hymn.

Logan tried to concentrate on the Scripture readings and Reverend Baker's sermon. He really did. But he was as antsy as his niece for the service to end so they could talk to Jeannette.

The instant the last note of the final hymn died away, he took Molly's hand and guided her through the crowd surging toward the exit. If they dallied, his neighbor could have second thoughts about hanging around.

But true to her word, she was waiting for them in the vestibule, standing by herself off to the side.

"Hi, 'Nette!" Molly pulled free of his hand and trotted over to the dark-haired woman.

"Hi, Molly." She got down on the girl's level and whispered in her ear. Molly's countenance brightened as she listened.

She rose as he joined them. "Good morning."

"Morning. I've been sharing your photos and texts with Molly. Sounds like the abandoned kitty is doing well."

"So far, so good."

"But at the expense of restful slumber." The faint shadows under her lower lashes were new.

"I can make up the sleep if I need to."

No ifs about it. But rather than risk insulting her appearance, he let it pass.

"Have you named our friend yet?"

"No." Her features flattened. "What's the point? I'm not keeping him."

"Can I name him?" Molly's face lit up.

"It might be better to let the people who adopt him pick his name, honey." Jeannette rested her hand on the girl's shoulder. "What if they didn't like the one we chose?"

A logical response—but why did he think there was more to her reluctance to name the kitten than the future owner's preference? The anonymity of a nameless creature allowed her to keep more of a distance—and arm's length appeared to be her modus operandi.

Molly cocked her head. "Well, I'm going to

call him Button. They can change it later. Or you could keep him." His niece gave Jeannette a hopeful look.

"No." His neighbor's response was immediate—and vehement. "I don't have time to take care of a pet. So . . ." She gave them both a smile that was a tad too bright. "What are your plans for today?"

"Chores—and we're going for a walk on the beach later with Toby." Logan left it at that. Molly might have more luck getting a positive response to an invitation than he would.

As he'd expected, she picked up his cue. "Do you want to come?"

He could see the conflict, followed by regret, in Jeannette's eyes—and knew what her answer was going to be.

"Sundays are very busy for me, honey. People come to tea in the afternoon, and I have to get ready."

"What about later?"

His niece got a gold star for persistence.

"I'll probably be tired—and I have to take care of the kitty."

"Welcome, folks." Reverend Baker joined them, putting an end to that discussion as he shook hands and gave Molly a pat on the head. "I'm not lingering to chat today. Father Murphy and I are running some supplies over to the Shabos' in between services, but I wanted to say hello. You knew about the fire, didn't you?"

281

Logan frowned. "What fire?"

He listened as the cleric gave him a shorthand version of what had happened yesterday.

"Man. That's the pits, after everything else they've been through."

"I couldn't agree more." Reverend Baker lifted his hand in greeting as Father Murphy entered and hustled over. "Morning, Kevin."

"Morning. Hello, folks." The priest nodded to him and Jeannette.

"You're ten minutes early." Reverend Baker tapped his watch.

"I wanted to grab a doughnut in the fellowship hall."

"I thought this was doughnut Sunday at St. Francis?"

"It is . . . but yours are free." The padre smirked at his fellow cleric. "Besides, as the good book says, it's blessed to feed the hungry. You'll find that in Matthew 25. And Isaiah 58:7 clearly says to share your food with the hungry. There are a host of other references to that subject too."

"I'm aware of that—but you may be stretching the message of Scripture a bit with doughnuts."

Father Murphy grinned. "Close enough."

The minister folded his arms, lips twitching. "You know . . . you may have a point—especially about the Matthew reference. It does mention doing good deeds for the least of our brothers . . . and here you are."

"Ouch." The priest grimaced, his eyes twinkling. "I should have seen that coming."

Reining in a chuckle, Logan looked at Jeannette. He didn't have much experience watching clerics interact, but these two were a hoot.

She appeared to be struggling to contain her own mirth as the two men bantered.

"Maybe we should have another joint Bible study with our churches this summer to help you bone up on your Scripture," Reverend Baker said.

"Hah. May I remind you which church won the Bible edition of Trivial Pursuit at the end of *last* summer's session?"

Reverend Baker gave a dismissive wave of his hand. "You got easy questions."

"For the record . . . that's not true." The priest directed his comment to the audience of three, then turned back to the minister. "But enough of this debate. We should move on to more important matters—like doughnuts and deliveries. Give me ten minutes and I'll meet you in the parking lot. You can wedge yourself into the back seat, next to the toilet paper."

"Gee thanks." Reverend Baker straightened his clerical collar. "You're lucky I'm such a great sport."

"Not on the golf course." He nudged the pastor with his elbow, and Logan hid a grin behind a cough as the padre winked at him and Jeannette.

283

"I'm glad I ran into you both today. I wanted to say thanks again for the tutoring, Jeannette, and for the job you gave Mariam, Logan. I understand Thomma is also training your pup."

"Yes—and doing an exceptional job. I think the man is a dog whisperer."

"Is that right?" Reverend Baker chimed back in. "I have another member of the congregation with a recalcitrant puppy. I wonder if she might want to enlist Thomma's aid once he finishes your job."

"Let's mention it to him during our visit. And now I'm off for a doughnut." Father Murphy lifted his hand in farewell and wove through the clusters of churchgoers in the vestibule toward the fellowship hall.

"I best be off too." Reverend Baker waved at another departing congregant. "I have to turn off a few lights in the church and stop in at the house. But first let me add my thanks to Kevin's. You two have gone above and beyond helping our deserving family."

"Mariam and Thomma have done far more for me than I've done for them, Reverend. Jeannette's the one who's gone above and beyond." Logan gestured toward the woman across from him.

"Indeed she has." The man took her hand. "May the Lord bless you both—and you too, young lady." He squeezed Molly's fingers.

As he returned to the sanctuary, Jeannette pulled out her keys. "I have to get home."

"If you change your mind about joining us for a walk—or you're in the mood for some visitors later—we'll be heading down to the beach about six thirty."

"Thanks. I'll keep that in mind. You two enjoy your day."

Molly watched her walk away, emitting a wistful sigh. "She's nice."

"Yes, she is."

"I wish she wasn't sad."

So Molly had picked up on that too. "What makes you think she's sad?"

His niece shrugged. "Sometimes her smile doesn't get up to her eyes."

Never again would he underestimate the perceptive powers of a five-year-old.

He surveyed the thinning crowd in the foyer. This wasn't the place he'd planned to broach heavier subjects with Molly, but if she was in a talking mood it might be wise to take advantage of the opportunity.

"I wonder why she's sad." He kept his tone conversational.

His niece studied the tips of her Sunday shoes. "She said she misses the people she loved. Like I do."

Throat tightening, Logan brushed back a strand of hair that had escaped from her ponytail. "Where did the people she loved go?"

"I don't know. Away."

285

That must be all she knew—but as long as they were talking about loss, he ought to follow his neighbor's advice about sharing what was in his own heart.

He dropped down to one knee beside her and tipped her chin up with one finger. "It's hard when people you love go away. I miss Nana and your daddy every single day. And I miss my own daddy too, even though he's been gone a long time. But they always stay in my heart." He touched the left side of his chest.

"Sometimes . . ." She sniffed and wiped her hand under her nose. "Sometimes my tummy hurts when I think about Nana. Like it's empty."

"Mine too."

She shuffled one of her feet and dropped her chin again. "I don't remember my daddy very good." Her soft voice quavered. "But Nana showed me pictures of him and told me stories."

"I know stories about your daddy too."

She met his gaze, the blue of her irises an exact match for her dad's—and his. "Could you tell me some?"

"Sure." Why hadn't he thought about doing that weeks ago? "I can start tonight while we take our walk on the beach." Where the seclusion and quiet would be much more conducive to building rapport than the busy vestibule of the church. "How does that sound?"

" 'Kay." She watched the people strolling

toward the doorway that led to the fellowship hall. "Can we get a doughnut?"

"I think that would be a fine Sunday treat." He stood.

But before he could follow his usual pattern and take her hand, she tucked her small fingers into his.

He froze.

That was a first.

And it had to be a positive sign—didn't it?

Or would everything go back to the status quo once they got home?

Impossible to know—and he was done predicting the course of his relationship with Molly. Nothing had gone as he'd expected, and the breakthrough he'd been certain he'd made the night she'd let him stay with her after he found her crying had ended up being a bust.

This could be the same.

But as they strolled toward the hall, a surge of warmth and optimism percolated through him, lifting his spirits.

Even if they weren't making any real progress, why not enjoy these small victories?

And who knew?

If he could string together enough brief positive moments, in the long term they would add up . . . and perhaps become a way of life.

At least he could hope—and pray—for that outcome.

• • •

Resist, Jeannette. You have plenty to do to clean up after today's tea. Quit standing here watching your neighbors trek down to the beach.

But she couldn't help herself.

Especially after they both glanced her direction as they walked along the perimeter of the lavender beds, Toby straining at the leash.

And the last vestige of her resistance melted after Molly stopped and pointed to the house.

She was probably asking about the kitten.

Why not let the child take a quick look at Button? What harm could there be in that? She—and her uncle—had been involved in the rescue, after all.

Before she could change her mind, she crossed to the door and pulled it open.

"Hi!" She waved at the pair as they approached the end of her property.

Logan and Molly pivoted in unison. Delight suffused the child's face, but beyond his obvious surprise, Logan's expression was harder to decipher.

"Would you like to peek in on Button?"

She couldn't hear what Molly said to her uncle in response to her question, but a few seconds later she was towing him toward the house.

Logan didn't appear to be resisting—and she'd be willing to bet it wasn't because he was all that interested in the cat's condition.

A delicious tingle ran up her spine . . . which she immediately squelched.

That reaction was *not* appropriate.

"Hi." Logan lifted a hand in greeting as he approached. "You made a little girl's day—and in the interest of full disclosure, a big boy's day too."

O-kay. That bit of candor had come out of the blue.

Since she hadn't a clue how to respond, she ignored his comment and motioned them in. "I'm keeping Button in the kitchen. It's the warmest room in the house, and the closest to his food."

Logan tied Toby's leash to the patio table umbrella—and the pup expressed his displeasure with a loud howl.

"Sorry, boy—you can complain all you want, but you're staying out here."

He responded with another plaintive yowl.

"He doesn't like to be by himself." Molly bent down and petted the dog.

"No kidding." Logan angled toward her. "If you want to retract your invitation in view of the noise machine here, I'll understand."

"No. You won't be here long." Jeannette stepped aside to usher them in, shutting the door behind them while Toby continued to protest at full volume.

Molly made a beeline for the box on the floor in the corner and squatted down beside it. "Ooh! He got bigger!" She reached inside to pet the kitten.

"He *is* growing fast. I think he'll be ready for solid food soon." Jeannette joined her.

She could feel Logan behind her, his presence almost palpable as the subtle aroma of his musky aftershave swirled around her. And the warmth of his breath on her cheek as he leaned close to examine Button sent her pulse soaring.

"He seems to be thriving. You're obviously taking excellent care of him."

"Th-thanks."

Oh, for pity's sake.

She sounded like a besotted teenager, not a thirty-two-year-old woman who'd vowed to avoid romance.

"You're paying a price for providing such diligent care, though." Logan swept a finger under her lower lash, his touch as gentle as the wing of a butterfly. "There are some smudges here."

Her lungs stuttered.

At this proximity, the silvery flecks in his blue irises shimmered like the sun dancing on the cobalt water of Hope Harbor. The faint web of lines at the corners of his eyes spoke of caring and compassion and laughter. Here and there in his sandy hair, a copper strand glinted in the early evening light beaming through the window. As for those generous lips—

Don't go there, Jeannette.

She edged back. "Uh . . . I should be able to

get more sleep soon. He won't need as many feedings once he's on solid food."

"Can I pick him up, 'Nette?"

The perfect distraction.

She redirected her attention to Molly. "I'll pick him up for you—but you can hold him. Why don't you sit at the table?"

Keeping her back to Logan, she lifted the kitten and its blanket, cradling the bundle gently in her arms as she walked over to Molly and set Button in her lap.

As the girl began to stroke him, the kitten emitted a soft purr.

"He's talking to me!"

"Yes, he is." Jeannette sat beside her, and Logan claimed an adjacent chair. "I wonder what he's saying?"

"Charley would know." Molly continued to pet the cat. "He talks to animals—like Floyd and Gladys. Can we get tacos again, Uncle Logan?"

"I think that could be arranged."

"Maybe we could have another picnic on the beach."

"I like that idea."

"You could come too, 'Nette."

She snuffed out the surge of longing that swept over her at that notion.

No, she couldn't.

Even this brief interlude was a mistake.

"I could think about that." She stood. "I better

get Button back in his box. He still likes to sleep away most of the day."

Logan rose at once, carefully plucking the kitten and blanket out of Molly's lap. "And we better get back to Toby or he's going to get laryngitis." He hesitated and arched his eyebrows, a spark of amusement putting a wicked gleam in his eyes. "On second thought . . ."

Despite herself, she chuckled. The man's infectious good humor was hard to resist.

"No . . . we'll suck it up and take him off your hands." He deposited Button back in the box. "You're welcome to join us for our walk."

"Thanks—but I have to clean up from the tea and set up for another feeding."

"Then we'll get out of your hair. Come on, Molly."

He hadn't pushed.

A surge of disappointment welled up inside her, but she tamped it down. She should be glad he'd let it go. With her resistance at low ebb, she could have compounded her mistake by capitulating.

She walked them to the door. "Enjoy the beach."

"It would be better if you came." Molly linked her hands behind her and lifted her chin. "If you were there, I could pretend I had a mommy. You'd be a good mommy, 'Nette."

Somehow she managed to dredge up a smile. "Thank you for saying that, honey."

But the job came with too many risks.

She motioned to Toby, who'd stopped barking when she opened the door but had started up again. "Our beagle friend is getting impatient."

"And Thomma isn't here with his magic touch to quiet the beast." Logan took Molly's hand and slipped past her. "Thanks for letting us see Button. Keep up the great work."

He didn't wait for her to respond as he freed Toby from the umbrella and led Molly down the path among the lavender beds, toward the rear of the property and the beach access.

Molly looked back once to wave.

Logan didn't—surprising after his earlier comment about her making his day . . . and that brush of fingers under her lashes.

The man was sending mixed signals.

And who could blame him?

She was sending mixed signals.

One day she asks him in, the next she avoids him like the plague.

That sort of inconsistent behavior would confuse anyone.

Yet one thing was clear.

The man was interested in her—and with a smidgen of encouragement, he'd ask her out.

A date with Logan.

Now that had intriguing possibilities.

From the shadows where she watched them disappear into the dunes, her mouth bowed of its own accord.

Not good.

She forced it back into a straight line at once.

There would be no dates in her future.

Nor motherhood.

That had been her decision three years ago, and she saw no reason to rethink it.

Well . . . that wasn't quite true.

Two reasons had spent the past few minutes in her kitchen.

However . . . she had to be strong about this. She'd survived the last loss—barely. But she might not be as fortunate the next time . . . if there was a next time.

And the only way to guarantee she was never put to that test was to avoid all relationships—a rule that hadn't been difficult to follow until a handsome doctor learning how to be a single dad had moved in next door and resurrected feelings best left buried.

Squaring her shoulders, she marched to the counter and pulled out the box of formula for Button.

She'd just have to rebury them.

Except there was one little problem with that plan.

She gripped the counter and admitted the truth.

The kinds of feelings Logan was rekindling were about as easy to contain as Toby's bark— and just as disruptive.

Unfortunately, while Thomma's magic touch

was taming the unruly beagle, as far as she knew, there were no romance-whisperers.

Meaning she was on her own to come up with a plan to deal with her sudden amorous leanings—and the loneliness they were leaving in their wake.

20

"Well, if it isn't our newest doctor and the latest artist in my gallery." Charley swept a hand over the back wall of the stand, where Molly's drawing was front and center. "You must be in the mood for tacos on this fine Tuesday evening."

Logan returned Charley's grin as they approached. "We're always in the mood for your tacos—as is everyone else in this town, from what I can gather. I'm surprised we didn't have to wait in line."

"Your timing was perfect. I just opened. Two orders or three?"

"Two. Why would I want three?"

"I thought you might have another beach picnic in mind."

"Not tonight." Geez. The man had a memory like an elephant. He should never have mentioned his thank-you plans for Jeannette the day of Mariam's accident, when he'd picked up tacos for their impromptu picnic.

"How are you doing, Molly?" Charley pulled an avocado from the cooler and began slicing it.

"Fine."

"How goes the search for a friend?"

"I finded one. Her name's Elisa, and her mommy

and grandpa and brother and uncle all went to heaven in a war."

"That's very sad." Charley paused and shook his head. "I'm glad she has you for a friend."

"Me too."

"Speaking of friends . . ." He set some fish fillets on the grill. "Here come two of mine." He waved a hand toward a pair of seagulls that swooped in and landed several yards away.

"Is that Floyd and Gladys?" Molly studied them.

"None other. You want to go say hello?"

"Will they fly away?"

"Not if you take it slow and easy so they don't get scared. You may have to practice a little, but if you stick with it, they'll let you get close. That okay with you, Logan? You can keep an eye on her while I finish up your order."

"Sure. Have at it, Molly."

Despite Charley's assurance that the birds would stay put, the interlude wasn't likely to last long if Molly invaded their comfort zone. But she'd get a kick out of trying to get up close and personal with them until they flew off.

"On the subject of friends, how goes it with Jeannette?" Charley began dicing some peppers.

Better set the record straight on that, in case the taco-making artist had any ideas about future beach picnics.

"To be honest, I don't know that I'd call us friends."

"No? How come?"

Not for lack of trying—but he left that unsaid.

"She's very protective of her privacy and her space."

"That's a fact." Charley tossed the peppers on the griddle. "I expect there's a reason for that."

"I do too—but she's not talking . . . to me anyway. Do *you* know why she's such a loner?" A long shot—but worth a try.

"She's never told me her story."

So much for his last potential source. If Charley and Marci didn't know any of the details of Jeannette's background, there wasn't much chance *anyone* in town did.

It was a shame she kept to herself, though. He could use her advice with Molly again, since last Sunday's walk on the beach hadn't led to the kind of heart-to-heart talk he'd hoped it would. His niece had sidestepped all of his attempts to reintroduce the subject of loss and feelings.

"However . . ." Charley flipped the fish, continuing as if there'd been no gap in the conversation. "I expect it's a very sad story. No one cuts off other people unless they've been badly hurt. Trouble is, those kinds of people are the ones who most need friends."

"It's hard to get close to someone who isn't receptive."

"That's true." He pulled out some corn tortillas. "But sometimes it's a matter of persistence.

Just hanging around or showing up can make a difference. You have the perfect excuse with Button."

Logan blinked. "How did you know about him?"

"Your neighbor happens to be one of my regular customers."

"Jeannette told you about the cat?" Strange she'd bring that up, since she'd taken it in under duress and intended to get rid of it as soon as possible.

"People tell me all kinds of things."

That didn't surprise him. Charley had an uncanny ability to engender confidences.

"I agree the cat sounds like a perfect excuse— but she made it clear she doesn't want us to drop in to see him."

"There are other ways to initiate contact. She does run a tearoom, you know. You could take Molly."

"I did that once—but Jeannette's busy at those teas. She wouldn't have any time to chat with us." He checked on his niece.

She was hunkered down not two feet from the seagulls, who didn't appear to be in the least perturbed by her touching-distance proximity.

It seemed Charley was right again.

"You could always drop by her booth at the farmer's market some Friday."

Neither of Charley's suggestions were bad.

Molly would enjoy both—and at the rate they were going, that sort of contrived meeting could be his only chance to see his neighbor.

"I'll have to think about that—though it's not like I'm in the market for another challenge. I'm plenty busy with Molly and the new job."

"Some challenges are worth tackling . . . and they often pay dividends far beyond what we can imagine." Charley finished assembling the tacos, wrapped them in white paper, and slid them into a bag. "Two orders, all set to go."

Logan handed over some bills and took the bag. "These won't last long."

"Music to a taco-maker's ears. You two enjoy your evening. Bye, Molly." He waved at the girl and turned to the next customer in the line that had formed.

"Bye." She called the farewell over her shoulder but remained by the birds.

"Come on, sweetie. These will get cold if we don't eat them fast."

After lingering a few more seconds, she rose and walked over to him. "Did you see how close I got to Floyd and Gladys?"

"Yes. They must like you."

"I just did what Charley said and went real slow and careful so I wouldn't scare them. He knows a bunch about birds."

Yeah, he did.

Also about people.

And his advice about the seagulls might also be appropriate for Jeannette.

His neighbor *did* need a friend, whether she realized it or not—and slow and easy could be the key with her . . . as well as with his niece. Perhaps his progress with both of them was meant to be marked in tiny increments rather than great leaps.

Not his usual dive-in-and-get-it-done style, but he could live with small steps forward—as long as they advanced.

He took another gander at Charley as they strolled back to their car.

Funny.

He'd been on the verge of giving up on Jeannette until he'd talked with the man.

But maybe he'd hang in for a while after all.

Because if he succeeded in breaking through her barriers, the dividends Charley had referenced might be well worth the effort—for both of them.

"Papa?"

At Elisa's tentative question, Thomma shifted around in his seat at the table on Anna Williams's patio.

His pajama-clad daughter stood ten feet away, clutching her Raggedy Ann doll in one hand, a book in the other, her demeanor somber.

"Yes?"

"Would you read me a story?"

He gritted his teeth and bit back a word Raca had

asked him never to use in front of their children.

His mother had put Elisa up to this.

And he was in no mood for stories—or reminders of his dead wife—after a long day on the boat. It was hard enough to cope with all of them living together in one large room, where there was no door to close to escape from his memories.

"Ask Teta."

"She's baking. She said to ask you."

"Maybe later. I'm busy now."

Not true. Now that their English lesson with Jeannette was over, he was doing nothing on this Wednesday except staring into the dusky distance and trying to figure out how he was going to get through the rest of his life.

Even Elisa recognized the lie.

Her eyes filled with tears and she backed up a few steps. "I told Teta you would say no." Her voice was a mere whisper.

The sharp prod from his conscience didn't improve his humor. "I didn't say no. I said maybe later."

"I'm going to bed soon."

"Another night then."

After lingering a moment, she trudged back to their temporary quarters.

Thomma let out a slow breath and closed his eyes.

He didn't want to hurt Elisa—but he couldn't change how he felt.

Too bad God hadn't taken him in the bombing along with the rest of his family. An absent father would be better than a cold one.

He had no idea how long he sat there, deep in his own misery, but at some point he heard someone settle into the chair beside him.

His mother, of course.

No doubt come to berate him again for his many failings as a father.

He kept his eyelids firmly shut. If he ignored her, she might get the message and retreat to the annex.

But as the minutes ticked by, she gave no indication she intended to leave.

He was going to have to deal with her.

Bracing, he opened his eyes.

She was looking into the distance, her expression placid rather than angry.

Not what he'd expected.

As if sensing his gaze, she turned her head. "Susan called on your cell phone. Father Murphy asked her to let us know we can move back into our apartment on Friday. He said if anything has to be replaced, we should make a list. The insurance will cover some of it, and the church will help with the rest."

"Now that we are both working, we can replace whatever is not insured ourselves."

"I told her that." She took a drink from the glass of water she'd brought out with her. "I put Elisa to bed."

Here it came.

"Thank you."

When she remained silent, he sent her a side-long glance. Why didn't she plunge in and bring up the subject she wanted to discuss? She'd never been reticent about broaching it in the past.

After another five minutes ticked by, he sighed.

Fine.

If she wanted him to initiate the discussion, he would. He was tired of her censure and her meddling. They needed to talk this out.

"You sent Elisa out here on purpose."

"I was busy in the kitchen, and she likes a bedtime story."

"You know I'm not in the mood for that sort of thing these days."

"Yes. I know." She set the water on the small patio table. "I'm worried about you, Thomma." There was no reproach in her inflection. No criticism. Only concern.

That was harder to take than her disapproval.

"I'll be fine."

"Will you?"

He had no idea.

"I hope so . . . in time."

"Time has passed."

"Not that much."

"Enough to see some improvement." Her tone remained gentle.

He clasped his hands tight in his lap. "I don't

know if I will ever get over all of the losses, 'Ami." His voice choked.

She reached over and laid her hand on his white knuckles. "It is a heavy load for a young man to endure. Perhaps too much."

He furrowed his brow. "What do you mean?"

"I have hoped, like you, that time would heal—but I am beginning to wonder if more is needed."

"You mean . . . like counseling?"

"That is one idea. Or there is a grief group at St. Francis. People who've endured losses of many kinds meet once a week to share their experiences and feelings."

His pulse stuttered as he scowled at her. "You have talked to the *priest* about this?"

"No. I ask Susan to read me the bulletin every week. The meeting notice is in there."

"I don't want to spill my guts to a bunch of strangers." The mere thought of it turned his stomach.

"You don't have to talk if you don't want to. You could go and listen in the beginning. You might hear some stories that will help you cope with your own situation."

"I don't see how. No one who lives in a world like this"—he swept a hand around the placid setting—"could possibly understand what I've gone through."

"I'm not certain that is true, Thomma. Each circumstance is unique, but loss is loss. And while we may be different than the other people who live in this town, hearts know no geographic or ethnic boundaries. Neither does the experience of grief. Will you think about it?"

His mother's request was reasonable—and he couldn't argue with her logic or her assessment of his mental state.

He did need help.

But a grief group?

"I can't make any promises, 'Ami. I don't think I would be comfortable in such a situation."

His mother scrutinized him for a moment, rose, and picked up her water. "I know you'd rather deal with this on your own, Thomma. Your father was the same. A very private person who never wanted to admit he needed help. But if you won't do it for yourself, do it for Elisa. I am grateful she found a friend in Molly, and that is helping her . . . but a friend does not replace a father. If this rejection by you continues, it will have long-lasting effects on her life. I know neither of us want that for her—nor would Raca."

She laid her hand on his shoulder, then returned to the house, a slight limp the only visible reminder of her sprained ankle.

Exhaling, Thomma twisted his hands together in his lap.

His mother was right.

She'd been right from the beginning

Elisa did deserve better.

And Raca would be disappointed in him.

But a grief group?

He grimaced.

All that touchy-feely nonsense was for wimps.

Or for people who are in over their heads—and sinking fast.

Hard as he tried to smother the nagging voice inside of him, it refused to be silenced.

So . . . why not consider her suggestion—down the road. Say, in thirty days? If he still felt as mired in grief a month from now, he could check out this group at the church. At least give it a chance.

If that didn't work?

He could try to find a counselor and hope he or she would be able to bring some clarity and logic to his muddled thinking.

And if none of that helped him?

He might have to put himself in God's hands and pray he'd have the kind of dramatic, attitude-changing encounter Saul had experienced on the road to Damascus.

But scarce as evidence of God's presence in his life had been of late, it was hard to dredge up much hope that the Almighty would grace his life with a miracle anytime in the near future.

21

"That was fantastic, as usual, Jeannette." Marci laid her napkin beside her plate in the Bayview Lavender Farm tearoom.

"I agree. Every bite was delicious—even if I'll have to supplement it later with a burger." Her husband grinned and took the bill off the silver tray Jeannette set on the table.

"Ben!" Marci sent him a horrified look.

Jeannette smiled. "Trust me—I hear that from most of the male customers."

"Do you get many men in here?" Ben nabbed a rogue raspberry on his plate.

"No. Luis comes with Eleanor on occasion, and my neighbor brought his niece."

"Logan came to tea?" Marci gaped at her.

"Yes." Now why had she shared that? Better add a caveat or the *Herald* editor might get the wrong idea. "It was a treat for Molly. Little girls like tea parties."

"Big girls do too." Marci sipped from her china cup. "So how is Logan? I don't see him much around town."

"I don't see him often either."

"I'm surprised, you being neighbors and all."

"He's probably busy with that niece of his, not to mention his new job." Ben extracted his credit card from his wallet and set it on the tray. "We were lucky to get someone of his caliber at the urgent care center. I couldn't have held on to both jobs much onger, with the Coos Bay practice mushrooming."

"I think it was providential." Marci rested her elbows on the table and steepled her fingers. "So many positive things have happened because he came."

"Like what?" Ben took a final sip of tea.

"He saved the clinic . . . gave Mariam Shabo a job . . . tapped into Thomma's magic touch with dogs—and the word is spreading about that, let me tell you . . . provided a companion for darling Elisa, who needed a friend . . . shall I continue?"

"No." Ben set his napkin on the table, chuckling. "We get the picture. In case you didn't realize it, Jeannette, my wife always sees the bright side of everything."

"Are you complaining?" A dimple appeared in Marci's cheek.

"Not in the least." He took her hand, tenderness softening his features. "Have I told you lately that you're the sunshine of my life?"

"Yes—but I never get tired of hearing it."

Jeannette took a discreet step back. "Thank you both for coming today, and enjoy the rest of your afternoon."

"We will." Marci's attention remained fixed on her new husband.

Jeannette retreated, checking on the newlyweds over her shoulder.

They were both still focused on each other, oblivious to the world around them.

It must be incredible to share a love like that.

Also scary.

Because if you loved, you could lose—as she well knew.

The Shabos would attest to that truth too. From what she could tell, Thomma might never get over the tragedy that had robbed him of most of his family. That could be the reason he was withholding affection from his daughter. Experience too much pain, and self-protection mechanisms kicked in.

But her heart ached for Elisa, who watched her father with such longing and confusion during every tutoring session.

Dwelling on troubling subjects while she had a tea to wrap up, however, wasn't productive.

She continued to the next table, forcibly redirecting her thoughts to the tasks ahead—settling the bills, seeing all her guests out, and feeding Button, who would be more than ready for his next meal.

A smile tickled her lips as she finished distributing the bills. The kitty was growing fast. Tomorrow she'd add solid food to the mix. Before long, he'd be ready for adoption.

And then he'd be gone.

Her mouth flattened.

Hard as she'd tried to keep her distance from the tiny fluff ball, he'd managed to worm his way into her affections with his soft, contented purrs . . . those big blue-gray eyes that watched her every move . . . and his trusting snuggle into the blanket after she settled him on her lap for feedings.

But that didn't mean she was going to adopt him, as Molly had suggested.

Instead, she would cut the ties—and the sooner the better. From now on, she'd approach the kitten's care as she had in the beginning—as a chore on her to-do list, nothing more.

It took another half hour for the last dawdling group to depart, but as soon as they did she locked the door, did some preliminary cleanup, and headed back to the house to change. Once she fed Button, she'd finish tidying up, reset the tables for tomorrow, and prepare the last-minute menu items that were best served fresh.

Ten minutes later, her elegant tea attire exchanged for jeans and a sweatshirt, she entered the kitchen and set about mixing the kitten's formula.

"I'll be with you in a minute, Button. It won't take long to warm this up."

After she set the bottle in a small pot of hot water, she replayed the messages on her answering machine. One cancellation for tomorrow, party of two, but otherwise a full house.

Business was good.

Today had also been good. The new lavender and goat cheese croustades she'd introduced to her tea menu had gotten rave comments, she was off the hook about offering the Shabos a place to stay now that they were back in their apartment, and the high school students who'd helped her with the lavender harvest last summer had signed on for another season.

Everything was going as well as possible in her life.

She tested the formula on her wrist.

Perfect.

"All ready, Button. I know you're hungry."

She set the bottle on the table and crossed to the box in the corner.

The little guy was sleeping.

Odd.

Usually when she bent down to pick him up for a feeding, he was wide awake and raring to go.

"Hey." She touched his head. "Wake up, buddy."

Nothing.

A tiny twinge of alarm radiated through her.

"Button?" She jostled him gently.

Nothing.

Pulse accelerating, she pushed aside the folds of the blanket he'd burrowed into.

He didn't react.

In fact—he didn't move a muscle.

That's when she knew.

Button wasn't sleeping.

He was gone.

Someone was sobbing in Jeannette's kitchen.

And given her solitary lifestyle—along with the absence of visitors other than her tea customers—it had to be her.

Logan hesitated at the back door. It had seemed like an inspired idea to pick up two Sweet Dreams cinnamon rolls while he'd been in town dropping Molly off for her sleepover with Elisa, then mosey over here and ask Jeannette to share them.

But surprising her in the midst of a meltdown could backfire.

On the other hand . . . if a woman who always maintained firm control over her emotions was shedding tears, there had to be a serious reason for it.

Maybe she'd welcome a shoulder to cry on.

Or not.

As he debated his options, another heart-wrenching sob tore at his gut.

Decision made.

No matter the consequences, he wasn't walking away.

Psyching himself up for whatever awaited him on the other side of the door, he lifted his hand and knocked.

The sobs continued.

He tried again.

Silence descended in the house.

Thirty seconds ticked by.

Sixty.

Was she going to ignore him?

Just as he was about to give up, the back door cracked open barely wide enough to give him a glimpse of one puffy red eye.

"I heard you crying." No sense pretending otherwise. She had to know the sound of her weeping had carried through the door.

She hiccupped a sob, and a tear trailed down her cheek. "B-Button died."

He clenched his teeth, biting back a term he rarely used.

A woman who—according to Molly—had lost people she loved . . . who avoided relationships of all kinds . . . who then took a chance on an abandoned kitten . . . would be devastated by another loss.

"I'm so sorry. May I come in?"

"Why? There's n-nothing you can do."

Not for Button—but his neighbor was another story.

"I'd like to see him." It was as valid an excuse as any.

She waited a few moments but finally swung the door open.

The full view of her face was like a punch in the solar plexus.

Both eyes were puffy and red rimmed, her complexion was pasty, and streaks of mascara trailed down her damp cheeks.

His first inclination was to pull her into a comforting hug.

But every taut muscle of her posture—not to mention the arms crossed tight over her chest—sent a clear keep-your-distance message.

He set the Sweet Dreams bag on the table and continued to the box.

"H-he was fine when I fed him before the tea." Jeannette stayed where she was, near the door. Away from Button.

Logan bent and examined the limp kitten.

He was gone, no question about it.

And there could be dozens of reasons why—none of which had a thing to do with the care Jeannette had provided.

She needed to know that.

He rose. "This isn't your fault, you know."

"I know."

Thank heaven she didn't sound as if she had to be convinced. Taking the blame for what had happened would have compounded her misery.

"You did your best for him." Small consolation, but what else was there to say?

"It didn't matter in the end." She sank into a kitchen chair and dropped her face into her hands. "Why does everybody and everything I love die?"

The broken question sent a jolt through him.

And what did she mean by everybody? Was that an exaggeration—or was she being literal?

If it was the latter, that would explain a lot.

He took the chair beside her. "Who else have you lost, Jeannette?" Asking the gentle question was risky. But she'd opened the door—and she might never do that again.

"My whole f-family."

She'd meant her previous comment literally.

His stomach twisted.

Curious as he'd been about her background, now that he was on the verge of finding out, he wasn't certain he wanted to know.

Because it was going to be bad.

Very bad.

As Charley had said, people didn't cut themselves off from others unless they'd been seriously hurt.

But he wanted to hear her story. Knowing what had shaped this woman could help him figure out how to help her move on.

"What happened?"

"It was an a-accident." She lowered her hands to the table. "Where's Molly?"

The non sequitur threw him for a moment. "Um . . . spending the night with Elisa. I'm picking her up tomorrow morning before church. The Shabos were able to go back to their apartment yesterday."

"I know. Why are you here?"

"I had a free evening, Molly was occupied, and I thought a cinnamon roll"—he tapped the bag— "and a walk on the beach would be a perfect Saturday night. I hoped you'd join me. I also wanted to get an update on Button."

"I have to . . . to take care of him." She glanced at the box, dread etching her features.

"I can do that for you, if you like." Later. After she shared whatever had happened in her life to cause a major meltdown over the kitten. "Jeannette—would you tell me about the accident?"

Her face was bleak as she looked at him, the sadness in her brown irises as deep as the fathomless waters beyond Hope Harbor. "I haven't talked about it in years."

"It might help if you did."

"That's what everyone said at the time. I tried. It didn't change how I felt."

"Did you lose a husband? Children?" Considering the profoundness of her grief, the death had to be on that level of magnitude.

"No."

Not what he'd expected.

"Then who did you lose?"

She appraised him. "Why do you want to know?"

Smart question. She was being cautious, protecting herself.

However . . . his interest had nothing to do with

morbid curiosity, if that was her concern. It was driven by a much more personal component.

But how to express that without scaring her off—and shutting her down?

"We're neighbors . . . and I'd like to think we're also friends." He didn't rush his answer, choosing his words with care. "Friends care about each other. They share their histories, like I shared mine with you." Reminding her of that couldn't hurt. "Friends also trust each other to keep confidences. Whatever you tell me will stay between us."

She frowned and bit her lower lip. "I don't know . . ."

He let several seconds pass. "I'll tell you what. Why don't I collect Button's things and take them—and him—over to my place while you think about it?" The delay was a gamble—but he'd rather not hear her story if she later felt she'd been coerced into telling it and ended up resenting him. "I'll bury Button tomorrow, if you like."

"Thank you."

"Do you want to come?"

She shook her head. "I'll help you collect everything."

They worked in silence, packing a bag with the bottles and formula and other items. When they finished, he tucked the package beside Button and picked up the box.

"I'll be back in ten minutes."

She nodded and opened the door.

He slipped through—and shifted into high gear. The longer he was gone, the higher the odds she'd stop him at the door with a "thanks for your help" greeting and send him home.

But that didn't happen. As he crossed her patio nine minutes later, the aroma of coffee drifted through the window.

She opened the door as he approached.

During his absence, she'd done some repair work on her face. The pallor remained, but the mascara smudges had been erased and the tearstains wiped away. Her eyes weren't quite as red, either, and the puffiness had subsided a tad.

"I put coffee on. I assume you prefer that over tea."

"I like *your* tea."

"Diplomatically put." She offered him the ghost of a smile. "But I'll have coffee too. Once in a while it's a nice change of pace."

He crossed the threshold. She'd put the cinnamon rolls on plates and added napkins, knives, and forks to each place. Two mugs waited beside a small coffeemaker.

"Where do you want me?"

"Either spot is fine." She moved to the coffeemaker and poured them each a cup. "Sugar or cream?"

"Black."

She set his mug on the table, added a healthy

dose of cream and a teaspoon of sugar to hers, and joined him. "Where did you put Button?"

"In the garage. I'll bury him in the backyard tomorrow morning."

She stirred her coffee. "Do you think Molly should see him first—or be there for the . . . burial?"

"Do you?"

Her brow pinched. "Sometimes that makes it more real. But she's already been through her Nana's death. That's fresh enough in her mind and should give her the gist of what happened without the ritual. Seeing where he's buried may be sufficient."

"I was thinking along those same lines." He took a tentative sip of his coffee. Not a bad brew for a tea drinker.

As if she'd read his mind, the corners of her mouth tweaked again. "I know how to make coffee. My dad loved his java, and even though I always preferred tea, he insisted I learn how to brew a decent cup."

"My thanks to your dad."

He waited, letting her set the pace, giving her a chance to organize her thoughts and tell him her story in the way that was most comfortable for her.

She broke off a bite of cinnamon roll with her fork but didn't eat it. "My comment about how seeing a body makes death more real is based on

321

personal experience. I didn't have that opportunity. It was just a memorial service."

Again, he wanted to reach out and touch her. Instead, he held on to his mug to keep his hands where they belonged. "Who did you lose, Jeannette?"

She drew a shaky breath. "Everyone."

She'd said that before, but it wasn't computing. How could a person lose everyone they loved in one fell swoop?

Even with the Shabos, three had survived the horrendous act of terrorism that had decimated their family.

"What do you mean by everyone?"

"I mean everyone. My entire family. Mother, father, brother, sister-in-law, niece—even my brother's d-dog." Her voice rasped, and she picked up her mug with both hands. Took a sip as her eyes began to shimmer.

Logan's stomach bottomed out as he tried to digest that bombshell.

The kind of loss she'd sustained was almost incomprehensible.

Yet she'd endured.

Meaning the slender woman sitting across from him had tremendous emotional stamina—perhaps more than she realized.

He remained silent while she composed herself. Hoping she'd continue the story without more questions from him—and he had plenty.

322

A few seconds later, she did.

"It was a plane crash. My dad was the pilot—but it wasn't his fault. The investigators from the FAA and National Transportation Safety Board found a mechanical defect in the aircraft Dad had rented. It was a new plane, but this was a factory error. The plane caught fire after the crash, and there . . . there wasn't much left to find by the time the emergency crews put it out." Her throat worked as she swallowed.

As Logan tried to process the horror of that scenario, she hit him with a second bombshell.

"I was supposed to be on the plane too." She swiped up a glob of icing that had dripped onto her plate. Wiped it off her finger with a napkin. "It was a thirty-fifth anniversary trip for my mom and dad. We were all going to Hilton Head. But the flu was decimating the staff at my school, and they asked me to delay my trip two days while they rounded up subs."

As the truth slammed home, his pulse stuttered.

If Jeannette hadn't agreed to stay behind, she would have died too.

He gripped his mug to steady his fingers. "I can't begin to imagine what you've been through."

"Don't try. It's not a place you want to go." Her voice hitched, and she motioned to his roll. "That's g-getting cold."

"I can nuke it again." But he wouldn't. His

323

appetite had vanished. "You told me a couple of weeks ago that you moved here because you needed a change of scene—now I can understand why."

"Most people back in Cincinnati didn't— but there was nothing left for me there except memories that made me sad. And I had the financial resources to start over somewhere else. I was the beneficiary of several insurance policies and wills, and those funds—along with the settlement money from the plane manufacturer—gave me the seed money for this place. Literally. Plus a fair amount to spare. Financial stability is one problem I never have to worry about." She took a tiny sip of coffee. "So now you know my story."

Yeah, he did.

And more—including the reason she shied away from relationships.

If you didn't care for people, you couldn't get hurt. Letting anyone—or anything—get too close could lead to loss . . . and pain.

As Button's demise today had affirmed.

Could the timing of that have been any worse?

If there had been any softening in Jeannette's resolve to keep her distance from others, the kitten casualty would convince her to shore it up—unless he did some fast talking and offered a compelling argument for a different course.

"After hearing your story, I can understand why

you want no involvements." He watched her as he spoke.

She met his gaze straight on. "I hoped you would. That's why I shared it with you. And please don't try to convince me to change my mind. The life I've created works for me."

"Does it make you happy?" He kept his manner conversational. Nonjudgmental.

"I'm . . . content."

"In every way?"

She gave him a wary look. "What do you mean?"

"I can see why keeping people at arm's length is safer for your heart—but it's kind of like that old saying about boats. While they're safe in harbors, that's not what they're built for. I think that's true of the heart too. It can't fully be alive without love."

Her chin rose a fraction. "It can't be broken, either."

"But like a ship that never sails, a heart that's never used isn't living up to its potential. Especially one as caring and giving and loving as yours."

Several beats passed, and when she spoke at last her tone was sad—but firm. "I appreciate what you're saying, Logan. And I'm flattered. But I've thought this through long and hard—and I still choose loneliness over the risk of loss."

He had no comeback for that.

With time—and tenacity—it was possible he could convince her to change her mind and give love another chance.

But perhaps that was selfish. Who was he to tell Jeannette how to live her life? After all she'd been through, after all the deliberation she'd given this, it was possible her choice was the best one for her.

Even if his instincts weren't buying that.

"Can I say I'm disappointed?" He tried for a smile but only half succeeded.

"I'll take that as a compliment."

"You should. And if you ever change your mind, I'll be right next door. All you have to do is ring the bell."

"I appreciate that."

"Well . . ." He stood. What more was there to say? "I think I'll take this home and heat it up later, after I take that walk on the beach." He picked up the cinnamon roll and slid it back into the bag she'd left on the counter.

She followed him to the door. "I'm sure I'll see you around."

"I'm sure you will. It's a small town."

He turned toward her, intending to say a simple good-bye—but at the longing in her eyes, the breath jammed in his lungs.

Sweet heaven.

Did she have any idea what a powerful invitation she was sending?

Not likely, since it didn't match her words.

Yet the unconscious message came straight from her heart.

And he couldn't ignore it.

His fingers crimped the top of the bag.

Maybe they were never destined to be anything more than neighbors.

Maybe she'd stick by her decision to avoid relationships and remain forever in the solitary world she'd created, with only her lavender plants for company.

Maybe she was strong enough to make it through life without the light of love to brighten her days and guide her steps.

But why not leave her with a hint of what she was missing?

Without giving the left side of his brain a chance to kick in and dissuade him, Logan shifted the cinnamon roll aside, leaned down, and pressed his lips to hers.

Her sudden, indrawn breath told him she was surprised.

He'd expected that.

What he hadn't expected was the sweet stirring of her mouth beneath his that told him she welcomed his kiss.

Jeannette might think she didn't want love in her life, but her ardent response said otherwise.

And that was hopeful.

It was also very, very tempting.

The urge to continue the kiss, to pull her close and deepen it until there was no doubt in her mind how much she attracted him, was fierce.

But that would be a mistake.

If she wanted more, she had to be the one to initiate it.

After giving himself a few more seconds to memorize the feel of her mouth against his, he slowly pulled back.

She stared up at him, her fingers clamped around the edge of the door. As if she needed the support.

"Just a preview of what's waiting next door if you ever change your mind." He cleared the huskiness from his throat. "Good night, Jeannette." He stroked a finger down her cheek, turned, and forced himself to walk away.

Only after he rounded the corner of the hedge and was out of sight of her house did he slow his pace—and try to convince his pulse to return to a normal rhythm.

Wow.

The lady knew how to kiss.

And he wanted more.

But he'd laid his cards on the table. Demonstrated the depth of his interest. The next move was up to her.

And if she never came around?

He exhaled.

Maybe someday he'd meet another woman with

potential—but he had a feeling no one would ever live up to Jeannette.

For now, though, all he could do was give her time and space . . . and pray she would find the courage to put her fears to rest and take a chance on love.

22

She ought to be in church.

But she couldn't face all those people today—not when she had to deal with a crowd later at tea.

For once, she'd have to visit with God here on Driftwood Beach.

Jeannette shoved her hands into the pockets of her jacket as a gust of cool wind whipped past. It wasn't the best day for a walk by the sea, after the fierce storm that had raged last night—both outside and in her heart—but with Logan picking up Molly from her sleepover this morning and going to church, she wouldn't have to worry about running into the threesome from next door down here at this hour.

Slowing her pace, she assessed the ominous clouds massed on the horizon. There could be more stormy weather in store. Maybe she ought to ditch the walk and go home, take a nap. With all the lightning and thunder last night, she hadn't clocked much shut-eye.

The storm wasn't the main reason you couldn't sleep, Jeannette.

Too true—and ignoring the root cause of her insomnia was as useless as trying to catch a mole crab.

That kiss was to blame for her tossing and turning.

No—that wasn't quite accurate.

Her restlessness had been due to far more than a mere kiss—though there had been nothing mere about Logan's potent lip-lock.

The real cause was the hibernating hopes and dreams and longings buried deep in her heart that her neighbor had stirred to life *with* that kiss.

And now that they were awake and clamoring for attention, what was she supposed to do with them?

Especially the longings, which were as unruly as Toby in his pre-Thomma days.

Jeannette kicked at a piece of driftwood.

This wasn't fair.

She'd arrived at her decision to live a solitary existence after much reflection and prayer. Her life was exactly as she'd planned it. Until the past few weeks, there had been no one in it to cause her one iota of worry or agitation.

Now she had plenty of both.

Sighing, she scanned the dark clouds.

So what's going on, God? You know I'm hanging on to my faith by a thread. Why are you making everything so hard? Why does life *have to be so hard? Why is—*

"Morning, Jeannette. You look as if you're contemplating the mysteries of the universe on this beautiful day."

She whirled around. Peered at the approaching figure.

Was that Charley ambling up the beach toward her?

Yeah, it was. No mistaking that distinctive pony-tail or the Ducks cap.

What on earth was he doing in her neck of the woods?

She forced up the corners of her mouth as he drew near. "For a minute I thought you were an illusion. I rarely see anyone on this out-of-the-way beach."

"I've been here often."

"Why haven't I ever run into you?"

"We must come at different times." He gave her one of the trademark smiles that illuminated his face.

That was possible. And she didn't get to the beach as much as she'd like to, anyway. The farm and tearoom took up most of her waking hours.

"It's kind of strange our paths crossed today. I usually walk on brighter days. I was hoping the sun would come out if I ventured down here."

"Sunny days are a treasure—but there's beauty in storms too. Volatile weather offers boundless inspiration for my painting." He swept a hand across the horizon. "Isn't that a magnificent example of God's handiwork?"

She didn't try to hide her skepticism as she surveyed the angry dark clouds. "That must be your artist's eye talking."

"Also the human one. Shall we stroll?" He fell in beside her without waiting for an answer.

So much for her solo walk.

And maybe that was okay, given the unsettled state of her emotions. Charley always had a few thought-provoking observations to offer, and perhaps one of them would help her sort through her jumbled feelings.

"As for the beauty in storms"—he picked up the conversation without missing a beat—"I suppose you have to work harder to see it. Sunshine and blue skies get all the positive press." After giving her a quick flash of his white teeth, he grew more serious. "But storms have amazing power. They can transform. Bring to the surface hidden treasures." He bent and scooped a small object out of the sand. "Like this."

She leaned close to inspect it. "Is that a key?"

"Yes. A very old one, by the look of it. Copper, I'd say, considering the lack of barnacles." He angled it toward the light as he examined it. "It must have washed ashore in last night's storm."

"I wonder what it's from?"

"A ship that was lost in a gale, I expect. It could have opened a sea chest . . . or the captain's quarters . . . or some storage compartment below deck. Like the first mate's private stash of rum." He tilted his head, humor lurking in his dark eyes. "A sailor may have 'borrowed' it to pilfer a few sips on a long sea voyage and dropped it

334

overboard to protect himself when he was about to be discovered."

"You have a vivid imagination. No wonder you're an artist."

"Doesn't take an artist to be open to possibilities." He weighed the key in his hand. "Too bad this can't talk. It would have some fascinating stories to tell."

"Many of them sad, I bet. Life was hard in those days—and that key wound up stuck on the bottom of the ocean for who knows how long. Not the happiest ending."

"But that wasn't the ending. It may have been tossed about by turbulent waters, but now the tides have brought it to our shore and it's getting a second chance at life."

"Its original purpose is gone, though. That's sad."

"Perhaps it has a new purpose, yet to be discovered."

The man definitely had a fanciful mind—and a boundless sense of optimism.

"If you say so."

He didn't respond—but after a couple more minutes of meandering along the hard-packed sand just past the surf line, he introduced a new topic. "I saw Logan and Molly going into Grace Christian this morning—and the Shabos passed me as they drove to St. Francis. I'd say we have some fine additions to our community in those two families."

"I agree." If that was a subtle attempt to find out why she hadn't attended services today, he was out of luck. "But they all have a sad history."

"That's true. Sometimes it's difficult to understand why God allows such tragedies to happen."

Strange that he'd bring up the very subject she'd been pondering as he joined her.

"I hear you."

"Yet good can come out of bad. Take the Shabos, for instance. Despite all their hardships, life may hold exceptional promise for them in this new country. Elisa will have opportunities she would never have had in her homeland—and who knows? She may end up contributing to the world in ways we could never foresee. The same with Thomma and Mariam. God has spared them for a reason."

"You really believe that?"

"Without question. Don't you?"

"I used to." Back when she'd trusted in God's design and accepted the bad along with the good—until the bad overwhelmed her. "These days, it's harder."

"Nothing important or worthwhile is ever easy. Like love."

She gave him a sidelong glance.

Where had that come from?

"Are you speaking from experience?" As far as she knew, Charley had never been married.

"Absolutely. What would life be without love?"

"Are you thinking of someone in particular?" She went for the subtle route rather than asking him straight out if he'd had a wife.

He saw through her, of course.

"Very diplomatic." He displayed his teeth again. "The answer is no. But I've loved many people. I also love my work—and all the creatures in God's kingdom. That love sustains me."

"But people—and creatures—die." She tried to erase the image of Button's limp form from her mind.

"Yet they live on in our hearts and remain with us in a very real sense. Plus, the absence of their physical presence doesn't diminish the impact they have on our lives. On the contrary. It sometimes grows after they're gone. That's a wonderful gift . . . and legacy."

He had a point—but it didn't take away the hurt of loss.

"It's not the same after they're gone, though. Memories aren't enough to chase away loneliness."

"That's true. So it's best not to be alone."

"You're alone. By choice, I assume."

"I may not have a wife, but I'm not alone. I have many friends in Hope Harbor who add joy to my days. I talk to them often, and I know if I ever need their help, they'll be there for me. The presence of God is also very real in my life. And then there's Floyd and Gladys—and my other

337

animal friends who offer love and comfort in a different way."

"None of that replaces people you've lost, though."

"Loss is a very real part of the human condition, no question about it. Nothing on this earth lasts forever. Lives are filled with endings—and beginnings. No matter how hard we try to maintain the status quo, the world changes around us . . . and changes our world in the process."

She couldn't dispute that.

Especially in view of all that had happened to *her* world in the past few weeks.

She fisted her hands in her pockets.

"And sometimes, while we might only recognize it in hindsight, changes that shake up our world can be positive." Charley stopped.

She did too—and turned to study the kindly eyes in the weathered, bronzed face. "Why do you always seem to have your act together?"

His smile was gentle. "Because it's not an act. I take life a day at a time, always staying true to who I am. While I appreciate my past, I live in the present and look forward to the future. I also fill my days with love, which is the great stabilizer."

"Except love can be snatched away from you."

As the words spilled out of her mouth, Jeannette frowned.

Why had she said that? It could provoke questions—and nice as he was, she wasn't about to share her story with Charley, as she had with Logan.

He didn't probe—suggesting he'd sensed her unwillingness to expound.

"Losing love is one of life's most difficult trials." For once, his usual smile was absent, and his dark brown irises were soft with compassion. "But wouldn't it have been worse never to have had it? Tennyson was a wise man."

Strange that she'd been thinking about that very same poetic passage not long ago.

"I'm not sure he was right about that particular subject." She shoved her hands deeper in her pockets.

"Ah—but think how much you would have missed if you'd never known love. How different your life would be."

He had a point. Much as she pined for her family, they'd enriched her world beyond measure. And they continued to do that, as Charley had said. To never have had them in her life at all was unimaginable.

But the loss had been devastating—and the notion of letting her guard down, allowing other people in, and risking more loss was paralyzing, despite Charley's pep talk.

Yet ruling out love also ruled out the potential for abundant joy—including the kind Logan might add to her life if she opened that door.

And based on last night's kiss, the man would be more than willing to test the waters if she gave him any encouragement.

"Are you still with me, Jeannette?" Amusement underscored Charley's friendly tease.

"Sorry. I zoned out for a minute. Everything you said makes sense—in theory."

"In practice too." He adjusted the brim of his cap and motioned toward a mottled silver-white harbor seal sunning itself on a rock offshore. "I see Casper has joined us."

Her lips twitched as the seal let out a loud belch. "Another friend of yours?"

"We're acquainted." He turned back to her. "I'll offer one other thought. God's timing isn't always ours. Sometimes he opens doors we aren't certain we're ready to walk through. And it's fine to be cautious. Not every door that beckons is divinely inspired. But at some point we do have to make a decision—because most don't stay open forever." He pressed the storm-tossed key into her hand. "A souvenir of the walk we shared."

"But you found it."

"Some treasures are meant to be passed on. Are you going any farther?" He motioned to the vast empty beach ahead.

"No. I have to get ready for tea."

"In that case, I'll leave you here." A ray of light broke through the dark clouds overhead, and he lifted his face to the heavens. "It appears you're

going to get your wish. Sunny skies are ahead."
He touched the brim of his Ducks cap. "See you
again soon, Jeannette. Have a wonderful day."

She stayed where she was for another minute or
two as Charley wandered down the beach, then
pivoted and slowly retraced her route.

Everything the man had said rang true—and life
without love was becoming lonelier by the day.

But how did you change course midstream?

How did you know if the door opening before
you was the one you were supposed to walk
through?

How did you banish fear?

If only God would write those answers in the
sky for her.

Since that wasn't how he operated, however,
she'd have to seek guidance through prayer—and
hopefully he'd give her some direction soon.

For Charley was right.

Doors didn't stay open forever.

He was *not* looking forward to the rest of his
Sunday morning.

As Logan pulled out of the parking spot in front
of the Shabos' apartment and Elisa and Mariam
waved them off, he glanced in the rearview mirror.

Molly watched the two figures recede, nose
pressed to the glass.

"Did you have fun?" He accelerated toward
101.

"Uh-huh."

"What did you do?"

"Played."

"What did you play?"

"Games."

He blew out a breath.

This sounded like a replay of their conversation from weeks ago, during Mariam's early days watching the girls at his house.

The taciturn Molly was back—and the news he had to share wasn't likely to change that.

In fact, it could exacerbate the situation.

A depressing thought if ever there was one.

His attempts at conversation on the short drive to church earned him more monosyllable answers.

Likewise on the drive home after the service, until he finally gave up.

But once they pulled into the driveway and he was taking off her seat restraints, he set the stage for the conversation they had to have. "Let's sit on the porch steps for a few minutes."

"I want to say hi to Toby."

"Okay. You can do that first. But don't open the cage just yet." He helped her out of the car and snagged her small overnight bag from the back seat.

"Why do you want to sit on the porch?" She squinted at him.

"Why not? The sun came out, and I have a cinnamon roll we can share."

"From Sweet Dreams?"

"Yes." He unlocked the back door of the house.

"I like those."

"I know." Even if the roll from last night hadn't initially been intended for her.

Toby greeted them with an indignant howl as they entered the kitchen.

He cringed.

Thank goodness Thomma was about done with his fence training. In another day or two, the beagle should be able to stay outside with no supervision, where he could cavort and dig and chase birds to his heart's content. No more leash—except on their trips through Jeannette's lavender plants to the beach.

And Thomma had also managed to get the random barking under control. The beagle only yapped these days if he had a reason.

Like being confined in his cage.

"I'll be back in a minute." Molly raced down the hall.

A few moments later, Toby's howls morphed to plaintive whines that almost sounded like "let me out, let me out."

But he could wait a few more minutes. Having the inquisitive beagle underfoot while he talked to Molly about Button would be too distracting.

Tamping down his nerves, he nuked the roll, poured Molly a glass of milk, and went out to the porch. Hard as he'd tried to psyche himself up for everything from stoic silence to a meltdown, who knew how she was going to react to the news of the kitten's demise?

But he was about to find out.

The door opened and closed behind him, and he scooted over to make room for her.

She chose the step above him instead, which ended up working better. It put them closer to eye level.

He held out the plate with the cut-up roll. After she took a piece, he set the plate down.

"Don't you want some?"

"Sure." He took a piece and forced himself to bite into it, but the sweet confection didn't tickle his taste buds as usual.

Too bad he hadn't brought out some water to keep the roll from sticking in his throat.

"What's wrong?"

He shifted sideways.

Molly was watching him, trepidation sharpening her features. She'd only taken a tiny nibble of her cinnamon roll. The bulk of it had been squeezed flat in her fingers.

More evidence of her keen ability to pick up moods.

And now that she was tuned in to his wavelength, there was no sense delaying the task before him.

"While you were at the Shabos', I went over to see Jeannette."

"Did Button die?"

At the solemn, out-of-the-blue question, he blinked.

How in the world had she figured that out?

And how was he supposed to respond?

Just tell her the truth, West. What other choice is there?

He took a fortifying breath. "Yes, he did. Jeannette took good care of him, but kittens that tiny aren't very strong yet. There are all kinds of reasons why they get sick."

"Where is he?"

"I buried him in the back." He motioned toward the rear of their yard, beyond the electric fence line. Out of Toby's digging range.

"Can I see?"

"Yes. I was going to take you back after we talked."

She set her mashed roll back on the plate and stood.

Apparently they were done talking.

Maybe they could continue the discussion in the yard, though.

Side by side, they trekked to the tiny grave in silence.

Once they reached the flat stone he'd laid on top, Molly squatted to touch it. "We should put his name here."

"I agree." He dropped to one knee beside her. "Why don't we do it together?"

No response.

After a moment, she stood. "Did you say a prayer?"

For a kitten?

"Uh . . . no."

"They said a prayer for Nana."

If a prayer made her happy, what was the harm?

"We could do that now. Do you want to say it?"

"A grown-up should do it."

Scrambling to come up with some appropriate words, he rose too and bowed his head. "Dear God, we commend our friend, Button, to your care. We know you created all the creatures on the earth and that you love them. We loved this kitten too. We ask you to comfort us—and Jeannette—as we say good-bye, and we ask your blessing on Button. Amen."

He checked on Molly.

Her expression was somber, but there were no tears as she walked to the edge of the yard and plucked a few of the yellow wildflowers that had sprouted past his property line.

She returned to the small grave and bent to arrange them next to the stone. "Is Button in heaven?"

He stifled a groan.

How was he supposed to answer *that* one?

"Um . . . I don't know, sweetie." But he doubted it. After all, animals weren't created in the divine image, like humans. Yet he needed to comfort this child who'd endured too much loss. "God wants all his creatures to be happy, though."

"I hope he *is* in heaven. I hope he's with Nana." She touched the flowers again, rose, and began walking back to the house.

"Sweetie." This wasn't how he'd expected—or wanted—the conversation to end. They should discuss what had happened.

But Molly had other ideas.

She turned at his summons but didn't rejoin him or respond. She just waited for him to speak.

"Why don't we sit on the porch for a while?"

"I want to play with Toby." She started forward.

"Molly."

She stopped again and half-turned toward him.

"Do you want to talk about Button?"

"Why?"

"Sometimes talking helps if we're sad."

"It won't make Button—or Nana—come back." She toed a divot of grass Toby had no doubt unearthed. "When people you love die, they're gone for always."

He couldn't argue with that.

"But you have me."

She lifted her head . . . looked at him . . . and walked away.

Pressure built behind his eyes as he watched her plod back to the house as if the weight of the world rested on her tiny shoulders.

She was too young to carry such a heavy load.

To be perennially glum. A girl her age should be skipping and chatting and laughing.

Yet in all the months she'd been with him, he'd never once heard a little-girl giggle.

That wasn't normal.

He rested his hands on his hips and exhaled.

Perhaps it was time to arrange for some counseling.

She circled around the plate with the cinnamon roll they'd left on the porch and disappeared inside.

He followed more slowly, bending to retrieve the uneaten treat as he passed.

Ants had already moved in to stake a claim, but several had gotten stuck in the gooey icing. They were attempting to extricate themselves from their sticky dilemma, but the harder they tried, the worse off they were.

He could relate.

A ray of sun peeked through the gray clouds scuttling across the sky, dispersing the gloom and revealing a patch of blue—suggesting the hours ahead would be bright despite the lingering effects of the storm that had raged last night.

If only that was true of his relationship with Molly.

An excited bark sounded inside as Toby celebrated his release, and Logan continued toward the door.

At least one occupant of this house was happy.

Hand on knob, he paused as a line from Reverend Baker's sermon this morning replayed in his mind.

"It's easy to get discouraged in the midst of life's storms. But God has our back—and when the raft we're clinging to begins to sink, he's always ready to extend a hand. All we have to do is trust him enough to take it and let go."

Could that be his problem?

All along, he'd been holding fast to the hope he could fix everything himself if he muscled through, instead of putting his troubles in the hands of the Almighty.

And he was getting nowhere—with Molly or Jeannette.

So why not add prayer to his daily agenda, see where that led?

It couldn't hurt.

Besides . . . he was out of ideas. None of his go-it-alone attempts to wedge open a door to their hearts had been successful.

But perhaps with God's guidance, he could find a way to help his niece and neighbor step out of the darkness of fear and grief and into the sunshine of hope and love.

23

She missed Logan.

Molly too.

And her conversation on the beach four days ago with Charley, along with that kiss from her neighbor last Saturday, had left her more confused than ever.

Keeping one hand on the wheel, Jeannette kneaded her forehead with the other as she drove through Hope Harbor.

If she listened to her heart, she'd scrap all the rules she'd made for her life when she'd moved here and take another chance on love.

If she listened to her brain, she'd add a moat to the tall hedge around her property and let no one in but paying customers.

Which was the right course?

Only God knew—and he wasn't sharing his thoughts, despite all the prayers she'd dispatched his direction.

Either that, or she was missing the still small voice of his response, as Elijah had.

Jeannette slowed as she drove past St. Francis church. From the street, a tiny sliver of the meditation garden in back that Father Murphy lavished with care was visible.

Might the serenity she'd heard people say could

be found there quiet her mind and help her tune in to any guidance from above?

Dare she drop in for a visit, even though she wasn't a member of the congregation?

Jeannette eased back farther on the gas pedal.

It couldn't hurt to pull into the parking lot and take a peek at the garden from the car. Father Murphy wasn't the type to make anyone feel unwelcome.

She hung a left, rolled past the church and attached rectory, and swung into a parking spot near the garden.

From here, she could see the sign beside the rose-covered arbor at the entrance.

All are welcome.

The invitation couldn't be clearer.

And since no one else was about on this Thursday noon hour, why not stroll through the beckoning archway and let the peace and tranquility seep into her soul?

She set the brake, picked up her purse, and left the car behind.

One step into the garden, she found herself immersed in a piece of heaven.

Lips curving up, she surveyed Father Murphy's handiwork.

A stone path followed a circular route through the well-tended space, where colorful flowers shared space with restful greenery. The soft tinkle of water from a fountain in the center provided a soothing background refrain that enhanced the harmony of the setting. A bird feeder hung from the sheltering bough of a towering Sitka spruce, and two wooden benches were placed along the path.

She ambled toward the one beside the small statue of Francis of Assisi and sank down, letting the peace envelop her.

Jeannette had no idea how long she sat there, but the faint hum of an approaching car engine at last prompted her to check her watch.

Wow.

Had she really zoned out for half an hour?

Hard to believe.

And while she was no closer to an answer than she'd been when she arrived, at least her soul felt refreshed.

She rose and returned to the parking lot, where Father Murphy was removing his golf clubs from the trunk of his car.

"Jeannette! I wondered who was enjoying my tiny slice of paradise." He beamed at her.

"That's an apt description for it." She dug her keys out of her purse. "I hope I wasn't trespassing."

"Not at all." He closed the trunk and slung his bag over his shoulder. "As the sign says, all are welcome. The beauty of nature is nonsectarian." He winked at her. "And the garden is a wonderful spot for contemplation and reflection. I often come out here to work on my homilies."

"I can see why. How was your golf game?"

He grimaced. "Sad to say, your fine minister won today's round. However . . . there's always next week. I can't change the past, but I have hopes for the future. That's the beauty of tomorrow—it offers you the possibility of a better day." He motioned toward the garden. "I hope I didn't run you off."

"No. I have to get home. But I enjoyed my visit."

"I'm glad. Come anytime. In general, you'll have the place to yourself." Hefting his clubs into a different position, he lifted his hand in farewell and sauntered toward the rectory.

She continued to her car, and as she took her place behind the wheel and slid the key into the ignition, the priest's comment about hopes for the future replayed in her mind.

It was kind of the same message she'd heard from Charley on Sunday.

Were those two kindly souls perhaps heaven-sent messengers? Was God giving her the guidance she'd requested via a taco-making artist and a priest?

Or was that a stretch? After all, the conversations she'd had with them could be nothing more than coincidence.

Yet it didn't feel like mere happenstance.

Whatever the precipitating factors, however, the end result was the same.

They'd forced her to think hard about the opportunity on her doorstep—literally—with Logan . . . and to reconsider the plan she'd outlined for her life.

But unless she could tame the paralyzing fear that gripped her in a choke hold, she'd never be able to risk taking the leap to love.

"You are being a good dog, Toby—yes?"

Mariam paused in her weeding of the overgrown flower bed behind Logan's house and reached out to pet the hovering pup.

He sat on his haunches, cocked his head, and gave her a goofy dog grin.

"I will take that as a yes. And you stay out of this garden, or you will have to answer to Thomma."

The pup might not have a clue what she was saying—but it was the same warning she'd given him every day since she'd started the project, and so far he'd left the plot alone.

She sat back on her heels and surveyed the garden. It had been long neglected, but someone in the past had planted it with care. Under the tangle of weeds, she was unearthing botanical treasures.

Not that Logan expected her to do this kind of labor. While he'd assured her he appreciated her efforts, he'd reminded her often that this wasn't part of her job description.

But the task kept her busy while the girls napped,

and the fresh air was invigorating. The exercise was also beneficial. Even back home, she'd always loved to tend her garden. And while the flowers here were different than the ones that flourished in Syria, digging in the earth and watching plants thrive gave her joy and fed her soul.

The rest would have to wait for another day, though. It was time to get the girls up, prepare a snack, and play some games with them until Logan returned from the urgent care center.

Also a joyful task.

Who wouldn't enjoy interacting with the two delightful girls?

Other than her granddaughter's own father.

A pang echoed through Mariam as she pushed herself to her feet and steadied herself on the chair she'd placed beside her.

Nothing had changed after their talk last week. She'd hoped a kinder, gentler approach would reach Thomma, but he hadn't mentioned their conversation once or warmed up to Elisa.

And she had no idea what to try next.

Toby bounded over as she brushed the dirt off her slacks, and she gave him a distracted pet.

Those two girls inside could use some of his boundless energy and enthusiasm. They were both far too solemn and quiet.

"You want to come in or stay outside?" Mariam tossed the question to the dog as she ascended the steps.

He dashed over and scrambled up past her.

She chuckled. "I guess that is my answer."

The instant she opened the door, he zipped through and charged down the hall.

No reason for her to follow and wake the girls. Toby would take care of that job.

As she closed the door and moved over to the counter, the beagle began to bark.

Mariam frowned.

He'd been much less prone to yap for no reason since Thomma had begun training him. Why would he revert to his old ways now?

"Toby! Kunn hadyaan!" Hopefully her son's magic command would quiet him and he'd come running for a treat.

It didn't work today.

She huffed out a breath.

Were the girls egging him on?

That wasn't their usual style—but who knew what the two of them were up to, after that cookie pilfering stunt they'd pulled earlier in the week? It was fortunate she'd found the stash they'd been hoarding in Molly's bedroom, or one of these days she'd have been dealing with two very sick youngsters after a cookie orgy.

"Toby! Come in here!"

He hurtled back down the hall and began dancing around her legs, barking at full volume.

She put her hands over her ears. "What is wrong with you today? Be quiet!"

He ran over to the hall, turned to her, and continued to bark.

When she didn't respond, he dashed back and nipped at her pants leg.

"Toby! Stop that!" She waved him off.

He tried again, this time tugging on the fabric. Like he wanted her to follow him.

"Fine. I'll come. I need to see what those girls are up to."

He ran ahead, disappeared into Molly's room—and fell silent.

At the threshold, she found him waiting beside the bed, panting as he twisted his head back and forth.

Now she understood what this was all about.

The girls weren't in the room.

A tingle of panic raced along her spine.

But they had to be here somewhere.

They must be playing a game. Hiding and waiting for her to find them.

"Elisa! Molly! Come out!"

Even as she issued the order, her stomach began to churn.

And the roiling worsened after she looked in the closet, peered under the bed, and broadened her search to the whole house with no results.

If the girls were inside, they'd hidden themselves well.

She did another circuit, noting details that hadn't registered on her first pass.

A slightly open drawer in Molly's dresser.

The absence of Molly's ratty blanket and Elisa's Raggedy Ann doll.

Crumbs on the kitchen counter.

As a suspicion began to form . . . and gel . . . she pulled open several drawers in Molly's room.

The clothing had been disturbed, and there were gaps.

Same with the clothes in her closet.

In the kitchen, she yanked open the refrigerator.

The jelly bottle and jar of peanut butter weren't in their usual places.

All at once the reasons for the secret stash of cookies became clear.

Mariam closed the door and slumped against the counter as suspicion morphed to sickening certainty.

The girls had run away.

This was a disaster.

As Logan sped out of town toward home, he tried to put the brakes on his racing pulse.

Failed.

Molly was gone.

How could this have happened?

Susan hadn't been able to get many details out of the distraught Mariam before she phoned him, but she'd promised to call the woman back and try again while he drove home.

Maybe the girls were somewhere on the

property. Or had ventured down to the beach. Or were hiding in the house in a spot Mariam hadn't checked, playing one of the make-believe games they liked to concoct.

Please God, let this have a simple resolution.

Even as he said the silent prayer, though, every instinct in his body told him they had, in fact, run away.

But why should that surprise him? He'd failed miserably in his efforts to connect with his niece, and she'd told him Elisa didn't think her father loved her anymore.

There couldn't be two better runaway candidates.

And while they were too little to get far on their own, there were people in the world who would find the temptation of two young girls alone hard to resist.

A wave of nausea swept over him, and he jammed the accelerator to the floor. If Lexie or one of her patrol officers wanted to give him a ticket, so be it. They were next on his list to call anyway if this wasn't resolved within ten minutes.

He zoomed down his street, tires squealing as he swung into the driveway and barreled toward the back of the house. After setting the brake, he leaped from the car and ran for the door.

Mariam was waiting for him in the kitchen, cheeks moist, worry scoring her features.

"So sorry." Her voice was shaky.

That answered his first question.

The girls hadn't turned up.

His phone began to vibrate, and he yanked it off his belt. Susan. He slapped it to his ear. "I'm home. Did you get any more information?"

"A little."

He listened as she explained in more detail what had transpired, along with the evidence that had led Mariam to conclude the girls had run away.

"Will you be available to translate? After I do a fast search myself, I'll be calling the police. They'll want to ask her some questions too."

"Yes."

"Did anyone contact Thomma?"

"Mariam tried, but he's not answering his cell. He's on the boat and must be out of range. She left a message."

"Okay. Stand by for other calls."

As he disconnected, he touched Mariam's arm. If the girls had snuck out during their nap, this wasn't her fault—and he didn't want to add another burden to the many she already carried.

"We'll find them. I look." He pointed to his eyes and swept a hand around the house. "Here and beach."

It was impossible to know if she'd understood all of that, but he didn't have time to try and explain.

He did a fast but thorough pass through the house, as he was certain she'd done. But no one other than him would have noticed a key clue.

Molly's Disney princess suitcase and backpack were missing.

His gut twisted.

That sealed the deal.

Short of hiking out to 101, though, there was only one other place the girls could have gone— and that was his next stop.

"I go to beach." He motioned toward the water. "Stay here. Call if you see girls." He tapped his phone and hers. "I'll be back in fifteen minutes." Angling his watch to her, he flashed the fingers of one hand three times.

She nodded.

He took off out the door, dashed around the hedge at the base of the driveway, and jogged toward the lavender beds behind Jeannette's house.

Slowed.

If the girls had cut through the farm, might she have seen them?

Not likely. If she had, she would have stopped them or called Mariam.

But it was worth asking.

He knocked on the back door. Waited. Knocked again.

No answer.

She must be out.

Giving up, he sprinted down the path at the back of the property that led to the beach.

In less than five minutes, he emerged at the top

of a dune that provided a sweeping view of the vast expanse of sand.

It was deserted.

So where were they?

That was a question he was going to need help answering.

Logan pulled out his phone and called the Hope Harbor police department.

As soon as he explained the situation to the woman who answered, she put him through to Lexie Graham Stone, who listened to the story, asked for a description of Molly and Elisa, and promised to be at his house within ten minutes.

"Is there anything I should do in the meantime?" Logan gave the empty beach another one-eighty.

"Find a recent photo of Molly and text it to me. Do you happen to have one of Elisa?"

"Yes. I took a shot of the two girls together a couple of weeks ago."

"Perfect. Send that one. We'll distribute it and the description you gave me of both girls immediately so police in surrounding areas can be on the lookout for them. Expect me soon."

Logan hit the end button, slid the phone back into his pocket, and examined his trembling hands as a wave of guilt crashed over him.

This was all his fault.

If he'd gotten Molly some professional help sooner, this might never have happened.

She was hurting and sad and scared, and much as he'd hoped his love would help her heal, it hadn't been enough.

And he should have admitted that weeks ago.

Now he could lose her for real.

The wind pummeled him as he stood at the top of the dune, and he lifted his gaze toward the heavens.

Please, Lord, help us find the girls. Molly's the only family I have left, and I've come to love her as if she were my own daughter. I know she doesn't believe that, but please help her realize how much I care for her—and give me another chance to prove it to her.

A drop of rain spattered against his cheek . . . almost like a teardrop.

As if God was crying.

A chill rippled through him.

Not the kind of reassurance he'd hoped his prayer would yield.

But he wasn't going to let negative thoughts undermine his resolve.

They'd find the girls, and they were going to be just fine. Scared, maybe. Chilly and dirty, in all likelihood. But otherwise unharmed.

And once they got this incident behind them, he and Molly were going to find a way to become the family they both needed.

Whatever it took.

24

Why on earth had a police car traveling at high speed just swung into Logan's driveway?

Mail in hand, Jeannette stared at the faint cloud of dust left in the wake of the cruiser.

That had been Lexie at the wheel, though the woman had been so intent on her driving she hadn't even glanced toward the lavender farm.

Yet the siren on the car hadn't been blaring.

What was going on?

Jeannette closed the door of the mailbox and shoved back her hair, still damp from the shower.

Should she go over? Offer her help?

Or would that come across as nosy, given her I-want-to-be-left-alone-so-keep-your-distance message to Logan in her kitchen last Saturday?

And if she *did* want to keep him at arm's length, she ought to march back into her house and close the door.

As she tried to decide what to do, the other Hope Harbor police car topped the rise down the road and accelerated toward her. It too swerved into Logan's driveway, Officer Jim Gleason behind the wheel, and disappeared with a crunch of gravel.

This wasn't good.

No ambulance or fire truck had been dispatched—yet—but two police cars didn't bode well.

And she couldn't pretend she didn't care.

She took a deep breath . . . let it out . . . and faced the truth.

Like it or not, Logan and Molly had managed to infiltrate her heart—and she couldn't turn her back on them during an emergency.

As for what that meant after the crisis was over?

She had no idea.

But she'd borrow a page from *Gone with the Wind* and worry about that tomorrow.

Jeannette shoved the mail back into the box and hustled up Logan's driveway.

The front door was open as she approached—and there was only one word to describe the scene inside.

Chaos.

Toby was barking and playing catch-me-if-you-can with Logan. Mariam was crying. Lexie was on the phone, one hand pressed to her free ear. Jim, leash in hand, was acting as running back for Logan as they tried to corral the beagle.

She scanned the room for Molly.

The girl was nowhere in sight.

A stomach-twisting sense of foreboding enveloped her.

"Jeannette!" Logan lost his focus on Toby for a millisecond, and the pup made his move.

But Jim was faster. He nabbed him and snapped on the leash. "You have a cage for this guy?"

"Yeah. First door on the right down the hall." Logan's gaze remained fixed on her as he crossed the room.

Only as he drew close, and the outside light fell on his face, did Jeannette pick up his pallor and the grooves of worry etched on his brow.

"What's wrong?" She braced.

He pushed through the door to the porch. "Molly and Elisa ran away."

"Oh no." She pressed her palm to her mouth.

"Oh yes." His tone and demeanor were grim. "From what we can gather, based on Susan's conversation with Mariam, the girls took off while she was outside working in the garden during their nap."

"You're certain it's a runaway situation?" Bad as that was, the alternative was worse.

"Ninety-nine percent. They packed a bag, made sandwiches, and took some personal items."

"How long have they been gone?"

"No more than a couple of hours."

"They can't have gotten far."

"Unless someone picked them up."

He didn't have to spell out what that could mean.

"Does Thomma know?"

"Mariam can't reach him. He must be out of cell range. She left a message for him to call ASAP."

"How can I help?"

"The fact you're here helps more than you know." He took her hand. Squeezed her fingers.

She squeezed back.

The barking inside grew muffled, and Jim reappeared. "The noise is contained—more or less."

"Come in." Logan opened the door and moved aside for her to precede him.

"Jeannette." The chief shook her hand. "I was about to pay you a visit. Have you been home all afternoon?"

"Yes."

"I knocked about twenty minutes ago, on my way to check the beach." Logan arched an eyebrow.

"That must have been while I was in the shower." She lifted a few damp strands of hair.

"Did you notice any unusual activity or see any strangers in the area this afternoon?" Lexie asked.

"No. It's been very quiet."

"I understand you watched Molly a few times. Did she say anything to you that would give us a clue as to why she ran away, or where she may have gone?"

"I know she was having some difficulty adjusting to all the changes in her life, but she never said anything about leaving. Other than telling me about her life in Missouri with her grandmother, and offering a few comments about the months she spent in San Francisco with Logan, she never mentioned any other places."

"Okay." Lexie directed her attention to Logan. "I've got a call into the Springfield PD, which has a K-9 unit with trailing capabilities, and I left a message with a private citizen in the Medford area who has a well-trained bloodhound and often assists law enforcement in search-and-rescue operations. However, travel time is close to three hours in the first case, three and a half in the second."

"That's too long. A ton of bad stuff can happen in three hours." A muscle twitched in his cheek.

"I know. That's why we're going to put together some volunteer search parties to begin scouring the area. We've also sent law enforcement in our vicinity the photo and description you provided, and I gave it to Marci at the *Herald*. She's sending an alert to the paper's email list and soliciting volunteers to join the search. As soon as Susan calls me back, I want to ask Mariam a few more—" She pulled her phone off her belt. "Here she is now. Excuse me."

Lexie crossed to Mariam, while Jim did a walk-through of the house.

"Let's go outside again for a minute." Logan took her arm and guided her back to the porch. Once away from all the activity inside, he faced her. "I can't believe this is happening. I knew she was unhappy, but I didn't think she was so miserable that she felt her only recourse was to run away." His voice rasped, and he swallowed.

"I'm sorry, Logan." She laid her hand on his arm. "And if it helps, I didn't get the impression she had anything like this on her mind, either. I wonder if Elisa put her up to it? There's a heavy load of sorrow in that child's life too. Do you have any idea where they might go?"

His eyes grew bleak. "No. I don't know enough about how Molly thinks to even make an educated guess. How sad is that?"

"It's not like you haven't tried to get her to open up and bond with you."

One side of his mouth rose in a mirthless smile. "I seem to be batting zero on that score across the board."

Lexie joined them on the porch, saving her from having to respond. "Jim's going to give the house and yard a thorough going-over. I'll head back to town and get the search parties organized."

"I'll go with you." Logan pulled out his keys.

"I know you want to be involved, but someone should stay here in case the girls wander back."

"I stay." Mariam dabbed a tissue around her lashes and joined them.

"Logan?" Lexie deferred to him.

"That's fine. I can't just sit around waiting for news, and Mariam's ankle isn't strong enough yet for her to search anyway."

"Sounds like a plan. Let's gather at the high school. We'll set up the command post in the gym. There's more room there to map out some grids and assign teams as people show up."

"I'd like to be on one of them." Jeannette wasn't going to sit around and wait for news, either.

"The more hands the better. I'll see you in town." Lexie didn't wait for a response.

"Are you certain you want to do this, Jeannette?" The twin creases above Logan's nose deepened. "I know you're trying to keep your distance."

"This is an emergency. I'm suspending my rules until we find Molly and bring her home."

He scrutinized her . . . and nodded. "I appreciate that. Would you like to ride with me?"

Yes, she would—but if she wanted to maintain the ability to preserve *some* distance, that wasn't the wisest course.

"If I take my own car, we can both come and go as needed. Why don't I meet you at the high school?"

"Okay. I'll see you there. And thank you." He squeezed her hand—and for one fleeting instant he seemed to be fighting the temptation to express his appreciation in a more personal way—but then he released her fingers and reentered the house.

Once she lost sight of him, she clattered down the steps and ran toward her own house.

She might not have any personal experience with runaways or missing children, but she knew one thing.

Speed was of the essence.

"Good job today, Thomma. Thank you."

As he finished tying off the last bowline to the cleat on the dock, Thomma looked over at Roark, who'd interrupted his conversation with today's customers to toss him that accolade.

His boss didn't say much, but he never failed to offer a few kind words at the end of a workday.

Thomma dipped his head in acknowledgment.

While Roark went back to conversing with the four men who'd chartered the boat for the day—with disappointing results—Thomma pulled out his cell phone, keeping one eye on the group in case Roark summoned him.

Not that there was much for him to do, other than clean the two fish the men had caught. An easy end to the day.

At least the customers didn't appear to be upset by the poor return, despite the hefty fee they'd shelled out for the privilege of a private fishing guide. Nor should they be. Roark couldn't make the fish bite—although some of their customers seemed to think he could coax them to do so at will and made no attempt to hide their displeasure if they returned without a large catch.

How could people worry about the number of fish they caught when that meant nothing in the grand scheme of things?

He shook his head in bewilderment and refocused on the screen.

There were four messages—all in the past hour. All from Logan's home phone number.

He frowned.

His mother must be trying to contact him.

But she rarely bothered him at work.

Why today?

And why with such urgency?

Pulse accelerating, he swiveled away from the group on the boat and returned her call.

"Thomma?" The tear-laced, frantic voice that answered a mere half ring in bore only a faint resemblance to his mother's usual in-control tone.

"What's wrong?" His fingers tightened on the phone, and he gripped the railing beside him.

"Elisa is gone. She ran away with M-Molly."

It took him a few moments to digest his mother's news—and to work through the implications.

When they sank in, his lungs locked.

In Syria, he'd lost his whole family, except for his daughter and mother.

And now Elisa was gone too.

This couldn't be happening.

"Thomma?"

"I'm here." He managed to choke out the response. "What happened?"

He listened as she told him the story in halting phrases punctuated with sobs.

"The police chief is organizing search parties now. They're meeting at the high school in town. I'm s-sorry, Thomma."

"This isn't your fault."

"I was supposed to be taking care of them."

"You were." He watched a happy family stroll down the wharf side of Dockside Drive, the little girl's hand tucked into her father's, her laughter ringing across the water as the man bent low and made a comment that tickled her.

That was the kind of relationship a parent and child should have—and the vignette in front of him underscored his epic failure as a father.

"Not well enough."

As his mother spoke again, he turned away from the family and looked toward the vast open sea that appeared empty but teemed with life below the surface. Life that would never see the light unless you fished deep and hauled it up.

Perhaps he should do the same with his emotions.

If he got another chance.

"The fault is mine, 'Ami." His voice broke. "If I'd listened to you, this wouldn't have happened. Maybe . . . maybe God is punishing me by taking away the child he spared, who needed my love."

"Don't talk like that." His mother's pitch

sharpened. "We will find them. You will get another chance."

Would he?

"Thomma." The weight of a hand rested on his shoulder.

"I'll call you back after I get to the high school." He ended the call and angled toward Roark.

"Is there a problem?"

His boss always used simple English with him and knew how to phrase questions and instructions so he would understand.

"My Elisa—she run away."

Roark's forehead wrinkled. "Go home. Now. Find her."

"Yes. Police look too. People also come to look." He motioned in the direction of the high school. "They meet at school. I go there."

"I'll come too after these people are gone." He nodded toward the customers.

Thomma's vision misted. He barely knew this man, and yet Roark was willing to step in and help after putting in a long day on the boat.

His mother would call this a blessing—and indeed it was.

One of many he'd failed to appreciate over these past few weeks.

"Thank you."

The man squeezed his shoulder. "This is what we do in Hope Harbor for our friends."

Thomma didn't understand every word, but *friend* came through loud and clear.

And as he turned to go . . . as he tried to psych himself up for whatever the rest of this day held . . . he prayed that despite his many lapses and lack of gratitude for the blessings that had been bestowed on them in the midst of tragedy, God would give him an opportunity to make things right with Elisa.

Yes, she would always remind him of the sweet, gentle woman he'd loved.

Yes, he would always mourn the loss of his beloved wife.

But while Elisa was part of Raca, she was also her own person.

And from this day forward, he would keep that front and center in his mind and do everything he could to cherish the sweet daughter God had entrusted to him.

If he was lucky enough to get a second chance.

25

They were getting nowhere.

And in less than an hour, it would be dark.

Logan retraced the beam of his flashlight around the inside of the large drainage pipe that emptied into the field his team was searching and straightened up, fighting back a wave of panic.

After three hours, none of the teams Lexie had assigned to grids radiating outward from his house had found a trace of the girls.

Yet Molly and Elisa couldn't have traveled on foot much beyond the perimeter of the area already searched. Not while lugging a suitcase and backpack.

Meaning that if they didn't find them soon, they'd have to consider other scenarios.

Like a runaway that had turned into an abduction.

He fisted his hands and took a deep breath.

Lexie had already mentioned the possibility of issuing an Amber Alert if evidence began to suggest that outcome—and they were getting closer to that step with every passing minute.

His phone vibrated against his hip, and he pulled it off his belt. The chief.

Pulse surging, he pressed it to his ear. "Any news?"

"Nothing yet—but the handler and dog from Medford are here. How close are you to finishing your grid?"

He gave the partially wooded terrain his team had been searching a sweep. Thomma was at the far end, Jeannette a few hundred feet away, and Steven Roark was in the opposite corner, visible through the trees. They were all close to being done.

"Ten minutes."

"Perfect. Since Thomma is on your team, why don't the two of you meet me and the handler at your house as soon as you're finished? We'll give the dog the scent and see where he takes us."

"We'll be there."

He pressed the end button and completed his quadrant of the grid at warp speed, scrutinizing the ground for any evidence that could suggest the girls had come this way—a lost hair ribbon, a dropped piece of clothing, small footprints.

Nothing.

It was almost as if they'd vanished off the face of the earth.

Suppressing that gut-clenching thought, he jogged over to Jeannette.

She gave him a hopeful look. "Anything?"

"No. You?"

"No."

"The dog and handler are here. Lexie wants Thomma and me to meet them at my house as soon as we're done."

"I'm finished."

"I think we all are." He indicated the other two men, who were walking their direction, and angled sideways so only she could see his face. "Thank you for helping today."

"It's what any good Samaritan would do—and Hope Harbor is full of those, based on the number of people who showed up at the high school."

He wanted to ask her if Christian charity was the only reason she'd volunteered, but Thomma and Roark joined them before he had the chance.

"Any sign of the girls?" A senseless question. One of the men would have given a shout-out if they'd unearthed some evidence of the youngsters' passage through the area.

"No." Roark shook his head.

So did Thomma.

Elisa's father looked as bad as Logan felt—complexion pale, eyes haunted, cheeks hollow, features taut.

Logan explained the latest development, and Roark added a few Arabic words to clarify for Thomma.

He extended his hand to Thomma's boss. "Thank you for volunteering."

"Not a problem. I'll go back to town and sign on for another grid. Hang in."

"Thank you." Thomma too offered his hand to the man.

Roark took it and said a few more Arabic words

that brought a shimmer to Thomma's eyes.

"I'll sign on for another grid too." Jeannette pulled her keys out of her pocket.

"Would you like to come back to the house with us instead?" Logan retrieved his own keys.

She hesitated but in the end declined. "I'll be of more use on a search team."

Logan wasn't certain of that.

He'd rather have her close by, where he could feel her presence and take her hand if this day got any tougher.

But from a practical standpoint, it was better to have her out looking for the girls.

"Okay."

A brief flash of—disappointment?—zipped through her eyes, gone so fast it was possible he'd imagined it.

"You'll stay in touch?" She fell in beside him as they walked toward their cars on the side of the road.

"I'll call if there are any breakthroughs at our end."

They formed a small convoy on 101 for a couple of miles, until he and Thomma peeled off onto the secondary road that ended at the undeveloped property beyond the lavender farm.

A Hope Harbor patrol car was already parked in front of his house, along with an SUV, when they arrived. A trim older man was talking to Lexie in the front yard, a large dog on a leash sitting by his side.

Logan swung into the driveway, Thomma behind him, and parked in back.

As he got out of the car, Mariam appeared on the porch, twisting her hands.

The woman looked as if she'd aged ten years in the past few hours.

"News?" She asked the question in English, switching to Arabic as Thomma slid out of the car behind him.

"No." Her son responded in English but continued his response in Arabic.

Lexie appeared around the side of the house, the handler behind her.

"Any updates from the other teams?" Logan doubted it. She'd have called him if there'd been a development—unless it had happened within the past few minutes.

She dashed that hope with a quick shake of her head. "No. We're expanding the grid. Jim's coordinating that while we focus on this approach." She motioned toward the man with silver-flecked brown hair, who appeared to be in his late fifties. "Logan and Thomma, Mark Roberts and his canine friend, Sherlock."

The man shifted the harness he was holding to his other hand and gave him a firm shake. Did the same with Thomma.

"I'm going to let Mark tell you what he needs

and how this works." Lexie turned the floor over to the handler.

"Let me get Susan on the phone and put her on speaker. She can listen in and pass the information on to Thomma and Mariam." Logan pulled out his cell, connected with the translator, and set the phone on the trunk of Thomma's car as he motioned Mariam closer. "Whenever you're ready, Mark."

"Lexie filled me in on the particulars. I know we're searching for two girls, but we have to concentrate on one at a time or we'll confuse Sherlock. What do you think the odds are they've stayed together?"

"High." Logan didn't hesitate. Unless they'd been forcibly separated, the two friends would stick close.

"Let's track the girl who lives here. That would be your niece, correct?"

"Yes."

"Is there anything in the house that would contain mostly her scent? Bedding, for example?"

"That would also have Elisa's scent. The girls take a nap together every day. But they each have their own pillow. Would that work?"

"Yes. The case would be fine. Do you know which exit the girls would have used?"

Logan leaned closer to the cell. "Susan, would you translate that for Mariam?"

The woman complied, and Mariam responded.

"She said it would have to be the front door," Susan relayed. "She was working in the garden by the back door the entire time she was outside."

"We'll start there. Why don't you bring the pillowcase out and we'll meet you in front?" Mark said.

Logan furrowed his brow. "Won't my scent confuse Sherlock if I touch it?"

Mark smiled. "He's smarter than that. Once I let him sniff you, he'll know you're not the person he's tracking and home in on your niece's scent."

"Got it. Give me three minutes."

Logan took the back porch steps two at a time, retrieved the pillowcase, and rejoined the group in front. Mark had unwound the long leash, and the dog was nosing around the area.

"Hang on to that for a minute." Mark reined in the dog and put the harness on him. "Okay. Set it on the ground and let Sherlock sniff you."

He did so, then backed off.

Sherlock gave the case his full attention.

Within seconds, the dog touched his nose to the cotton rectangle, laid down beside it, and made eye contact with Mark.

"We're set." Mark hooked the leash to the harness, and gave Sherlock a treat. "As I understand it, the adjacent lavender farm has been thoroughly searched, and you have a team on the beach. So while your niece has been to those places, there's no reason for us to track in that area. Correct?"

"Yes." Lexie pulled out her phone. "Any other direction, however, is fair game."

"Got it. Sherlock—search now."

The dog didn't wait for a second invitation.

He was off like a shot, nose to the ground, barreling straight down the driveway, tugging at the long tracking line.

"Susan—tell Mariam to wait here. Thomma and I are going to follow the handler."

Once the woman complied, Logan ended the call and set off at a jog after Mark, Thomma on his heels.

Lexie was ahead of them, staying a dozen yards behind the man and dog.

Sherlock paused at the bottom of the driveway to sniff the entire area, then started around the hedge toward Jeannette's.

At a command from Mark, he sniffed some more . . . and took off down the road that led to 101, staying on the shoulder.

Yes!

He had the trail!

Logan's spirits took an uptick.

Since he'd never walked this direction with Molly, Sherlock had to be picking up the route the girls had taken after they'd left the house together.

And despite the fact they'd been gone close to

six hours, how far could they get with a suitcase and backpack in tow? Yes, teams had searched this area—but it was possible the girls had made it a short distance past the farthest grid that had been combed.

Wherever they were, though, Sherlock would find them.

Unless the dog somehow lost their trail.

Not likely, based on everything he'd ever read about bloodhounds—but a terrifying possibility nonetheless, regardless how remote.

In the distance, a rumble of thunder reverberated through the air, and a chilly breeze sent a shiver rippling through him.

Stormy weather appeared to be in store.

And as the small group followed the dog into the deepening dusk, Logan prayed that Molly and Elisa had taken refuge somewhere safe and warm and dry.

Molly wiped her nose on her sleeve and sniffled.

It was getting really cold . . . and her socks were wet from crossing the creek . . . and the sandwiches were soggy 'cause Elisa had dropped them in the water . . . and it was getting dark . . . and they were lost.

A tear rolled down her cheek.

If only she could go home.

But home was with Nana—and Nana was gone.

A rumble of thunder shook the ground.

"I s-scared, Molly." Elisa took her hand and moved closer in the shadowy space.

"Me too."

"We go home?"

Molly peered through a crack in the wooden slats and held tight to her blankie. "I don't know where home is."

"We ask?"

She couldn't do that.

Nana and Uncle Logan always said never talk to strangers—and everyone was a stranger.

But there wasn't anyone around here anyway. Nobody lived in this old shed they'd found in the woods.

Another tear trailed down her cheek.

"You said you wanted to run away too." Molly sniffed. Elisa didn't always know all the words she said, but her friend usually understood her.

"I want my Teta." She hugged her Raggedy Ann doll.

"What about your papa?"

Elisa bit her lower lip. "He be mad."

Uncle Logan would be too. Running away was naughty.

Maybe, if they did go back, he wouldn't want her anymore. Nobody liked naughty children.

What if he sent her to an orphan's home, like the one on that TV show she'd seen, where you had to eat something called gruel for breakfast and sweep floors all day, like Cinderella?

Molly hiccupped a sob.

Uncle Logan wouldn't do that—would he? He'd always been nice to her. Bought her ribbons, took her to the beach . . . gotten Toby for her. He'd gone to tea at 'Nette's with her too.

Maybe after he got done being mad, he'd let her stay, even though he hadn't wanted her in the beginning.

She shivered and wrapped her blankie around her fingers. It would be warmer in the pretty bedroom with the fairy princess bedspread at Uncle Logan's house. Sleeping there was nice. And it was fun playing on the swing set he'd just put up in the backyard.

Besides, if they left for always, she'd never see Toby or 'Nette or Mrs. Shabo again.

Or Uncle Logan either.

All at once, her stomach felt funny. Kind of like it had after they told her Nana had gone to heaven.

Except . . . Uncle Logan wasn't in heaven.

He *might* go, though—like Nana . . . and her daddy . . . and Button.

If that happened, she'd *have* to live in an orphan's home.

She wadded up her blankie and squeezed it tight.

But not everybody went to heaven right away. The boys and girls at that place Uncle Logan had taken her to during the day in the big city had mommies and daddies. They weren't orphans.

Maybe Uncle Logan would be her uncle for a

long time before he went to heaven. Maybe until she was a grown-up.

"Molly?" Elisa sounded like she was going to cry again.

"Yes?"

"I miss my Teta."

She kind of missed Uncle Logan too. He was even better at reading bedtime stories than Nana, especially when he used funny voices for some of the people.

And that night he'd laid down with her when he was sad and lonesome had made her feel special. Like she was important to him.

Molly frowned.

Would he be sad if she was gone?

Would he be more lonesome than before?

Maybe he was used to her now. Maybe he needed her to help him be happy.

Maybe . . . maybe he even loved her.

"Molly." A shiver ran through Elisa. "I cold."

"Me too."

A crack of thunder boomed through the night, and she cringed as rain began to beat against the roof.

"We go home." Elisa edged closer. It wasn't a question anymore.

"It's dark."

"We go that way." She pointed in the direction they'd come.

Molly bit her lip.

That might work.

If they got back to the big road over the hill, across the creek, and followed it, they should be able to find their way back. They'd stayed by that road after they turned off Uncle Logan's street.

But they'd have to be careful if they saw any strangers. Nana and Uncle Logan had told her even people who seemed nice could be bad.

" 'Kay. But let's wait for the rain to stop."

"I don't want to stay here all night."

"The rain might be done soon."

But walking home in the dark would be very scary.

And what if they got lost?

What if they never got home?

Molly tried not to cry.

Yet as another crack of thunder shook the walls of the shed behind her back, she couldn't stop the tears that trailed down her cheeks.

Running away had been a big mistake.

A slash of lightning illuminated the entrance to the high school gym and rain began to pummel the roof as Jeannette dashed inside to get her next search assignment, Roark on her heels.

They joined a small group gathered around Jim Gleason, who was on the phone.

"Got it. I'll pass that along." He slid the phone back into its holster. "Listen up, folks. That was the chief. The dog is following a trail, and she wants to pursue that approach for the remainder of the night. Since it's easy to miss an important clue in the dark and rain, she's suspending the volunteer search until further notice—probably first light. If you'd like to be on the call list should we have to resume, put a check mark next to your name on the sign-up sheet over there." He motioned toward a table against the wall.

Roark headed that direction, as did many of the others who'd returned to the command center after completing their grid, while Jim fielded questions from a Coos Bay news crew.

Jeannette scanned the crowd, spotting several familiar faces. Tracy and her husband, Michael, from the cranberry farm. Luis Dominguez. BJ, still dressed in her construction attire, and her husband, Eric. Lexie's husband, Adam.

So many people in the town had turned out to help. Marci and Ben and the two clergymen had also been on the volunteer list, but they must be out working their grids.

Charley walked in the door, lifted a hand in greeting, and crossed to her. "Any updates?"

She repeated what Jim had said. "I understand the logic behind the decision to wait until morning to continue, but it's not sitting well."

"I know what you mean. When people we care about are hurting or in need, we want to help in any way we can. And I can see that you care deeply about Molly—and Logan."

She squinted at him.

Apparently the feelings she'd only acknowledged to herself a handful of hours ago were obvious to others.

Or at least to Charley.

"I may ask Jim if there's anything else I can do until the search resumes." She glanced toward the officer.

"Or you could call Logan, see if he could use some moral support."

"Charley! Can I see you for a minute?" Jim called from across the room where the map with the search grids was displayed on a large board.

"A few prayers wouldn't hurt, either." Charley touched her arm and walked away.

Jeannette hesitated.

She could sign up to help with the search in the morning—or she could call Logan, as Charley had suggested, and offer him a hand to hold, an empathetic ear, a reassuring touch.

In other words, she could offer him her heart.

God, what should I do?

An unsettling rumble of thunder was her reply.

She knew what she *wanted* to do.

But it was risky.

Very risky.

She was already more involved with the duo next door than she'd ever planned to be, and if anything happened to Molly—

Her lungs stalled, and she clutched the back of

a folding chair as the truth ricocheted through her.

Whether she backed off now or chose to get closer, it would be Cincinnati all over again if this night didn't have a positive outcome.

Because a burrowing beagle, an endearing little girl in need of TLC, and a man of character and integrity who honored his promises despite the cost to himself had shattered her defenses.

Jeannette let out a shuddering breath as the safe, predictable world she'd created crumbled around her.

She shoved her trembling fingers into the pockets of her jacket—and as they brushed the key Charley had found during their walk on the beach, several of his comments replayed in her mind.

"No matter how hard we try to maintain the status quo, the world changes around us . . . and changes our world in the process."

"Sometimes, while we might only recognize it in hindsight, changes that shake up our world can be positive."

"Love is the great stabilizer."

Perhaps their resident sage was right.

Yes, she was more vulnerable now than she'd been six weeks ago, but her life was also richer, more vibrant, and filled with possibilities—*if* she had the courage to embrace them.

And as she exited into the rain and ran for

her car, one final thought from Charley looped through her mind, ramping up the urgency of the decision she faced.

Most doors didn't stay open forever.

26

It was raining hard now, but Sherlock wasn't stopping—and neither were they.

Logan turned up the collar of his jacket as he and Thomma followed Lexie, the dog, and his handler.

They had to be at least two miles from the house at this point, past the farthest grid anyone had searched, paralleling 101 away from town, twenty yards back from the shoulder.

How had the girls managed to . . .

"We have something."

As Mark called out and aimed his flashlight toward a large bush, Logan's phone began to vibrate.

He ignored it and broke into a jog, as did Lexie and Thomma.

It took him no more than a second to identify the abandoned Disney princess suitcase through the foliage.

"It's Molly's."

Lexie pulled out her phone. "I'll have one of our officers pick it up. Mark, does the scent end here?"

"No." Sherlock was already straining at the tracking line. "It continues along the same path."

Meaning they hadn't been snatched. They'd

simply ditched the suitcase after it became too cumbersome to lug around.

Logan exhaled.

Thank you, God.

"That's good news," Lexie confirmed. "I'll wait here until the officer arrives, then catch up with you."

Logan and Thomma fell in behind the man and dog again.

Another quarter of a mile down the road, the rain tapered off as the trail veered inland, toward a copse of trees.

The going got rougher, and a hundred feet in the dog alerted again on the edge of a small creek.

"Do either of you recognize this?" The handler called the question over his shoulder.

Logan dashed forward, Thomma at his side.

A limp, bedraggled lavender ribbon was caught in the tall grass.

"Yes. It's Molly's."

"Let's leave it until the chief arrives. Why don't you put a couple of those rocks next to it to mark the spot?" The handler motioned to several large stones beside the water.

Logan complied as the dog strained at the leash.

Mark waited for him to finish before letting Sherlock move forward.

The dog splashed through the creek and continued into the trees.

Less than a hundred yards later, he sat.

Mark lifted his flashlight higher.

And there, in the arc of light, stood two dirty, wet little girls holding hands and staring at them with wide, fearful eyes, one clutching a doll, the other clinging to a blanket, a backpack slipping off her shoulder.

Every muscle in Logan's body went limp.

Thank you again, God.

Mark clicked off the flashlight as Logan and Thomma surged forward.

"It's me, Molly. Uncle Logan." His voice was as shaky as his legs.

Thomma spoke too.

Logan dropped to one knee in front of his niece and wrapped her in his arms as tears streamed down his face. "Oh, sweetie. I don't know what I'd do if anything happened to you. I love you so much."

Her arms crept around his neck as the words spilled out of his mouth, and he hugged her tighter, this child who'd entered his life out of the blue . . . transformed his world . . . and touched his heart in unexpected ways.

When he at last eased back, she scrutinized him with her usual solemn expression as the moon peeked out from behind the clouds. Then she lifted her hand, and with one finger traced the trail of a tear down his cheek.

"I didn't mean to make you cry." Her voice was soft. Uncertain.

"But it's a happy cry, not a sad one, now that we found you and you're fine. I was so worried, sweetie. It's very scary when someone you love disappears and could be in trouble."

She dipped her head and fiddled with the edge of her ratty blanket. "I didn't know y-you loved me."

Her statement smacked him in the face.

All these months, he'd done everything he could to demonstrate his love . . . but had he ever said the words?

Not that he could recall.

And while showing was important, maybe actions didn't always speak louder than words.

Maybe there were times when words were needed too.

"I'm sorry I never told you that." He brushed a damp strand of hair off her forehead. "But it's always been in my heart."

"Excuse me, folks." Mark drew closer. "I've got Lexie on the line and she wants to know if she should dispatch the EMTs."

"Hang on a minute." Logan backed off and gave Molly a fast once-over. "Are you hurt anywhere, sweetie? Did you fall or get cut?"

"No."

"What about Elisa?" He sized up the other girl as Thomma knelt beside her.

"No. But we're cold—and h-hungry."

"We can fix both of those fast." He angled toward Mark. "No EMTs necessary."

The handler relayed that news and ended the call. "She said to wait by the road. The officer who's retrieving the suitcase will take her back to the house to get her car, then they'll come by and pick us up. ETA is less than ten minutes."

A shiver rippled through Molly, and Logan slipped his arms out of his jacket, wrapped her in it, and swung her up into his arms.

Thomma did the same, pulling out his phone once Elisa was settled against his chest.

"Are you calling Mariam?" Logan retrieved his own phone.

"Yes. She be happy."

So would Jeannette.

He checked the call he'd ignored a few minutes ago. No message—but it was from his neighbor.

One tap . . . one ring . . . and she was on the line.

"We found them."

"Oh, Logan . . . " She expelled a breath. "I've been praying."

"So have I."

"Are they okay?"

"Cold, wet, tired, scared, hungry—but otherwise no worse for wear. Where are you?"

"Home. They called off the volunteer search until morning. Where are *you?*"

"Less than three miles away. We should be back in about ten minutes."

"Be prepared. There's a news crew from Coos Bay in front of your house."

"Thanks for the warning. We'll pull around the back to avoid them. I assume Lexie will make a statement. Do you want to come over?"

"I'd rather not run that gauntlet."

"Later, maybe?"

She hesitated. "It's almost ten—and you'll want to spend some time with Molly before you put her to bed."

"Tomorrow?"

"That could work. Give her a hug for me in the meantime."

"Will do."

After they said their good-byes, Logan weighed the cell in his hand.

Jeannette hadn't committed to visiting them—surprise, surprise.

Not.

First Button dies, then a child she's come to care for goes missing.

She was either retreating to the safe world she'd created at the lavender farm—or struggling to vanquish the fear that was holding her back from taking another chance on love.

Not much he could do tonight to press his case. Molly had to be his first priority.

But come tomorrow, Jeannette was jumping to the top of his list.

And as their small group trooped back through the woods toward the road to await their ride home, he was going to follow the same rule with her that he'd followed with Molly tonight.

He wasn't just going to show her how he felt.

He was going to tell her.

Mariam lifted the pot of beans off the stove, pulled open the oven door, and divided the chicken-and-potato casserole into two portions—one for her family, one for Logan and Molly. Usually Logan refused her offers to leave dinner for them after she prepared a meal at his house for her family, but tonight she would insist.

Lunch had been hours ago, and while Logan appeared to be a fine doctor, based on the contents of his refrigerator, he wasn't much of a chef.

Besides, cooking had kept her hands and mind occupied during the stressful hours until the children had been found, and he might as well benefit from the results.

The beams of headlights illuminated the backyard, and her pulse stuttered.

They were here!

She finished dividing the food and removed her apron as Toby pranced about the room, pinging with excitement.

Hopefully the newspeople waiting in front would stay there and let their two families have some peace.

She hurried to the back door and pulled it open as the two police cruisers came to a stop.

Thomma hadn't said much on the phone a few

minutes ago, nor had she pressed him for details. All that mattered at this moment was the well-being of the two girls.

But if today's events hadn't been the wake-up call her son needed to realize how precious Elisa was to him, perhaps there was no hope.

Gripping the edge of the door, she closed her eyes.

Please, God, let this be a turning point for him—and let Elisa respond to his overtures. Please let it not be too late for them to salvage their relationship. You know far better than I how much they need each other.

Logan and Thomma got out of the first cruiser, and the police chief slid from behind the wheel. She spoke to Logan, then strode back down the driveway while the dog and handler exited the second car.

The two men, the girls in their arms, walked over and shook his hand before heading for the house.

As Logan stepped back to let Thomma enter first, Mariam held out her arms for Elisa. "Oh, *tafalay alhulu.*" And that was more than a generic endearment. Elisa *was* her sweet child, always obedient and loveable. Running away had been a cry for help—and attention.

She hugged her tight, fingered her shirt, and inspected both girls.

"Clothes wet. Need change."

402

"Yes." Logan walked toward the bedroom. "Come."

She followed.

In Molly's bedroom, he pulled out tops and pants for both girls. "Bath first."

He led them to the bathroom. "You help?" He arched an eyebrow at her.

"Yes. I be quick."

Moving at top speed, Mariam filled the tub and got both girls cleaned up fast. Though she tried to talk with them, neither had much to say.

Perhaps Elisa would open up to her later, at home—or better yet, talk to her father.

Once both girls were warm and dry and dressed, she led them back to the kitchen, where Logan and Thomma were drinking coffee.

Thomma stood as soon as they entered. "We go home now."

"Yes." She retrieved their food, and motioned toward the covered dishes in the oven as she looked at Logan. "For you."

For once, he didn't refuse.

"Thank you."

"I come tomorrow?"

Logan hesitated.

"Better keep . . ." Mariam searched her vocabulary but came up with no word for routine. "Keep same." After today's excitement, it would be best if the girls got back to normal as soon as possible.

Based on Logan's nod, he seemed to get her gist. "Yes."

She picked up their dinner and motioned for Thomma to take Elisa's hand.

He did better than that.

After crossing the room in two long strides, he bent and swung her up into his arms.

Mariam's spirits rose.

Perhaps her prayers were about to be answered.

Logan followed them to the door, and as Mariam turned to say good-bye, Molly sidled close to her uncle and tucked her hand in his. As he bent to pick her up, she lifted her arms and smiled. A real, no-holds-barred smile that banished the hurt and grief that had always darkened her eyes.

It appeared those two had mended their fences.

Now if only Thomma could win back the little girl in *his* arms.

Logan closed the door behind the Syrian family and shifted Molly in his arms. "What do you say we eat some of the dinner Mrs. Shabo left for us?"

"Can you hold me first?" She tightened her grip around his neck—like she never wanted to let go.

Fine with him.

"Sure." He carried her into the living room and sat in the overstuffed chair he'd brought from his apartment in San Francisco. It was large enough to accommodate both of them—though Molly had never initiated a lap-sitting session.

Toby trotted in and plopped down at his feet.

For several minutes they sat in silence, Molly cuddled up against his chest as he stroked her back and waged a mental debate about how to proceed.

Should he introduce the subject of her afternoon adventure—or hope she'd tell him about it on her own?

But what if she never brought it up? Should he let it go?

Maybe.

After all, it wasn't as if there was any secret about why she'd left. She and Elisa were both unhappy and grieving.

Thomma's daughter had Mariam, of course. But while the woman loved her deeply, it wasn't the same as a father's love—and Thomma, for whatever reason, had closed himself off emotionally. Rejection by your own father would be devastating . . . and nothing could make up for that—even the love of a doting grandmother.

As for Molly—she'd lost everyone she loved, and the conversation she'd overheard in San Francisco had convinced her she was an unwanted intruder in her uncle's life.

It was no wonder the two girls had run away.

In hindsight, the bigger surprise was why they'd waited so long.

His niece burrowed closer, emitting a contented sigh, and he swallowed past the lump in his throat.

Running away hadn't been the latest transgression in a litany of stunts from two ill-behaved children.

It had been an act of desperation—and despair.

But based on Molly's behavior since the rescue—and since he'd verbalized his love for her—the two of them might finally be on the road to the kind of relationship he'd envisioned for them.

Perhaps they didn't have to talk about her running away or—

"We were going to Missouri."

Molly's soft comment pulled him back to the moment.

Apparently they *did* need to talk about this.

"That's far away."

"It didn't take very long to get here."

"But we were on an airplane." Not that the different speeds between modes of transportation would mean much to a child. Better to ferret out her reason for that destination. His mom was gone, and they had no other relatives in the town. "Why did you want to go back there?"

"It was my happy place."

A simple answer that summed up everything.

Everyone wanted to find their happy place— and his mom would have created that for Molly.

"It was my happy place once too." He finger-combed a few tangled strands of her hair. "Thinking about it makes me smile."

"Me too. That's why I wanted to go back. I told Elisa about it, and she wanted to go too."

Careful how you phrase your response, West.

"Sometimes I wish I could go back there too. But it wouldn't be the same as I remember. What usually makes a place happy is the people who are there."

Her shoulders drooped. "I know. And Nana isn't in Missouri anymore. She's in heaven."

"And in your heart. No matter where you go, she'll always be there."

"But I can't sit on her lap anymore."

"No." That was reality, and trying to sugarcoat it wasn't going to help. "But sometimes, after people we love go to heaven, God gives us new people to love—and new laps to sit on."

Several beats of silence ticked by.

"I like sitting on your lap."

At the shy admission, pressure built behind his eyes. "I like holding you on my lap."

She played with a button on his shirt. "Maybe . . . maybe you and me can stay together so we don't get lonesome anymore."

"I'd like that."

"If you get sad at night again, it's okay if you come sleep with me."

"Thank you. I'll remember that."

She twisted in his arms to search his face, tiny creases denting her smooth brow. "Do you really love me?"

"With all my heart."

"You didn't at first."

"Yes, I did—but I never had a little girl live with me before, and I was scared I wouldn't know what to do or how to make you happy. I had to figure it out."

"That's what 'Nette said."

God bless his neighbor!

"She was right."

"I like her."

"Me too."

"I think she's lonesome, like us." Molly continued to watch him.

"She might be."

"Do you think she could live with us? At night, we could all sleep together."

Logan snuffed out the mental image of Jeannette in his bed and cleared his throat. "I don't know if that would work. She has her own house. And usually people who live together are married."

Her eyes lit up. "If you married 'Nette, would she be my mommy?"

"Yes." *Change the subject. Now.* "Aren't you getting hungry? I hear some growls. Unless you're hiding a bear inside there." He tickled her tummy.

She giggled . . . and his lungs locked.

That was the sound he'd been waiting to hear for months.

"Yes. Mrs. Shabo cooks good. Better than you."

"That wouldn't be hard." He stood, balancing her on his hip as he smothered a yawn. The long, traumatic day was catching up with him.

"Are you sleepy?" She held on tight as he bent to scratch behind Toby's ear.

"Getting there. After we eat, I think we both should go to bed."

"Do you want to stay with me tonight, so you won't be lonesome?"

The two of them in her twin bed? Until morning?

It wouldn't be the most comfortable night of his life.

But it might be one of the best.

"I think that would be perfect."

She smiled at him, no trace of worry or sadness in her eyes. "I love you, Uncle Logan."

"I love you back." Somehow he managed to choke out the words.

And as he carried her into the kitchen, the beagle at his heels, Logan's heart overflowed.

After months of effort, he and Molly were finally on the road to their happy place.

One down—one to go.

"I'll do the dishes while you put Elisa to bed." Mariam rose as the family finished their late dinner and looked at him across the table.

Thomma didn't need his mother's prompt. He'd planned to take on that duty tonight, had been thinking about what he'd say to Elisa once the two of them were alone.

The words still hadn't coalesced in his mind, though.

He'd been hoping for some guidance based on Elisa's conversation during dinner, but despite his diligent efforts, his daughter hadn't cooperated. Even his mother hadn't managed to elicit more than a sentence or two.

Elisa had eaten her dinner mostly in silence, casting him frequent surreptitious glances.

Like she sensed something was different but didn't quite know what.

He intended to clear up her confusion now.

Setting his napkin on the table, he rose. "Are you finished, my little one?"

Elisa stared at him, and in his peripheral vision he saw his mother freeze.

No wonder.

He hadn't used that term of endearment for his daughter since the day his world had exploded in Syria.

Elisa sent his mother an uncertain look.

"Go with your father. I'll give you a good night hug here." She did so, offered him a nod of approval, and busied herself clearing the table.

Thomma held out his hand to Elisa.

After regarding him for a moment, she slid off

her chair and slipped her fingers into his. "I have to brush my teeth."

"You can do that while I get your pajamas out."

She followed along beside him to the bathroom and disappeared inside.

It took him a few tries to find the drawer where his mother kept her pajamas—yet more evidence of his lack of interest in his daughter.

But perhaps he could lay the groundwork for a new start tonight.

He was waiting when she returned, her night-clothes in hand. "Want me to help you put these on?"

She shook her head. "I can do it myself."

And she did, with quick efficiency, turning her back on him as she changed.

Like he was a stranger.

A twinge echoed in his heart, but her treatment of him was no more than he deserved. After all the months he'd pushed her aside, he *was* in many respects a stranger to her.

She tugged the top into position, folded up the clothes Logan had loaned them, placed them in a neat pile on the chair in the room, and climbed into bed.

Thomma tucked her in, dimmed the light, and sat on the edge of the mattress, heart hammering.

God, please help me as I try to mend the damage I've done.

Summoning up his courage, he took Elisa's

411

hand. "I'm glad you and Molly decided to come back today."

The conclusion that the girls had changed their mind about running away was a supposition—but they *had* been retracing their steps when Sherlock found them.

"Why?"

So his assumption had been accurate.

That was a positive sign—unless Molly was the one who'd decided to return and had convinced his reluctant daughter to go with her.

"Because it wouldn't be the same here without you."

She hugged her Raggedy Ann doll tighter, watching him. "You wouldn't miss me."

His stomach knotted.

What else could she conclude after his behavior these past few months?

But hearing it verbalized gave her despair a stark harshness that ate at his gut.

"Yes, I would." He stroked his fingers down her cheek and met her gaze. "I know I haven't been a good papa for a long time, and I'm sorry for that. I've been very sad about all the people we love who went to heaven, and about leaving our home in Syria. Sometimes, when you're that sad, it's hard to think right. You forget about what you have now because you're thinking so hard about everything that's gone. That's what happened to me."

A few seconds passed.

"I miss Mama a lot too." Her voice was a mere whisper.

Curious that she knew he'd been fixated on Raca in particular, given all the family they'd lost.

"I know you do, little one."

"Sometimes I look at the picture Teta gave me and pretend she's here."

His mother had given Elisa a photo of Raca? Which one?

"Will you show it to me?"

She hesitated. "You won't keep it, will you?"

He frowned. "No. Why would I do that?"

"Teta said it might make you sad and you might take it away."

Would he have deprived his daughter of a photo that gave her comfort?

He'd like to think the answer was no . . . but it was hard to say, considering his mental state since the tragedy.

"I promise I won't take it away. Maybe we can look at it—and remember her—together."

She studied him, kneading the edge of the blanket between her fingers . . . then rolled over, opened the drawer in the bedside table, and pulled out the photo. She tilted it toward him, keeping a tight grip on the image. As if she didn't trust him.

Another punch in the stomach.

Taking a fortifying breath, Thomma leaned

413

close to examine the dog-eared photo. It wasn't one he'd ever seen, but the setting was familiar. The shot had been snapped at the wedding of some friends of theirs, less than a year before the bombing. Raca was holding Elisa on her lap, her eyes bright with laughter as if someone had just made a humorous remark, her whole being radiating life and joy and optimism.

It captured her perfectly.

He blinked to clear his vision.

Someone must have given this to Mariam—and if that was how she'd acquired it, there wasn't much chance she had anything but the print she'd passed on to his daughter.

But it could be scanned. *Should* be scanned before the edges got any more ragged from handling.

"I would love to have a copy of this picture, Elisa. It's exactly how I remember your mama."

"You could ask Teta if she has another one."

"I will—but if she doesn't, I could make a copy of yours."

She tucked it close to her chest. "I like to keep this here."

"You could come with me while I get the copy made. You don't have to give it to me."

"I guess so." She traced a finger over the image in the photo. "Mama was pretty."

"Yes, she was." He managed to keep his voice from cracking.

"Can she see us from heaven?"

"I don't know—but I'm sure she can feel how much we love her."

"She loved me this much." Elisa spread her arms wide . . . then let them droop. "Like you used to."

Past tense.

As if he too was dead.

And in truth he had been—in every way that counted.

"I still love you, Elisa." The sentiment sounded empty even to him. Words without action meant nothing.

But going forward, there would be plenty of action to back them up.

"Are you mad at me for running away?"

"I'm more mad at myself."

Her brow knitted. "Why?"

"Because if I'd been a better papa, you wouldn't have wanted to leave." He brushed her hair back with trembling fingers. "I'm sorry I haven't told you every single day that I love you, and given you hugs, and read you bedtime stories, and kissed you good night. From now on, I'm going to do all those things—if that's okay with you."

She emitted a tiny, shuddering puff of air. "It's okay."

Her expression didn't change. No smile chased away the somber demeanor he'd come to expect from her. But God willing, that would come in time—after she was certain her papa was really back.

He leaned toward her and pressed a gentle kiss to her forehead. "Good night, my little one."

Rising, he smoothed out the blankets and reached over to flip off the lamp.

"Papa?"

"Yes?" He paused, his fingers on the switch.

She slowly held out her precious photo. "You can make a copy."

As the significance of her simple gesture registered, the room blurred—and hope filled his heart.

Despite all he'd done to hurt this child, she'd accepted his apology, trusted him to honor his promise, and was willing to give him a second chance.

And as he took the photo, thanked her, and bent to give her another kiss, he sent a silent prayer of gratitude toward the heavens.

While his life hadn't played out as he'd hoped, and there would be many challenges ahead, he had much to be thankful for.

And here in Hope Harbor, with the love of his daughter and mother to sustain him, he would remember each and every day to count his blessings and to focus on what could be rather than on what might have been.

27

Logan hadn't contacted her all day.

And why should he, after her vague response when he'd called last night to tell her the girls had been found and invite her over?

The man wasn't going to come begging for her attention. If she wanted to explore where their memorable kiss might lead, the next move was up to her.

Jeannette settled the last lavender wreath into its box, added it to the other two that hadn't sold at the Friday farmer's market, and gave the empty booth one last scan.

She was out of here.

And much faster than most of the other vendors. Rarely did she have much unsold merchandise to haul home, and the photos and lavender netting she used to decorate her booth were easy to take down. Fifteen minutes flat, she was ready to roll.

"You've got this routine down pat."

She swiveled toward Marci, who waved as she jogged over.

"Comes from practice." She set the wreaths into the trunk and closed the lid. "It helps that vendors are allowed to pull their vehicles up to the booth after the market closes. That expedites the proce What are you doing down here on a Friday nig

417

"I'm writing a story for the next issue on the myrtlewood booth, and I need a few photos to go with it—which I almost didn't get. I forgot the market was closing an hour early tonight so the town could set up for that 5K run tomorrow morning. Not that it would have been a big deal if I had to wait a week. I'll probably bump the story to leave space for the big news in our little hamlet, anyway."

"You mean the runaways?" What else could it be?

"Yes. I'm going to focus on the inspiring turnout of local citizens to assist with the search and tie it back to the outpouring of support the town gave to the idea of sponsoring a refugee family. We're blessed to live in such a special town."

"I won't argue with that."

"So how are Logan and Molly doing?"

Marci was the third person today to ask her that question.

Why did everyone in town think she had inside information about her neighbors?

"I haven't talked to Logan since last night."

"Oh." Marci regarded her. "Well, I'm assuming everything's fine. I saw his car at the urgent care center as I drove here. If there were any issues, I doubt he'd have gone in today."

He'd been at work all day?

That could explain why she hadn't heard from

him—although he'd gotten off two hours ago, and he'd had plenty of time to—

"—you think of him?"

Drat.

She'd been zoning out on conversations since the market opened—as more than one customer had noticed.

"Sorry. I, uh, was distracted for a minute."

"I said, now that you've gotten to know our new doctor, what do you think of him . . . off the record?"

She busied herself sweeping a few cookie sample crumbs off the counter of the booth. "He seems very nice."

"More than, from everything I've heard. Did you know he made a house call for Rose Marshall from the garden club? She has the flu and felt too sick to drive, so he swung by after work earlier this week."

No, she didn't know that.

But she wasn't surprised.

Logan West was the real deal.

"I thought house calls had gone out with the dodo bird." Jeannette kept her tone conversational as she brushed off her hands.

"My point exactly. If you ask me, he's a keeper—just in case you happen to have any ideas along those lines." Marci grinned and gave her an elbow nudge. "By the way, I haven't forgotten about the feature on the farm and tearoom. You're up next. Gotta run—Ben and I have a dinner date." With another wave, she bounded off.

Lips flexing as the energetic editor disappeared into the crowd, Jeannette circled her car, slid behind the wheel, and twisted the key in the ignition.

As she slowly drove down Dockside Drive, taking care to edge around the vendors loading their vehicles, she couldn't dispute what Marci had said about Logan.

He *was* a keeper—if you were in the market for one.

But last night had been scary. If the situation had gone south, she would have been right back where she'd been in Cincinnati—all because she'd let herself get too close to the doctor next door and his charming niece.

Thank heaven she'd dodged a bullet on that one. Everyone was fine.

This time.

Tomorrow could be a different story though.

However . . . if she backed off, eventually her emotional attachment to them would fade.

It was an easy solution—*if* that was the outcome she wanted.

The very question she intended to ponder long and hard during the weekend ahead.

"She's home!"

At Molly's excited announcement, Logan

fumbled the lightbulb he'd been screwing into the kitchen fixture.

Somehow he managed to grab it before the glass shattered on the floor.

Good grief.

He hadn't even been *this* nervous during his first surgery assist.

And why was Jeannette home an hour early? The market never closed until eight.

Whatever the reason, he'd better shift into high gear and get over there or she'd be deep into some baking project for tomorrow's tea.

He finished securing the bulb and descended the stepladder, trying to rein in his pulse as doubts began to nip at his confidence.

What if the approach he'd decided on didn't work? After all, it wasn't the usual tactic guys used to woo a woman. That would involve flowers and invitations for high-end dinners and dates for dancing or movies or concerts.

Those were all fine—and they'd come later . . . if the lady was willing.

But he wanted this straightforward, with no frills. He'd be honest about the life she'd have if they did date and if the relationship got serious.

And he was also going to tell her exactly how he felt—not a usual pre-dating strategy, but it seemed appropriate in this case.

Especially after Molly had reminded him last night that despite all his efforts to win her affection, he'd somehow forgotten to say I love you.

"Are we going over now?" Molly skipped into the kitchen, Toby on her heels.

"Let's give her ten minutes to unpack the car."

"I can carry the brownies."

"That works." He handed her the small white bag of goodies he'd picked up at Sweet Dreams. "And bring a doggie treat for Toby."

The pup gave a happy yip at the mention of his name and followed Molly over as she trotted across the room to retrieve one.

Eight minutes later, after buttoning Molly into her jacket, donning his own, and tucking their beach blanket under his arm, he clipped on Toby's leash.

"Let's do this."

Taking Molly's hand, he exited onto the front porch, locked the door, and led his entourage around the hedge, toward the back of Jeannette's house.

"The light's on! She must be in the kitchen." Molly pulled him along.

"Why are you so anxious to see her?"

"I like her a whole lot."

That made two of them.

And he was hoping it would escalate into much more than that.

Holding tight to Molly's hand, he stopped at her back door, took a deep breath . . . and tried to shore up his flagging courage.

What if this went south?

What if she refused his invitation and shut the door in their faces?

What if he couldn't—

"Ouch." Molly wriggled her fingers loose. "You're squishing my hand."

"Sorry."

She squinted at him. "Are you scared, Uncle Logan?"

His niece was way too intuitive.

"Why would you ask that?"

"I squeeze my blankie real hard when I'm scared."

She was also too smart.

"I'm fine." Without giving her a chance to ask any more questions—and before his nerves kicked into overdrive—he rapped on the door.

Half a minute later, Jeannette pulled it open, her eyebrows peaking as she took in the group assembled on her doorstep. "This is a surprise. But I'm glad you're here. Now I can give you a hug in person." She bent and drew his niece into her arms. "I'm so happy you came back."

"Me too." Molly returned the hug, then wiggled free and held up the bag. "We're going to the beach, and we have brownies. Want to come?"

Jeannette stood and tipped her head. "Isn't it kind of late for a walk on the beach?"

"I came prepared." He retrieved the small flashlight he'd tucked into his pocket to guide them home if they lingered for the whole sunset show. "And I'll second Molly's invitation. We'd love to have you join us."

"I don't know . . . I just got back from the farmer's market and—"

"Please." Logan gave her his most persuasive smile. "We won't be there long."

She hesitated.

"Please, 'Nette."

After a moment, her taut features softened in capitulation. "I guess I can go for a few minutes. Let me get my jacket." She crossed the room, retrieved it from the coatrack, and rejoined them.

"Can I hold Toby's leash, Uncle Logan?"

"Sure. But keep a tight grip. We don't want to lose him." He passed the strap over to her, and girl and dog moved into the lead as they walked through the lavender gardens and set out on the path over the dunes.

Jeannette waited until the distance between them grew to a dozen yards, then spoke in a soft voice. "Everything okay?"

"Better than okay. We've had some false starts, but I think this is the real thing. She's like a different little girl since we found them."

"Any idea why?"

"Better than an idea. I'll give you the whole scoop once we get to the beach. In the meantime . . . tell me about your day. How was the farmer's market?"

"Sales were excellent, and there were a couple of interesting customers."

He listened as she relayed a humorous story about a man whose wife had always wanted to spend a night on a lavender farm and who'd tried to rent a room for their anniversary in three weeks.

"I explained to him that I wasn't a B&B and that most of the lavender wasn't in bloom yet, but after he kept pushing I suggested he bring his wife to tea instead and book a night at the Seabird Inn in town—a very romantic spot, from what I hear. He said he was going to run that idea by his wife." She brushed some wind-tossed strands of hair back from her face. "You have to admire a guy who's willing to make an effort to please the woman in his life."

Duly noted—and encouraging.

"Your idea sounds like a perfect compromise." They crested the last dune, and he stopped. A gold-and-rose wash colored the sky above the horizon, and the setting sun cast a gilded swath of light across the water.

"It's beautiful here." The corners of Jeannette's mouth rose as she surveyed the view.

"Yes. It is."

She looked at him . . . and he kept his attention riveted on her to leave no doubt about his meaning.

A slight flush spread across her cheeks, and she

lowered her lashes. Shoved her hands into her pockets.

Before she got spooked and hightailed it back to the safety of her house, he took her arm and urged her forward. "Let's go down to the beach."

He found a spot not far from the water and spread out the blanket.

"Can we eat the brownies now, Uncle Logan?" Molly held up the white bag.

"Let's wait for a while. You can play with Toby first." He unclipped the dog's leash, and the beagle took off along the sand, staying back from the surf—one of the pluses of the breed. They might like to dig, but they weren't fans of water—meaning he didn't have to worry about sudsing up a wet dog later.

Nor did he have to worry much about Molly getting too near the water. She'd stick close to Toby.

He motioned toward the blanket, and Jeannette sat. He joined her, waiting until his niece was out of hearing distance to return to the subject his neighbor had introduced on the walk down.

"With Molly occupied, this is a perfect opportunity to give you the scoop on why she and I finally clicked."

Based on the sudden tension in her features, some nuance in his inflection must have put her on alert that the conversation was about to turn personal. "You don't have to. I don't want to pry."

"It isn't prying to ask questions about people who are important to you. And I'd like to think Molly and I fall into that category—because you're important to us."

She swallowed and shifted her position to sit cross-legged. "You know I have an issue with getting close to people."

"Yes—and I understand why. If you love again, you could lose again. I think that's one of the reasons Molly didn't warm up to me. She lost her father . . . and her Nana . . . and Button. What if she lost me too?"

"Yet you won her over."

"Thanks to what I told her after we found them."

"Do I want to know what that was?"

"I'm not sure—but I'm going to tell you anyway." He locked onto her gaze. "In all the months she lived with me, I did my best to show her how much I cared for her. But I neglected to put that into words. I never said I love you—until last night. And that made all the difference."

She sucked in a breath, alarm flaring in her eyes. "I'm not—"

"Wait." He held up a hand. "Don't panic. I'm not going to declare my undying love for you on this beach tonight. It's too soon for that. But I *am* going to tell you that I care for you, that I think we have great potential, and that I'd like to see where a relationship could lead. I do come with a ready-made family, however." He motioned toward Molly and Toby. "That's why I brought them along tonight. If you sign on with me, you sign on with them. That means we won't have the typical kind of courtship two single people with no attachments would expect to—"

"Uncle Logan!"

He gave her a rueful grin. "See what I mean?" He cupped his hands around his mouth and directed his attention toward Molly. "What's wrong?"

"Toby won't come." As she called out her response, she pointed to the pup, who'd run much farther away than usual.

Logan rose. "I'll be back in a minute. Will you wait?"

After a brief pause, she nodded. "Yes."

He wasn't certain about that.

Yet she was still there when he checked over his shoulder as he jogged down the beach.

But now that he'd laid his cards on the table, would she fold—or play the hand she'd been dealt?

Logan was forcing her hand.

By backing up that toe-tingling kiss with a candid declaration of his interest, he'd put the ball in her court.

As Jeannette watched the man and girl in the distance, Molly detached herself and ran back toward the blanket.

"We need Toby's leash." She bent to retrieve it,

then smiled. "I like it when you come to the beach with us."

"I do too."

"Maybe you could do it more so you don't get lonesome."

Her throat tightened. "I'll think about that."

"I told Uncle Logan you should come live with us too—but he said people who live together are usually married."

Not as much in today's society . . . but it was never too early to begin instilling solid values in a child.

"That's true."

"If you want to marry Uncle Logan, it's okay with me."

"Um . . ." She glanced at her neighbor, who was chasing Toby and would probably have apoplexy if he was privy to this conversation. "A man and lady are supposed go out on dates and get to know each other first—and I'm very busy with my farm."

Molly's face grew serious. "But flowers aren't the same as a family."

No, they weren't.

But if they died, they didn't take part of you with them.

A tear brimmed on her lower lid, and she reached up to swipe it away.

"Don't cry, 'Nette." Molly touched her cheek. "I was kind of scared to love Uncle Logan too,

429

but I like loving him better than being afraid. And me and you and him could make a new happy place together."

"Molly! Where's the leash?"

She jumped to her feet. "I gotta go. But love is better than lonesome."

As Molly dashed off, Jeannette fished a tissue out of her pocket, her fingers once more brushing the key Charley had found on this very beach.

A key that had been through turbulent waters but received a second chance at life—and an opportunity to find a new purpose.

Kind of like what was happening to her.

Strange.

She thought she'd already found her new purpose, with the lavender farm and tearoom.

But perhaps there was supposed to be more.

Perhaps God had brought her here not simply to launch a new career but to bring an honorable man and his precious niece into her orbit.

Now it was up to her to decide whether to break free of their pull or align her trajectory with theirs.

In the distance, Logan clipped the leash on Toby, took Molly's hand, and began walking back.

She watched them approach, the tall, handsome man and the little girl who'd lost so much but who'd chosen love over loneliness—and who'd given her an example to emulate.

And with a sudden, blinding flash of clarity, she knew what she should do.

Yes, loss was hard—especially on the scale she'd endured.

But loneliness was too.

Yes, opening her heart again was a risk—but what was the worst that could happen?

She'd be alone again—like she was now.

In the meantime, though, she could store up a treasure trove of memories that would sustain her every day of her life.

Starting today.

As the threesome drew close, Logan handed off the leash to Molly and continued toward her.

"Sorry about the interruption." He dropped down beside her again.

"No worries. It gave me a chance to think about what you said."

He drew up his knees and linked his fingers around them. "I debated whether I should be that upfront, but since my kiss apparently didn't bowl you over, I figured I better back it up with words." He offered her a sheepish shrug. "It worked with Molly, and I was running out of ideas with you. I hope I didn't scare you off."

"Nope. And for the record—your kiss did bowl me over." She scooted closer, and his eyebrows rose. "Your niece also just passed on some astute wisdom. She said flowers aren't the same as family, that love is better than lonesome . . . and

431

that maybe the three of us should make a happy place together."

"She's a smart kid."

"Yes, she is."

"Are you telling me you agree with her?" His tone was cautious.

"Yes." She watched an ember spark to life in the depths of his cobalt irises. "But while I agree with you that words are important, I do think they have to be backed up by action. Like this." Jeannette leaned close and pressed her lips to his.

He was all in the instant he got over his shock, pulling her tight against his solid chest, one hand cupping her head.

Somewhere in the background, above the sound of the breaking surf and the caw of the gulls, she heard Toby's happy yip of approval and Molly's giggle.

But her focus was on the man expressing his pleasure at her decision in a most delightful fashion.

And Jeannette held nothing back as she responded to his kiss.

It was possible, of course, that somewhere along the way their paths would diverge. That her instincts could be wrong, and Logan and she weren't destined to create the happy place together that Molly had mentioned.

Yet in the waning light of day, as the setting sun painted a glorious canvas on the western horizon, she was as certain as she could be that someday down the road, she'd look back at this moment with sweet remembrance as the start of something big.

Epilogue

"Sorry to leave?"

As her new husband crossed to the sliding door of their Kauai beach cottage, wrapped his arms around her from behind, and bent to nuzzle her neck, Jeannette sighed. "Yes—and if you keep that up, we'll miss our plane." She shimmied against him.

"You keep *that* up, I guarantee we'll miss it." His response came out in a low growl, suggesting he was only half kidding.

"In that case, I better stop—or we'll have to forego phase two of our honeymoon."

He groaned. "I'm not sure how I let you talk me into that plan."

"Like you said that night on the beach in May, you're a package deal—and I don't want Molly to feel excluded right at the beginning of our new life together."

"I think I'm regretting that comment."

"That's your hormones talking."

He went back to nuzzling her neck. "Guilty as charged."

"Hey—Disneyland will be fun. Think of it as an extended honeymoon."

"With a five-year-old in tow?" He lifted his head and gave her a get-real look.

"Oh, I have a few ideas that could stimulate some romance. And since you splurged and booked us a two-bedroom suite, we'll have plenty of alone time after Molly goes to sleep—which should be early after a full day at the park."

He gave her a slow smile. "I like how you think, Mrs. West. Still . . . Disneyland won't compare to this." He swept a hand over the palm trees and blue horizon that dominated their view.

"I know. It's hard to believe this is the same ocean we see at home every day, isn't it?"

"Yes." He shifted next to her, draping an arm around her shoulders. "Just shows how a different perspective can alter your view of the world."

That was true—about many things.

Including love.

And in every case so far since she'd taken a leap of faith and dismantled the barricades around her heart, the view had been better.

"The current landscape is hard to beat." She leaned against his solid strength.

"True. Sunny skies, tropical foliage, and warm sand between your toes aren't too shabby on a December day." He stole another kiss.

"I was speaking more broadly. Like the land-scape of my life."

"The landscape of my life has improved too. And this past week has been—" His voice rasped, and he traced the line of her jaw with a finger that didn't feel quite steady, all traces of levity gone. "Being here alone with you has given me a glimpse of paradise."

Jeannette's vision misted, and she turned into his arms, resting her hands on his chest as she regarded him, this man who'd brightened her world with his kindness and understanding and integrity and trustworthiness. Who wasn't afraid to show—*and* tell—her how he felt. "Thank you for saying that."

"I meant every word."

"I know you did—and I feel the same."

He fingered a lock of her hair as two faint creases appeared on his brow. "You've made a huge number of changes because of me, though. You know I would have been happy to sell my place and move into your house. You didn't have to upend that part of your life too."

"I wanted to. I like the idea of putting some physical distance between my business and personal life—and the Shabos were thrilled to rent the house. Plus, now that we've cut a walkway through the hedge, Molly and Elisa can go back and forth whenever they want. What's better than having your best friend live next door?"

"Having her live in the same house." His eyes softened as he leaned close to brush his lips over her forehead.

Her heart melted as she leaned into the kiss—which quickly intensified.

Hmm.

At this rate, they *might* miss their plane.

One of them should put the brakes on, but—

A knock sounded on the door.

Logan ignored it.

When the interloper rapped again, however, he eased back. "It's probably the porter, come to get our bags." He was close enough for his words to leave a whisper of warmth on her skin.

"We better answer."

"Yeah."

After a few beats, he released her. "I'll take care of this. Meet me on the lanai for one last moment with our beautiful view?"

"And maybe one last Hawaiian kiss?"

"That could be arranged."

She watched him walk to the door, then slipped outside, where the sweet scent of plumeria perfumed the air.

Leaving this magical place would be hard.

But as she waited for the man who'd banished the shadows from her life, she smiled.

Anywhere would be magic with him.

And no matter what tomorrow held, she had today—and the abiding love she'd found with Logan was a blessing that would sustain her all the days of her life.

Logan tipped the porter, accepted the man's best wishes on his marriage, and closed the door so he could rejoin his wife.

Wife.

The corners of his mouth lifted.

It was still hard to believe.

But there was plenty of proof it was true. A marriage certificate. Wedding photos. An amazing honeymoon. And a large number of witnesses. Half the town of Hope Harbor had shown up at Grace Christian to watch them exchange vows.

Thank goodness he'd had the foresight to build optional unpaid leave into his contract with the urgent care center. He hadn't needed it for Molly, as he'd half expected, but it had definitely come in handy for a two-week honeymoon a mere seven months into his tenure.

Well, a ten-day honeymoon and a four-day trip to Disneyland.

Jeannette's idea.

He'd much rather have two full weeks in a tropical paradise with just the two of them—yet he loved her even more for her unselfish gesture.

As did Molly.

He pushed through the sliding door, his cell pinging with a text as he joined Jeannette.

She motioned toward it. "Are you going to check that?"

"I'd rather ignore it." The longer he could keep reality at bay, the better.

"It may be from the airline. Could be a departure time change."

If so, maybe they could carve out another few minutes here alone before the world impinged.

He pulled out his phone and skimmed the text. "It's from Molly—via Thomma."

"Everything okay?"

"Yes. She says, 'I packed my suitcase for Disneyland. Me and Elisa are having fun. Toby is being good. I can't wait to see Cinderella's castle. I love you, Uncle Logan. You too, 'Nette.' "

Jeannette smiled. "She sounds happy—and excited."

"Yes, she does. She's a different child these days."

"So is Elisa. She and Thomma seem to be on much better footing." She slipped her arm around his waist, the rustle of palm fronds and the chirp of a myna bird the only sounds breaking the peaceful stillness. "It was kind of the Shabos to watch Molly while we were gone."

"I know. Mariam is a wonderful nanny. And with all the inquiries she's had from young parents, she won't have any difficulty lining up more work once the girls start school next fall."

"Thomma seems happier too, since he got that job at the high-end kennel in Coos Bay. Between that and the private dog-training clientele he's developed, they've both found their niche."

"A happy ending all around." He tugged her into the circle of his arms.

"The best." Her lips curved up.

His gaze dropped to them . . . and he dipped his head to—

The phone pinged again.

Logan blew out a breath and closed his eyes.

"You better get it." Laughter lurked behind her words.

"Yeah."

Resigned, he pulled out his cell and skimmed the text. "Molly says she forgot to send us the photo Thomma snapped of the picture she drew."

He clicked on the icon, and as the image filled the screen, he stopped breathing.

A woman with long dark tresses and a man with golden-brown hair were walking down a beach, a little girl with reddish locks between them. They were all holding hands, and a spotted dog trotted ahead of them.

They looked like a happy family.

And the icing on the cake?

The sky was bright blue.

"What is it, Logan?" Jeannette touched his arm.

He angled the cell toward her, not trusting himself to speak.

Her features softened as she examined it. "I love that she sees us like that." She lifted her chin and studied him. "But there's more to it, isn't there?"

"Yes." He swallowed past the lump in his throat and told her about the picture Molly had drawn months ago with the dark sky. "I prayed for it to turn blue."

Her own eyes began to shimmer. "That's what love can do. It chases away the dark clouds and turns gray skies to blue. Your love did that for me too."

Blinking to clear his vision, he tapped in a quick response to Molly, pocketed his phone, and drew Jeannette toward him again, this woman who'd vowed to keep love at bay but who'd trusted him with her heart.

And he would never, ever betray that trust.

"Do you have any idea how much I love you?"

"No more than I love you." She twined her arms around his neck. "I was hoping there'd be a flight delay so I could demonstrate."

"Hold that thought for a few hours. In the meantime . . . let me give you a preview of what *I* have in store for *you* for the next, say, fifty or sixty years."

He touched his mouth to hers, in a gentle kiss that he quickly deepened at her ardent response.

And as the world faded away . . . as he lost himself in her sweet embrace . . . one final, rational thought registered.

All those months ago, when he'd upended his world to accommodate a child, he'd known his life would never be the same again—and he'd assumed most of those changes wouldn't be for the better.

But God did indeed work in mysterious ways.

For who would have predicted that all the upheaval of those early months with Molly would lead him to a woman who touched his heart as no one ever had? Who filled his world with unimagined joy and endless possibilities? Who had been exactly what he needed to find his own happy place?

And every day, for as long as he lived, he would thank the Almighty for guiding him to a little town on the Oregon coast with a name that had more than lived up to its promise.

Author's Note

Thank you for visiting Hope Harbor—where hearts heal . . . and love blooms.

If this is the first time you've dropped in, I hope you enjoy your stay. If you're returning, welcome home.

And Hope Harbor does feel like home, doesn't it? It's the kind of place where everyone can find hope and a new beginning. Where people are benevolent and willing to help their neighbors. Where love and healing are in the air.

I'm so grateful that readers have come to care for this charming Oregon seaside town as much as I have.

In practical terms, that means sales are good—and more books are coming! Hope Harbor will remain what *Publishers Weekly* has called "a place of emotional restoration" for the foreseeable future.

I'd like to offer my deepest thanks to all the people who have encouraged me in my writing journey, especially my husband, Tom; my parents, James and Dorothy Hannon (Mom would have loved this story, and I know she's cheering me on from heaven); and my publishing partners at Revell—Dwight Baker, Kristin Kornoelje, Jennifer Leep, Michele Misiak, Karen

Steele, Cheryl Van Andel (this is the last cover of mine she worked on before retiring), and Gayle Raymer.

Please return with me to Hope Harbor in April 2020, when charter fisherman Steven Roark from *Driftwood Bay* and a local teacher find themselves on opposite sides of an issue that threatens to disrupt the placid existence of the seaside community.

In the meantime, if you like romantic suspense, *Dark Ambitions*—book 3 in my Code of Honor series—will be out in October 2019. For those who've been reading my suspense novels for a while, we'll be revisiting Phoenix, Inc.—the PI firm from my Private Justice series. That's where Rick goes for help when a mystery drops into his lap—and the newest member of the staff . . . a female investigator . . . is assigned to his case. Sparks fly, in more ways than one—so be prepared for another thrilling adventure that will keep you up until the wee hours!

IRENE HANNON is the bestselling, award-winning author of more than fifty contemporary romance and romantic suspense novels. She is also a three-time winner of the RITA award—the "Oscar" of romance fiction—from Romance Writers of America and is a member of that organization's elite Hall of Fame.

Her many other awards include National Readers' Choice, Daphne du Maurier, Retailers' Choice, Booksellers' Best, Carol, and Reviewers' Choice from *RT Book Reviews* magazine, which also honored her with a Career Achievement award for her entire body of work. In addition, she is a two-time Christy award finalist.

Millions of her books have been sold worldwide, and her novels have been translated into multiple languages.

Irene, who holds a BA in psychology and an MA in journalism, juggled two careers for many years until she gave up her executive corporate communications position with a Fortune 500 company to write full-time. She is happy to say she has no regrets.

A trained vocalist, Irene has sung the leading role in numerous community musical theater productions and is also a soloist at her church. She and her husband enjoy traveling, long hikes, Saturday mornings at their favorite coffee shop, and spending time with family. They make their home in Missouri.

To learn more about Irene and her books, visit www.irenehannon.com. She enjoys interacting with readers on Facebook and is also active on Twitter and Instagram.

Center Point Large Print
600 Brooks Road / PO Box 1
Thorndike, ME 04986-0001 USA

(207) 568-3717

US & Canada:
1 800 929-9108
www.centerpointlargeprint.com